Kip's Monster

Also by this author
Scrap Metal
Brothers Of The Wild North Sea
Cold Fusion
The Tyack & Frayne Mystery Series

Kip's Monster

Harper Fox

FoxTales

FoxTales Publications
www.harperfox.net

Kip's Monster
Copyright © 2018 by Harper Fox
ISBN 978-1-910224-19-9

Cover art by Harper Fox
Image licensed through Shutterstock

Chapter One
My Birthday Tea

"Oh," said Gran, emptying a packet of custard creams onto a plate on the table. "Another package came for you, too. Spoiled rotten, you are."

For my birthday, Gran had bought me a cologne I'd stopped wearing when I was eighteen. I had three unopened bottles of it in my wardrobe upstairs. This would make a fourth. She'd also, in a surprisingly modern twist, got me a voucher for an online music store. My sister Jules had taken a break from hating me long enough to buy me a beautiful cashmere sweater I'd admired last time I'd been in town. Considering their resources—pension and pocket money—I thought Gran wasn't wrong. The remains of my family had done their best to spoil me today. "Thanks, Gran. They're really nice presents."

"Well, I know you like your New Spice. Smells completely different on you to the way it does in the bottle."

"Must be my body chemistry."

"Aren't you going to open your parcel?"

Warily I pulled the brown paper package towards me. The label on it had been typed, and there was no return address. Only the string said anything about the sender: a length of fragrant hemp garden twine, tied with precision and flair. "It's probably just the brackets I ordered for the guttering."

"No, it's too light for that. Too soft, as well."

She'd had a good feel, then. Taking pity on her curiosity, I undid the twine. The package opened easily when I ran a finger under the sellotape strips, and I found myself looking at a T-shirt from Black Sabbath's legendary 1973 tour of the UK.

A diehard fan, my dad. He hadn't called me Oz after Ozzy, Lord of Darkness—our family name was Osman, that was all—but Oz I'd been, from birth to my first ride on his shoulders at Ozzfest 2001, and onwards and upwards to my distinguished career as a data-entry clerk for the local council. I smoothed the fabric under my hand. "I don't know how he's had the balls to send me this."

"Don't say *balls*, Oz," she corrected me absently. "Who do you think sent it?"

"My good-for-nothing father. Obviously."

"I'd think again, if I was you. There's a note.

The note was sticking out from between the folds of the shirt. It was headed with my old university's crest, and then *Department of Environmental Science.* Then came a few lines of beautiful, elegant scrawl. *Dear Oz-Man, don't stop loving what you love. Happy birthday to you. Best always, Kip.*

Gran took the note from me. She turned it sideways, then upside-down. Her complaints of failing eyesight usually just meant she was tired of holding her book and wanted me or Jules to read to her while she counted tiny stitches on her knitting needles. Eventually she deciphered the message. "Terrible handwriting, that lad has. What do you suppose he means—don't stop loving what you love?"

I leaned my elbows on the kitchen table. In the garden, a grey wind was blowing the leaves around. Gran's house had been built in the 1950s, when small towns often had on their outskirts a building known as the police house, a place they would offer to the local bobby as part of his pay. My granddad had been the last village constable, and had exercised his right to buy when the time came, leaving his widow with a roof over her head, if little else. The house was a council build, the same as the rest of the estate, and made of the same breezeblocks and concrete render, but stood apart in a kind of paddock of its own, the better for the northeast-coast winds to pull it apart. Already there were tiles off the roof. If I didn't fix up the guttering, no-one would. "He means," I said tiredly, "that I shouldn't stop loving Black Sabbath just because they're my dad's favourite band. He probably also means that I shouldn't have packed in my engineering degree at uni just because my dad did it before me, or stopped following in any of that treacherous arsehole's footsteps just because they were his. But Kip has no idea, Gran, and nor have you, so please don't start."

"Do you not like the T-shirt, then?"

That really wasn't the issue. I picked up the shirt by the shoulders, though, and held it to the chilly winter light. Vintage shirts like this came up online from time to time, and Kip and I had wasted happy half hours in the uni canteen, calculating what we could buy for the same price. Four or five lots of groceries, or even—not that either of us had ever thought we'd get that far—an instalment payment on our student loans. The cotton had been worn to softness, but the *Sabbath Bloody Sabbath* logo stood out fresh and clear, as well as the knight in armour, the devil and the angel. "I love it," I said without meaning to, and clapped a hand to my mouth.

Gran beamed in satisfaction. "Go and try it on, then."

"I haven't got time. I'm on split shifts today. Got to be back in the office by half four."

"No, you haven't. I called you in sick so you wouldn't miss your birthday tea."

I stared at her in dismay. Any hope that she might have been kidding died with the last ray of afternoon sunlight on her horn-rim specs. "Gran, no."

"It's one day. The world won't end."

"You can't do this. You don't know what they're like. They time you when you go to the loo."

"No wonder your tummy's been upset."

"This isn't funny. I need that job."

"You're not going to lose it. I know your supervisor, the one who sits behind his desk with his little stopwatch. Your granddad arrested his dad a few times for selling stolen phones and laptops down at the car boot. He was quite nice to me when he worked out who I was. Quite polite."

I buried my face in my hands. "Oh, shit."

"Don't say *shit*, Oz."

"Sorry. I really am. But..."

I heard the sudden scrape of her chair on the lino. Then came a shuffle of slippers—then, unexpectedly, a caressing touch to my shoulder. We weren't a hugging family. "Take the afternoon off," she said gently. "Everybody knows you work your heart out for me and Jules. Not like your dad."

Weirdly—because I was fine about it all now, really fine—I couldn't bear her to mention him. I made a blind grab for the other thing she'd said. "What do you mean, my birthday tea?"

"Why do you think I bought the custard creams? There's a cake in the cupboard too, your favourite one from Morrison's. I've invited Mrs Patwardhan from down the road, and Sally and Emma Higgs who you used to go to school with."

"Sally Higgs always hits on me, Gran."

"Well, you're a handsome boy. And she's not the sharpest. Takes a while for the penny to drop." She gave me a half-pat, half-slap. "Go and try your T-shirt on! I know everything's different this year—not like your twenty-first, when your dad was here and we could afford to give you a bit of a blow-out. But it's still a party. Try to come back looking less like you just got kicked off *The Apprentice.*"

***

I stood in front of my bedroom mirror, trying to work out when Ozzy the Oz-Man had turned into John Osman of Filing and Records, third floor of the Civic Centre, desk six, row eight. There were thirty five rows. I'd never tried counting how many desks sat to the left of mine: on winter mornings, the distance between me and the grimy window seemed infinite, a bleak inner sky no bird could cross in flight. Suddenly my tie felt like a garrotte. I unfastened it and pulled it off—carefully, because despite Gran's manoeuvres, I'd have to go in later to make up my hours—and began to unbutton my shirt.

A handsome lad, in Gran's opinion. I'd put a bit of weight on, sitting on my backside for a year at desk six, but that was what the men in our family did: spent their teens whip-thin, then filled out to fit their sturdy frames, carrying it off with charm and a scapegrace grin that made it hard not to forgive them. My dad had carried it off best of all.

Hard, but not impossible. I shrugged out of my shirt and hung it out of reach of Slasher, Gran's aptly named cat. Kip must have bought the T-shirt a while ago and kept it in his flat: when I pulled it over my head, I was for half a second enveloped in Kip scents and Kip memories.

Books and coffee. Just the faintest trace of the ciggies he'd given up for me when we'd started to get serious. A dirty habit, I'd told him, and when he'd just looked at me blankly as if ordinary human standards of dirt and cleanliness didn't apply to him, I'd added that I didn't want to see him gasping his last of COPD in his mid-thirties the way my mother had done, when I'd been fourteen and poor Jules only five.

I hadn't breathed a word about my mam in years until then. He'd gone white, stubbed out his fag and come to wrap his arms around me. He'd quit on the spot, without a regret as far as I could see. God, I'd loved him! My hands not quite steady, I pulled the T-shirt straight. It was a perfect fit, as if he'd held me in his mind's eye when he'd chosen it. My cheap, sensible, badly cut office trousers looked even worse for the contrast, and I tugged them down and stepped out of them, reaching for a pair of jeans instead. I ruffled my hair until it stood up in trendy spikes. There. That was how I'd looked before my dad had turned my world to fragments of shit and broken glass. When I'd still been a promising engineering student, and Joe Kipton's Oz-Man.

I'd loved Kip, and he'd quit smoking for me, but he was an alcoholic. Not in the temporary way some students go through when first let off the leash, but quietly, seriously, with the dedication of a priest. He kept it off the roads and away from the lecture halls, and God knew he was a sweet-natured drunk—sweeter, if possible, half-cut than sober—but it went all the way with him, right down to the core. *I have to have something*, he'd said to me one night when I'd gone to haul him home from another session at the union bar. *I know I'm pathetic, Oz, but I've just got to have something.*

I could understand that. I hadn't even minded, although part of me wanted to say *you have me.* I was sorry, and I worried about him, but I believed him when he said he could handle it. He was smart, far brighter than I was. Already he'd put forward a theory about the loss of biodiversity in our local river systems which had made his whole department sit up and take notice. For me, looking at him had been like sunshine flashing off a mirror, or diamond or ice. Even Jules, who these days loved no-one, had eaten out of his hand.

As if on cue, a key scraped in the lock of the front door. A flurry of footsteps shook the stairs, and then the door of the room next to mine banged open and shut. I counted down from ten. You could usually tell how bad a day she'd had by how fast and how loudly her music went on.

Bloody hell. Five seconds, and the volume off the scale. I strode onto the landing. Her bedroom door was jumping lightly in its frame from the force of the bass. I grabbed the handle and shoved the door wide. "Jules, for God's sake!"

She froze like a rabbit in headlights. I'd caught her halfway out of her school uniform. Her blouse was in a heap against the wall, as if flung there with all her strength. She was still the same skinny kid who'd blighted my life since I was nine, but to my shock she'd developed breasts—not little teenage buds but a proper pair. She gave a shriek, dived full-length onto her bed and rolled herself up in a blanket. "Fuck off, Oz," she spat when she could manage it, pushing up against the headboard. "It's my *room*. You should *knock*."

She was dead right, of course. But percussion was shaking the walls, and sometimes she made me so angry I could barely speak. I grabbed her MP3 player off the dressing table and hit pause. "It's not your room when you act like it's got no walls. This is Gran's house. Show some bloody respect."

"Gran's deaf. She doesn't mind. It's only you who minds, you boring old fart. Anyway, like I didn't have to listen to years and years of your boring old-fart music, the Grateful Who or Twat Sabbath or whatever. And another thing..."

She'd obviously decided to go all-out. I rested my hands on my hips and looked at the carpet. When she paused to draw breath in her litany of my sins, crimes and inadequacies, I interrupted her. "I should've knocked. I'm sorry, okay?"

How she hated an apology. She was too good a kid not to respond, and it always took the wind out of her sails. She curled up tighter on the bed. "No, it is not bloody well okay. What are you doing here anyway? You should be at work."

"I'm taking a few hours off. Gran's invited a couple of people over. I'm having a birthday tea, apparently."

Finally she met my eyes. I could see in hers our shared memories of this time last year, the riverboat Dad had hired for my twenty-first, the champagne and twinkling lights, and dancing on-deck with Kip until I'd almost fallen into a happy, cake-stuffed sleep in his arms. "What a thrill," said Jules. "Who's coming?"

"Just Mrs Patwardhan and the Higgses. And you, I hope."

"Oh, God. Forget it. I've got homework."

"When do you ever let that stop you?" I let go a sigh, and lowered my voice: Gran's deafness, like her failing vision, was very selective. "Look, I don't fancy this party much, either. But she's set it all up. She's doing her best."

"I'll consider it." She frowned. "What's happened to you? You don't look like quite so much of a relic as usual."

"Ta. I got a new T-shirt, that's all. I like the jumper you bought me. There's some kind of weird button on it, though—do you know anything about that?"

"Probably just the security tag. They must've forgotten to take it off after I paid. You can flip it off with the flat of a knife-blade. I'll show you later on, if you're too old and boring to manage it yourself."

Unease pricked my nape. But she and I were back on some kind of even keel, and that was too rare for me to want to rock the boat. "Pick your clothes up off the floor," I said vaguely, not feeling I could retreat without some words of brotherly advice. "And... look, don't throw another wobbler on me, all right? Gran needs to buy you a bra."

"Oz, can you please fucking stop it?"

"If you can stop swearing, I'll try. Stop what?"

"Trying to play Mammy as well as Dad. Gran bought me half a dozen bras, nice ones. But they just make the bloody things look bigger, so I don't want to wear them. And she gave me the talk about periods and having it off, and I've got a cupboard full of tampons and sanitary towels. If you must bloody know. Okay?"

I wasn't. I'd had to start looking out of the window halfway through this declaration. For weeks I'd been putting off tackling all that stuff with her, trying to think of an approach that wouldn't leave me sounding like a perv or a bull in a china shop. What did I know about teenage girls? Still, I'd really thought it my duty. Why hadn't it occurred to me that Gran might have it all in hand? "Sorry," I said to her roughly. She was puce with embarrassment, but still valiantly giving me the finger. I raised one to her in return, and we exchanged a kind of fuck-off salute.

I let myself out onto the landing. Then I stuck my head back around the door. "Did she really call it the having-it-off talk?"

"No. She said *intercourse*. But she kept getting it mixed up with the period thing and pronouncing it *intercurse* instead. *When a lady has sexual intercurse, Juliet...*" She burst into hooting giggles. This triggered a sudden explosive fart, which just made her worse: she curled up, shrieking and howling.

I closed the door and left her to it. The racket she was making, like every other noise in this thin-walled house, resounded up and down the stairs. Poor Gran probably gone deaf to preserve her sanity. I shook my head and leaned my arms on the banister. Very softly, barely above a whisper, I said, "Jesus Christ."

Promptly Gran appeared in the doorway to the kitchen. "Don't say *Jesus Christ* like that, Oz."

"Right. No. Sorry, Gran."

***

"That T-shirt suits you, Oz."

I'd helped Gran lay out plates, napkins and seven sets of her cracked and battered best china. She must have been more confident than I was that Jules would come down. Even then we were one set too many, unless she'd managed to rustle up another neighbour from somewhere. Probably she'd just lost count. I pulled gently at the T-shirt's hem and made an upside-down inspection of the 666 and the supernatural crew. "I dunno. These things cost a fortune. I should probably send it back."

"Don't do that. Just thank him for it when you see him."

We were sitting in a state of party-readiness in the front parlour. This was Gran's room for special occasions. If I squinted right, I could conjure the memory of my granddad's coffin laid out on the long oak table. Instead I focused on the seventh teacup, innocently waiting on its little chintz saucer. "Oh, Gran. No."

"Why not? He's a lovely lad. I would, if I was your age." She settled back in her chair, folded her arms and gave me a wrinkly, lecherous grin. "I still might."

My heart was beating fast beneath the *Sabbath* of my shirt. I jumped to my feet and went to the window. "You actually invited him? He's coming here?"

"Sit down, Oz. Even Jules knows better than to stand with her nose pressed to the glass when she's waiting for her boyfriend."

"Her *what*?"

"Your sister is thirteen years old. Kip is a nice young man, and you were happier with him than I've ever seen you in your whole life."

I spun to face her. "You don't know what you're doing. I broke up with Kip when Dad left because..." My voice shook, and I swallowed hard. "Kip's wild. He drinks too much. And yeah, he's great, but he's got no idea how people like you and me live. His parents are worth a mint, and—"

"Didn't you say he never speaks to his parents?"

"Yeah, but that's his choice, not theirs. They love him. As soon as he turns twenty five he'll inherit some kind of trust fund, and that's it. He'll be rich. He's got that safety net, so it's okay for him to mess around at uni and drink his head off. Not like me."

The spectacles gleamed enigmatically. "No, not like you. You've got to work for a living."

"Exactly."

"To show Jules that somebody round here's willing to earn their keep and help put a roof over her head. To give her a good example."

"Yes!" The old lady was usually far from this understanding. Maybe she'd finally started listening to me.

"It's really important now. If Jules doesn't see that one man in her family is capable of putting his own selfish bloody needs aside and doing what's right, she'll never learn." I eased down off my high horse. "She doesn't really have a boyfriend, does she?"

"Of course not, unless you call Sunil Patwardhan parking his bike outside and gazing moonily up at her window a boyfriend. I just wanted to see your face." Before I could draw breath to respond, she took off her glasses and looked at me in dead earnest. "But it's going to happen, Oz. People do have boyfriends. And they're not always tidy and nice."

She had a way of silencing me. I stood staring at her. And somebody knocked on the door.

Chapter Two
Kip

I didn't run. My mouth had gone dry and I could barely breathe, but I'd got used to hiding a thing or two over the past year. I was fairly sure I could open the door to my ex without falling over my feet, stammering or bursting into tears.

Gran's little front hall had become very long, though, and as I made my way down it, I vaguely registered sounds from upstairs, a series of thuds, creaks and rattles I'd heard on a couple of memorable occasions before. I couldn't pay them proper attention. My whole world had come to a burning central point beyond the door.

I pulled it wide, and found myself face to face with two uniformed police officers, one male, one female. The woman's kindly face was familiar. With the recognition came a click of memory to memory. The sounds I'd heard from upstairs had been my little sister climbing out of the bathroom window at the back of the house.

The kitchen had a flat roof, and from there it was an easy drop into the garden. Jules knew all the exits. She was too smart to try for the back gate, but I hadn't got round to repairing the fence at the side. How the hell was I meant to, with everything else on my plate? I had maybe ten seconds before she dodged out through the loose plank and escaped into the lanes. "'Scuse me," I said to the constables, darted past them and ran outside.

I cut Jules off en route to the fence. Her day at school must have been very bad: she'd regressed into an ancient dinosaur onesie that barely fit her anymore, complete with feet and tail. I caught her by the green-crested hood. "Don't even try," I said, reeling her in. "What've you done this time?"

Her face was a mask of fury. I scarcely recognised her. What had I been supposed to do—hold the plank aside and let her go? I slackened my grip, hearing the fabric tear, and she promptly tried to elbow me in the gut. "Stop it, you little sod. I don't want to hurt you, but I'm not about to bloody well let you go."

She wrenched away. I grabbed her wrist, and she loosed a wild shriek. "You *are* hurting me! You are. You're breaking my arm!"

The female officer came round the corner at a jog. "Oh dear," she said. "It's like Jurassic Park out here. Come on now, love—we just want a chat with you, that's all."

She was a lot better at this than I was. She laid a hand on Jules's shoulder and gently spun her round. The dinosaur knew when the jig was up and stopped fighting.

The constable steered her, soaking feet, bedraggled tail and all, back into the house through the front door.

Gran was waiting in the parlour. She didn't seem concerned that her granddaughter had just been hunted down by the police. She got another two sets of cups and saucers out of the sideboard—not the best china for the poor coppers—and nodded at them genially. "Nice to see you again, Claire. I don't know your friend there. He must be new. I'll just pop the kettle on."

She was back a few moments later, the cashmere sweater in her hands. "Have a seat, officers," she said, indicating the chairs around the table. "Jules, you come and sit here by me. The security tags look different to when our Jenny was doing her teenage shoplifting, or I'd have cottoned on sooner."

I bristled. My mother's name was sacred to me. No-one had asked me to sit down, so I stayed where I was in the doorway, folding my arms. "Mam never did anything like this."

"Oh, hush, Oz. Just because it would never occur to *you*." She paused, head on one side, considering. "It *doesn't* seem to occur to the boys, does it? They do their graffiti and break a few windows. Maybe it's hormones, when the girls get to that age. Needing to gather berries or something. Line their nests."

Bollocks, I'd have said, anywhere else than in my gran's best parlour. But the sergeant was looking thoughtful. "That's an interesting theory, Mrs Woods. Hormonal compulsion to petty theft in young teens. I might bring that up with the crime-prevention team at our next meeting. Do you, er... Do you think there's much more upstairs?"

"Not that I know of. But go and have a look if you want."

"Do you know what? We've only had the one complaint with security footage to back it up, and that was about this jumper. I don't think we'll bother with upstairs—not today, anyway." She picked the jumper up off the table and examined it. "This wouldn't fit you, Juliet. Who did you steal it for?"

Jules gave a kind of grunt. She tossed her head so that the absurd crested hood of her onesie flew up and forward to hide her face. Gran sighed. "You're on thin ice, miss," she said, and pulled the hood back. Then she tenderly took hold of Jules's chin, turned her face and tucked two strands of hair behind her ears. "Talk to Sergeant Claire. She's giving you a chance, and so am I. But you only get one."

"All right." Tears were coursing down Jules's face. She poked a finger in my direction. Her hand was shaking, and that went through me, but this was all still bullshit. I was sure her drawers upstairs were packed with loot. And Gran was wrong: I'd never vandalised a wall or broken anyone's window. I'd been a good son. "I got it for him," Jules croaked. "He had a big party last year, presents and a riverboat and everything. And this year there's nothing. I wanted to get him something nice."

"Oh, don't you make *me* the reason for this," I broke in, far more harshly than I'd meant to. Gran, Sergeant Claire and her colleague all turned to me in surprise.

"Well, for God's sake. This is what happens if you keep letting her off the hook for things, Gran. Nobody will ever punish her for anything, just because her dad shipped out and abandoned her. She's gonna keep getting worse and worse."

Claire was old school. She looked to be in her late fifties, and her face was hard to read, but very patient. She even had a little notebook and pencil. She gave the notebook a few considering taps. "You're Juliet's brother, aren't you? John Osman."

"Oz," I corrected automatically. "Yes, that's right."

"Then... didn't your dad ship out and abandon you too?"

The question hit me like a brick. Just for a second, though: I'd learned deflection over the last year too, and bigger things than a wily copper had tried to break me with sympathy. "Of course not," I said flatly. "The party last year was for my twenty-first." All paid for by dad, some bloody incomprehensible last gesture before he vanished—along with our income and our family home—a fortnight later. "If a parent leaves a grown-up, it's not abandonment. That's just... leaving."

Claire was nodding. "Fair point. Well, Mrs Woods, since this is a first offence and we've recovered the goods, we'll leave it at that for today. I'm sure Juliet understands that we won't be as lenient next time."

Gran gave Jules a push. "Did you hear the sergeant?"

"Yeah."

"Then what do you say?"

Jules was still crying. They weren't crocodile tears, or dinosaur ones either: they were as real as she was. Humiliated, snotty and distraught. Abandoned by her one surviving parent at the age of twelve. "Thank you," she managed, and I should have been so bloody sorry for her, just like everybody else. Even the brisk young constable who'd come along with Claire, all badge and business, was shaking his crew-cut head sadly at a silver-framed photo of our mother on the mantelpiece.

This was ridiculous. I *had* seen Claire before. "This isn't the first time," I burst out. "Not the first time she's done something. You were getting into your car outside the house a few weeks ago. And you were talking to her in the school yard when I went to pick her up the other day. You weren't in uniform, but that was you. Why are you letting her get *away* with all this?"

The sergeant and Gran traded glances. "It's a fair cop," Claire said resignedly after a few seconds, possibly thinking she was funny. "Yes, I know Juliet. She's truanted from school a few times—like lots of kids without parents, she's getting bullied. Children are horrors sometimes. It's like they can smell weakness. Blood in the water. Does that explain things, Oz?"

"Yes. No. Why did nobody tell me?"

"Your grandmother thought you had enough on your plate with your job."

"But I'm Jules's older brother. I'm the... the..."

"The man of the house," Gran finished for me. "You're trying to be, at any rate. But Juliet's in my custody, not yours, and it's up to me to deal with her.

Now, if you don't mind, officers, we're expecting some guests."

She was bones of steel and heart of gold, my gran. I knew that. On some level I knew that she was all I had, and without her, Jules and I would truly have been abandoned and alone. But I hadn't given up everything— my education, my career, my feckless, beautiful boyfriend—to be set aside and told that my sister was none of my business. I drew a breath.

Someone in the room was angrier still. Jules's tears had stopped. She had got to her feet and was glaring at me, fists clenched. "You bastard, Oz!"

"Juliet Osman!" Gran grabbed her by the tail as she lunged at me, overturning the milk jug. "Stop this at once."

"I won't stop. You heard him. He *wanted* me to get arrested. Even though you and these coppers here said it was all right, he wanted me to get punished. He was *disappointed*!"

"Oh, Jules, I was not. I didn't know about the truancy thing, okay? Or that you're getting bullied. Nobody tells me anything."

But that was too little too late. She was on fire with betrayal as well as rage. "I'll tell you something now," she spat. "Maybe our dad wouldn't have pissed off to his nice new American family if his only son from this one hadn't been gay. Did you ever think about that? Maybe it was *all your fault*."

A dreadful silence fell. I must have left the front door open behind me. Everyone but Jules was staring past me into the hall. Slowly I turned round. There, obviously taken captive on his way up the garden path, was Kip. A Higgs sister was hanging adoringly on either arm. "Oh dear," said Mrs Patwardhan brightly, pushing past them into the parlour and looking around. "Have we come at an awkward time?"

Jules shot across the room like a bullet. "Kip," she shrieked, and flung her arms around his waist. The impact shook him free of Emma and Sally Higgs, who stumbled back in dismay. Jules buried her face in his shirt and exploded into sobs. "Kip! Kip!"

Reflexively he caught her. He'd always been so good with her. It was as if he saw straight into her, saw her gaping hole. And he didn't waste time trying to fill it or cover it over, for his benefit or hers: just agreed that it was shit that her dad had chosen his new family over her, absolutely fucking shit. And after that, when the hole gaped, when the wind blew through it and shrieked in Jules's voice, when she threw things and swore and climbed the walls in her pain, he just let all that happen too. When she was done—when the gale had blown itself out—he would take her to the amusement arcade on the sea front, or out for fish and chips, or load her into his rusting Mazda MX-5 and dash her up and down the A1 with the top down, come rain or shine.

A Mazda was parked outside the house now. The things were so low-slung that the hedge concealed it, but the long nose poking past the gateway was a different colour from the one I remembered. I'd told him over and over that he could've saved his money and bought one good car instead of a series of clunkers, but he'd enigmatically said that wasn't the point. He'd called each one of these cars his Love Machine. The first time I'd heard the name, I'd been curled in the fragrant warmth of the passenger seat in a layby on the coast road, waiting with him for the AA. I'd recoiled in disgust, and he'd looked at me wide-eyed and told me the cars were called that because he just loved them so much. With any other guy I'd have laughed, but he literally did mean no more and no less than that. I wished this was the kind of world where I too could chuck myself into his arms and howl. Instead I pushed my hands into my pockets. "Hi, Kip."

"Hi, Oz." He gave me a onceover that made my skin tingle. "You look good in your shirt. Hello, Gran. Er... can I take Jules upstairs, if the police officers are done? Then Oz can look after his guests. I'll be back down in ten, Oz."

He made a tiny gesture with his head. I'd grown used to reading him, and this meant that I should meet him in the garden. I turned to Gran, who was nodding frantically. She was a proud old girl, and had never cared much about what the neighbours thought, but this social encounter—police in the parlour, a weeping kid in a dinosaur suit—had spiralled beyond her control. "Thanks, Kip," I said. "Yeah. That would be great."

***

I did my best with my guests. I sat them down, helped Gran pour and hand around the tea, cut my cake, smiled for a photo with Sally Higgs even though I knew she'd post it on Facebook and change her status to *it's complicated*. I kept an eye on my watch. At the end of the ninth minute, Jules reappeared. By some miracle she was washed, brushed and presentable, in jeans and a retro cheesecloth shirt she'd adored for years, then abandoned because she said it made her look fat. Unwanted pity moved in me like gravel. She was unforgivable, and this time unforgiven. She tried to meet my eyes, and I avoided her, turning to Gran instead. Gran, who'd learned to read Kip too, and had read me like a book my whole life, made a tiny gesture of her own.

I slipped outside. Winter had seized our stretch of coast with its usual bleak hunger, but I didn't pause to grab a jacket or to register the bite of cold on my skin. Kip was waiting under Gran's wind-stunted apple tree, the one place in the garden out of sight of all the windows. I realised that I'd seldom seen him without a ciggie or a glass in his hand. I remembered him on the steps outside the union bar, airily explaining some point of marine ecology, his cigarette a firefly in the near dark. He looked oddly naked now, as if he didn't know what to do with his arms. Then he held them out to me as if he definitely did.

I strode into them. I laid my brow on his shoulder and shut my eyes. His embrace closed and he rocked me, and I shouldn't have let him, because every breath I took of him—coffee and books, just like the T-shirt, with a tang of laboratory chemicals on top—was stolen, forbidden, wrong. A luxurious cashmere jumper, security tag still attached... Maybe he felt the same. He gave me a rib-cracking squeeze, roughly kissed my head and let me go.

There were two plastic chairs beneath the tree, Gran's idea of garden furniture. Awkwardly we sat down. "Here," he said, unfastening his jacket. "Put this on. It's perishing out here."

"What about you?"

"I'm okay. I've got a sweater."

Whereas I had a vintage T-shirt, already dampening in the mist-fretted wind from the sea. I took Kip's jacket and shrugged into it, trying not to shudder with pleasure at the residual warmth from his skin. "You shouldn't have bought me this. It was way too expensive."

"Oh, it's not the one we were looking at last year. Loads cheaper than that."

He was an effortless liar, especially when the lie was a benign one, a sweeter pill to swallow than the truth. It was one of the reasons I'd left him: I'd had enough of lies, even sugared ones that easily slipped down the throat. "Kip, it's the exact same shirt."

"Well... Okay, yeah. But he'd reduced it."

"At least you could've saved a bit of money on the postage. Why send it, if you were coming here anyway?"

"I wasn't that sure of my welcome."

We sat in wind-rattled silence, the tree's bare branches clicking and creaking overhead. I wanted to take his hand, but we weren't boyfriends anymore, and you didn't do that to another lad who was just your mate. Not even that, maybe, after our year-long estrangement. "Thanks for sorting Jules out," I said eventually. "What did you do?"

"She just needed her nose blowing. She let me brush her hair, and she put that old shirt on she used to like so much. When did she start to think she was fat?"

About the same time everything else went to shit. "Dunno. About a year back. It's just a girl thing, isn't it? Hormones."

"Boys get it too. Dysmorphia, it's called—where you look in the mirror and can't see the real person there, no matter how hard you try. You see someone fat, or someone ugly, or whatever hurts you the most."

I swallowed. "God. Do you think Jules has that?"

"If she does, your gran will know. I don't think so, though. She's just really unhappy." He paused, leaning forward to rest his elbows on his knees. "And she is so sorry for what she said. That crack about your dad leaving because you were gay. *So* sorry."

"She doesn't have to be. It doesn't matter." Kip's eyebrows went up, and I ploughed on. "I hear worse from her than that all the time. It's water off my back. Look, it's her job to freak out and say dreadful things—she's thirteen. It's my job to put up with it."

He took this in. "Speaking of jobs," he said gently after a while, "how's it going?"

"Oh, you know. Pays the bills. Will you believe that old turkey inside had the nerve to call me in sick today? So I could enjoy my birthday tea."

He gave a snort of laughter. "She hasn't changed much, then. Listen, I... I was at a meeting with the department heads the other day. Old Leighton-Smythe was talking about that project going on near Kielder— Eden of the North, was it called? He said there'd be loads of jobs for good engineering graduates in a year or so's time. He mentioned your name. Said it was pretty much a sure thing, if you could finish your course."

I knew all about EON. An equivalent of the Cornish Eden Project for the northeast, huge Buckminster domes being built in the forest near the reservoir. My hands itched. I loved those shapes, those steel hexagons, the way they fitted together. I had half a dozen ideas about the challenges the domes would face in a northern environment: the cold, the wind, the same basic forces that had shaped me. "Right," I said, shifting in my seat, wincing as the cracked old plastic nipped my thigh. "Thing is, that's a bird in the bush. I've got a job in my hand right now, and I've got to keep it. Anyway, never mind me. What were you doing in a meeting with the department heads?"

"Oh. Nothing much. My prof thinks I could do my PhD, that's all, and she's trying to recruit me for her conservation study, the Tyne Valley biodiversity thing. That's why she dragged me along."

"You're gonna do your doctorate? That's brilliant."

"Yeah, it would be. Except she'll only take me on if I give up my... my hobby."

I stared at him. "Oh, Kip. Are you still involved with all that?"

He flashed me a rueful smile. "Worse than ever, I'm afraid. I spent six weeks last spring in southern Alaska, and in summer I hitched a ride with some Canadian kids going back to Okanagan Lake for their holidays. If you want the absolute truth, I just got back from Wales. Missed quite a bit of term. No wonder Prof Wilson has her doubts."

I stifled a groan. Kip's hobby had been a bane of mine, not just Prof Wilson's, literally since the day I'd met him. He'd ambushed me outside the engineering halls, where Leighton-Smythe had me and a handful of his other pet undergrads working overtime on an experimental filtration pump for sewage. The handsome lad from Environmental Science had introduced himself as Joe Kipton, on a mission from Prof Wilson to beg or borrow an expensive piece of underwater sighting kit.

What he'd really meant, of course, was *steal.* Our underwater scope had disappeared for weeks, along with Joe Kipton, leaving me to face the wrath of Engineering and Environmental combined. When he came back and learned how badly I'd got my arse kicked, he took me out to dinner and told me all about his trip to Scotland in search of the Loch Ness monster.

I should have been enraged by him—or baffled by his lunacy—but instead I'd been charmed. It had taken me months to work out that his search for the creatures he called *cryptids* was more than a harmless leisure-time pursuit. He was completely obsessed. "All right," I said reluctantly. "Alaska must have been Bigfoot. And Canada... Ogopogo, right? The lake monster?"

"You got it."

"Any luck?"

"Definite footprints in the woods outside Ketchikan. We drew a blank in Canada. Nobody in Engineering will let me near their scope anymore."

"Are you surprised? What's in Wales?"

"ABCs, a real cluster. That was pretty exciting."

Anomalous big cats. You couldn't live with Kip for long and not learn the jargon. Or the sheer wild hopelessness of his endeavours. Kip had painted a motto on the ceiling of his bedroom in his tiny student flat. He'd done it in phosphorescent paint so as not to outrage the janitor. At night, flat on my back in his bed, the message had glowed down at me: *absence of evidence is not the same as evidence of absence.* I'd come to associate the letters, their eerie green light, with sensations of the most exquisite pleasure.

But all Kip's motto really meant was that nothing could be proved. That he'd engaged himself—his brilliant mind, the department resources he pinched over and over again until he found himself on a final disciplinary warning—in a giant waste of time, a bottomless pit of stubborn, unshakeable self-delusion. It all tied in, I'd decided, in my undergrad's wisdom, to the cigs and the drinking, his addictions. His daily escapes from reality. "You know," I said cautiously, because I might have had the right to nag him back then but had certainly lost it since, "a PhD with Wilson would be quite something. She hardly takes anyone on."

"I know."

"How did the ABCs go, then? Did you get any footage? Prints?"

"Loads. It was a really good trip."

"But?"

He let go the tiniest sigh. "But it turned out to be someone's huge black Maine Coon cat. We actually caught it. The kid who'd lost it was really glad to get it back."

I couldn't help it. A gurgle of laughter escaped me. He and his nutcase friends had spent weeks of term-time tracking some kid's missing cat. I put my face in my hands, trying to shut myself up—God knew I'd never wanted to hurt him—but I couldn't stop. I hadn't laughed like this, or very much at all, for the best part of a year. My eyes began to stream. Suddenly Kip gave a roar of his own. He flung an arm around me, almost upsetting me out of my plastic chair. And that was how Gran found us half a minute later, both helpless, hooting and yawping with laughter. She looked down on us sadly. "It's cold out here, Oz," she said, "and Jules is acting like a tragedy queen for letting Kip alone with you this long. You'd better both come in, if you've finished your heart-to-heart."

Chapter Three
Trouble With Angry Teens

All our guests had left. It was such a familiar scene, Kip helping out at the end of a party, drying the glasses Gran washed, handing them to me to put away, while the dusk gathered and the house became a frail island of light and warmth.

He and Gran had been the best of friends, which had made my decision even harder. We finished clearing up. Gran closed the curtains. I was noticing things tonight: the nicotine stains in the fabric, although she hadn't touched a cigarette in years; the yellow blaze of the overhead bulbs in their glass shades. She'd never embraced what you'd call mood lighting. *Just one more electric flex to trip over, Oz.* All my childhood nights here, all the Sunday evenings Kip and I had spent with her in front of the telly, had passed in that unforgiving, somehow comforting glare. She sat down at the kitchen table and picked up her knitting. I noticed for the first time in months how small the kitchen was, how shabby.

She deserved so much better. My imagination tried and failed to place her somewhere else, in a little country cottage or a beach-front apartment in Marbella, but I thrust away the idea that she might be exactly where nature intended: nothing in my world, natural or otherwise, could possibly be right. She, Jules and I had all been cheated and dumped. The task of fixing that lay on my shoulders alone. "Right," I said, drying my hands on a tea towel. "Time I got back to work, if I still have a job."

She emitted a small sigh. She looked inexpressibly *Gran* tonight, as if some clever artist had conjured up the archetypical English grandmother, specs and flowered pinafore and blue-rinsed perm. Other people's grans didn't look like this, I'd observed. They were young and trendy, got their highlights done and went to Zumba. "I know I can't turn the clock back," she said sadly. "But I can't imagine anything nicer than if you two boys were to sit down and have a chat with me tonight. The long dark nights do get lonely."

"How can you be lonely?" I asked, nevertheless sitting down in my usual place, watching Kip sitting down in his. "Jules is here all the time."

"Jules is doing her homework."

That hardly answered the question. Was hardly true, either: I could see Jules through the half-open door into the living room, curled up in an armchair. She had some textbooks spread out on the coffee table, but her head was bobbing to the beat from her headphones. Sensing my gaze, she pulled a sheepish, defiant face, then cast a look of unmistakeable adoration in Kip's direction. I picked up an imaginary pen, made my palm into a notebook and began to scribble. *Get on with it.*

She stuck out her tongue at me. Relieved that we were back on some kind of normal footing, I returned my attention to Gran. "You really should've told me she was playing truant."

"I was going to. At the weekend, you know, when you were less busy. I didn't want to distract you from your work."

"It's data entry for the council, Gran, not nuclear codes. I really do need to know stuff like that. I..."

"Kip," she said brightly, as if I'd suddenly ceased to exist. This was one of her gifts. She did it so neatly that you could hardly take offence at the interruption. "You know that family's not always easy, don't you? How are things with yours?"

He almost concealed a twitch. She plugged people into the mains when they least expected it, too. "Oh, you know. About the same."

"And did you get in touch with your parents, the way you said you were going to do when I last saw you?"

"Hoi," I said. "Gran, don't put Kip on the spot."

He gave me a sweet smile. "It's all right." It had only taken him a heartbeat to collect himself, but for once I'd seen the process. "They're doing really well, Gran. My dad closed a massive deal in Japan a couple of months back, and Letitia sold one of her sculptures for some fantastic amount. So they're off touring the Far East, having a great time."

She nodded in apparent satisfaction. "And how's lovely Kipton Manor?"

"Fine, as far as I know. The staff take good care of it while Mum and Dad are away."

"I'm sure they do. I'd love to see it one day. Just imagine!"

Kip clearly could. He brightened. Imagination was his thing, the dancing daemon that lured him around the globe in search of his cryptids and monsters. "We'll totally do that. We'll all go—you, me, Oz, Jules. We'll go out by train—that's the best way—and Perkins will pick us up from the station in the Bentley. Dad will bore you to death with tales from the stock market, but Letitia will show you everything."

"The rose garden, and the pond with the fountain, and the place with the funny little bushes all cut short?"

"The box-bush labyrinth, yes. Her studio, too, if she's in the right mood. She's sometimes pretty shy if she's got a new sculpture going on, but that's how it is with really gifted people, I suppose. Dad's the same, in his own way. Not shy, but just... talented. Amazing, off the scale. They both are."

"Of course, for us to visit, you'd have to be speaking to them."

This time the twitch was a jump, too hard and painful to hide. "Gran," I said warningly. "Let him alone."

"Why, Oz, you used to say to me yourself that you didn't understand how Kip could possibly have such nice parents and not appreciate them. How if they'd been

yours, and you'd had all that security and all that money—
"

"*Gran!*" Christ, I couldn't bash her over the head with a pan. I'd spend the rest of my life in jail, and bad as things were, I was still hoping for better days to come. "Kip, I never said those things. Not like that, anyway."

He was making a placating gesture with one hand. "I know, man. You'd have had a good point if you did, though. I know how it must look from the outside."

I hadn't always been on the outside. "It's none of my business now. Or my gran's."

"Don't worry about it, okay?" He pushed back his hair, which was as usual tumbling into his face in rich curls I'd once loved to touch. "You're both right. They're great people, so great that it's been a problem for me. You know, your parents are these high-flying saints, and you're... well, nothing much. A bit of a waste of space."

"That's nonsense, Kip. You've got a PhD in your pocket if you can just stop chasing shadows."

"That's right. So things are going to be different from now on. I always felt like I wasn't good enough—couldn't ever be, no matter what I did. It's never been that I wasn't speaking to them, Gran. They were just better off without me, so after I left for uni, I never got back in touch."

She poked her knitting needle through a loop of acid-green wool. "But now you will. So you and me and Oz and Jules can visit Kipton Manor."

He grinned. "Among other reasons, yeah. Getting onto a PhD programme ought to be enough, even for them."

"That's right. You'll be Dr Kipton then." She leaned sideways far enough to poke me with the blunt end of one needle. "Dr Kipton! Doesn't that sound nice? Oz, I bet you never thought you'd be going out with a doctor."

Kip and I sat staring at one another in the more-than-hush that followed. The boiler thumped into action. Gran's needles clicked. She looked serene as a UN peacekeeper who'd just resolved the differences between warring nations. No point in reproaching her: the diplomat's work was done, leaving only a little old lady who'd sat back to get on with her knitting. "Kip," I said, when I could get my lower jaw working again, "I really didn't mean to... I never even thought about—"

"Me neither," he broke in, coming to my rescue. "Not at all."

There was something very different about the future Dr Kipton today. Through my blood-rush of embarrassment, I tried to work out what had changed. Wait, though—I'd seen it before, hadn't I? Out in the garden, when I'd first had a chance to look him over. The lack of cigarette had been one thing. But he'd been here for hours, and at no point slipped off to the bathroom to return looking shamefaced but more cheerful. Hadn't offered Gran a sherry to excuse the appearance of a quart of White Russian from one of his capacious pockets. His eyes were lucidly clear.

Once more he took pity on me, on my train of thought which had derailed outside the station. "Packed it in, haven't I?" he said, lacing his fingers on the table top and holding my gaze wryly. "It's been... Let's see. Three months, three days."

"But... that's great, Kip. Really, really good. How did you..."

"Oh, don't ask. There's no magic. Just the daily grind of—well, of not drinking." He unclasped his hands and reached across the table to lay one warm fingertip on my knuckles. The shabby little room faded out for me. There was no Gran, no bright-eyed, sharp-eared Jules next door. "The thing is," he said, "although I really never did think about... you and the future Dr Kipton, I wouldn't have come here today if I hadn't been sober. I know why you had to ditch me. I understood that from the start."

My throat ached. "Oh, Kip."

"I mean it. Your dad was gone, and the last thing you needed was a wild-eyed nutcase who chased all his shadows with a glass in one hand and a joint in the other. And I don't know how much difference it makes to you—if you'd ever, ever give me another chance, but... Well, I wanted to let you know." He drew back his hand, and I just barely stopped myself from grabbing it. "Look, don't even think about it now. Your gran's right. You really do have enough to cope with, what with your job and the house and poor Jules getting bullied at school."

I didn't care about any of those things. Suddenly, unforgivably, I really didn't. I remembered what it was like to be twenty years old and out in the world unsupervised for the first time. I'd bedded five lads in as many months. Then I'd met Kip, and my urge to screw around had vanished overnight, melting into the *absence of evidence* glow. Unforeseeably, flirty, fickle Kip had seemed to feel the same.

Then an alarm bell pinged in my head, the same sound I'd heard when checking a schematic for inconsistencies and flaws. There might be wiggle-room in his field of study—acres of it in his off-duty hunt for shadows—but there was none in mine. An engineer had to make sure each bolt was in place, fastened tight. He'd heard me ask Gran about Jules playing truant, but... "How did you know about that?"

"About what?"

"The bullying. The policewoman who was here... She'd finished talking about that before you arrived."

Kip and Gran exchanged a guilty glance. He pulled a face, and I could read it as if he'd written her a note: *I won't drop you in it if I can help it, old lady, but the water's getting hot around here.* She rolled her eyes. *Oh, go ahead. We're busted now.* "To be honest," he said, as if it had never occurred to him to be anything else, "I found out from Gran."

"What? When?" Neither showed any signs of answering. I bumped the heel of my hand off my brow. "Fantastic. The local cops and my ex find out about my sister before I do. For God's sake, Gran—why not get yourself a Facebook account and do our family laundry in front of the whole planet?"

The dreadful old woman just smiled. Did she think selective senility was going to work for her, as well as the occasional deafness and sudden bouts of inability to see? She left it to poor Kip to say, after a mortified pause, "Actually, it was your gran's FB where I read about it."

Somebody here was having a laugh. My gran was eighty two. "You... You're on Facebook?" I ran out of ideas—adequate ones, at any rate. "You haven't even sent me a friend request."

"I did too, John Osman. Yummy Grandmummy 69. You declined me—marked me as spam, an' all. I know you did because you were sitting beside me on the sofa at the time." She peered at me over the top of her specs. "And as for the laundry, young man, I have my groups on Facebook, and they're a big help to me."

I scarcely dared ask. "Groups?"

"Trouble With Angry Teens. Grannies Who Love Too Much."

Oh, she was pulling my leg. "There is *not* a group called Grannies Who..."

"No, of course not. But you'd swallow the idea of a group called TWAT?"

A year ago today, I'd still been enough of a kid that I'd have fallen off my chair and under the table, creased up by my own stupidity. I'd been quick enough to find poor Kip's ABC hilarious. Was that what the year had taught me—to laugh at anyone's misfortunes but my own? I pulled out my mobile and tapped in a search for Yummy Grandmummy. I asked, not knowing why I kept sticking my head in the lion's mouth like this, "Why 69?"

"There are lots of yummy grandmas, believe it or not. I asked Sunil, and he said I should use 69. Apparently it's funny. He wouldn't tell me why."

"My sister is not to go out with Sunil Patwardhan." Oh, there she was. She'd chosen a profile pic from her thirties or forties, when she'd looked—quickly I put my thumb over the thumbnail—startlingly like my mum. Quickly I scanned her timeline. Oh, great. Chapter and verse on all Jules's troubles and wrongdoing, with what I had to admit was an outpouring of compassion and support from other elders saddled with their grandchildren. "I'd have helped you," I muttered, "if you'd bloody well asked."

She cupped a hand behind her ear. "Say again?"

"Kip isn't in any of your groups, Gran. Your profile's on public setting. You're broadcasting to the whole world."

"Oh, am I really? Oh, dear."

She was completely unrepentant. Kip came round to my side of the table and looked at the screen over my shoulder. "She is on public, but she doesn't have many friends. They're all just people like her."

"Plus you."

"Well, I accepted her friend request."

"What about Jules's privacy? She's only thirteen."

"She never mentions her name. And... can I borrow your phone for a sec?" He took it out of my hand and tapped the screen. "She's got location-sharing switched off. Nice one, Gran."

That was pretty sophisticated. I looked at her. "Sunil Patwardhan again?"

"He's a good boy, Oz."

Kip went back to his chair. He didn't sit down: picked the chair up instead, and carried it through the narrow gap between the end of the table and the wall, being careful not to knock Gran's collection of straw donkeys off their shelf. He set the chair down beside me. The gesture startled me so much that I forgot all about Yummy Grandmummy 69. "The point still stands, though," Kip said, whether to me or to Gran I wasn't quite sure. "The point Oz was trying to make. Or was it me? I can't remember."

He'd lost me. I didn't really mind. Being lost with Kip had always been such a wild ride. "What point?"

"You didn't need another rogue element in your life. You couldn't have a boyfriend like me, getting wasted every night. It took me ages to work that out, but once I did, I... I stopped."

I couldn't look at him. I examined the insides of my cupped palms instead. "For me?"

"I'm not meant to say that, am I? I'm meant to say I did it for myself. And I don't think for a second that subtracting the booze and the drugs from my life equals being your boyfriend again and everything back to normal. But we had some good times, didn't we?"

"God, yes."

"I thought I could maybe help you out with some stuff, like entertaining Jules and patching things up around here. So—yeah, I did it for you in a way. It was easier than packing in the fags. Nicotine's the real bitch to quit."

I waited for Gran's mild reproof. *Don't say bitch, Kip.* She'd always treated him as just another grandchild, to be praised or scolded like us. But an uncharacteristic silence was emanating from her end of the table. Finally I raised my head. Her chair was empty. She'd made herself scarce without a sound. She was in the living room, her back turned, apparently taking the deepest interest in Jules's homework. I waited until I could speak without a treacherous wobble in my voice. "I missed you."

"I missed you too. Like stink."

My heart lifted and lightened for the first time in months. "More than the fags?"

"Well, that was touch and go."

"Thanks. You make it sound like you'd be coming back as Gran's odd-job man or Jules's carer, though."

He shrugged. His half-smile was in place, but there was yearning written all over him too. "Well, I've missed having someone to look after. And I liked our odd jobs."

"Me too. If you did come back, though, I'd want it to be as my..." I hesitated. *Boyfriend* sounded frivolous, for a man with a steady job and bills to pay. Still, as Gran kept pointing out, I was hardly a pensioner yet. "As my boyfriend. Obviously."

He lit up like the sun. Without thinking, I got to my feet. His arms were open for me again. Closing my eyes like a diver on the brink, I let him pull me down into his lap. How childish I'd felt when he'd first invited me there, and how soon I'd got over my awkwardness, the sense of being all elbows and knees! How often after that I'd availed myself of the pleasure, on battered student-flat sofas and in pubs when the seats had run out, in the back of overcrowded taxis and cars... It should have felt stupid to me now, grown up as I was, but it didn't. It just felt sexy and safe and good. I opened my eyes to find his earnestly on mine, their shadows in abeyance, full of questioning hope. I laid one hand on his face and leaned in.

Jules burst into the kitchen. The door bounced off the wall, deepening the hole already gouged there by the knob. "Yes!" she yelled, tossing her notebook in the air and beginning a wild dance. "Oz and Kip are sitting in a tree! Oz is sitting on the Kipster's knee!" She leapt from foot to foot, then shot over to grab poor Kip by the head and plant a squelching kiss on his brow, which was more than I'd had the chance to do. "You're back! Now there'll be some fun around here again. Honestly, Kip, it's been like the bloody grave."

I tried to assert myself. "Don't say *bloody*, Jules."

"Bloody, bloody, bloody, bloody! Kip and Oz are more than buddies!"

"Are you sure you want this gig, Kip? You can see she's insufferable."

"I can see that, yes." He gave me a squeeze. He flashed a smile at Gran, who had come to stand in the doorway, nodding benignly as if she and she alone had brought this all about. "I do still want the gig, though. Yes, please."

Chapter Four
In A Tree

Being back with Kip was everything I'd dreamed of on grim Monday mornings at desk six, row eight. I could see it all so clearly now. What a pompous little dick I'd become! My dad had left, and I'd overreacted. I was proud of myself for this insight. Still level-headed, though. Still responsible. I'd hang on to desk six until a better chance came along, but with Kip at my side, I could at least see that the chances were there.

Then there was the sex. We went at it like a pair of Kip's ravening ABCs, shaking the walls of his flat. We weren't virgin terrain to each other anymore, no longer clumsy and tender and awkward, but it was fantastic, of course. I loved every minute.

He took me out to the pub where a lot of the sciences staff congregated for lunch at the weekends, and there we saw Professor Leighton-Smythe, who came over to our table without asking and didn't need reminding of my name. Not at all—he shook my hand heartily, told me about a new programme for undergrads in full-time work. Evenings and weekends, residential crammer weeks. Tough to do a whole degree that way, but I should manage it easily with just my last year to complete. EON was still hiring. The engineering halls and labs would be open to me, provided I undertook to loan no equipment of any kind to Joe Kipton.

Kip, cradling his orange juice, just smiled. He could see my fresh chances bursting around me like fireworks too, I could tell. He had lit the fuse. I was so bloody happy—wildly, edgily happy, with an excitement to meet and match that of Jules when I waved her and Kip off for their first spin in the MX-5. And Kip was as good as his word: turning up clear-eyed and early at Gran's to help me fix the guttering and the missing tiles on the roof.

He didn't even talk to me about his monsters. And again I felt proud, because if he was turning my life around, maybe I was doing the same for him. We worked, loved, laughed, and everything was just the way I'd dreamed it would be if only Kip could stay clean.

Yep. Amazing. Definitely the best five and a half days of my life.

Chapter Five
Bollards

My phone began to ring right in the middle of my performance review.

Normally I'd have switched it off. Little tick though he was, Supervisor Cedric had a right to forbid personal calls in office hours. The juniors used to joke about it, and this past week I'd even felt like joining them. *Entering the office. Going dark for comms.* Reception was terrible anyway. Was it the extra sheet of concrete in the walls, a Cold War measure installed in the days when people still thought they'd want to survive a nuclear strike? I tried for an apologetic glance as I pulled the phone out of my pocket. I didn't really care, though, not the way I'd have cared the week before. I'd continue to give my best to this mind-numbing work until the day I could leave it forever, but if Cedric had issues with my three extra minutes in the toilet—Gran was right, stress did play havoc with my guts—he could take a running jump. I had a warm tingle in my spine at the prospect of telling him so. My blood was up, the doors to my future open.

"Personal calls aren't allowed, Mr Osman."

"No, Cedric—er, Mr Beaver." Christ, why wouldn't he let us use first names? Cedric wasn't too bad, a nice old-fashioned sound to it, but what made him think that *Beaver* was ever going to cause anything but explosions of childish laughter every time he left a room? "Sorry. Won't happen again."

It promptly did. I banged my thumb down on the cutoff key, but not before a tinny bar or two of *Paranoid* had shrilled through the air. That was odd. Gran knew the rules even better than I did. A mottle of purple was rising from beneath Cedric's collar. "Sorry, Mr Beaver. I'm going to have to return this."

"You're going to have to *what?*"

He'd definitely come off worst in his recent skirmish with the old lady. Now he was about to show me who was the man, even if his dad *had* been a fence for minor electrical goods down the market. *At least I still have a dad*, he could have told me, and won the fight forever as I crumpled to the floor in defeat. Nothing so pitiful would ever have occurred to him, though. He was a proper grown-up, with grown-up concerns.

And so was I. "That was my grandmother," I said flatly. "She knows not to call when I'm at work. If she has, it's an emergency, so I have to phone her back."

I didn't even bother to leave the room. I got out of my hot seat and went to the window. The 1950s councillors must have reinforced the glass in here too:

when Gran picked up, there was so much static on the line that I was only getting about four words in ten.

The first four were *Kip, car* and *police station*. Then there was a flurry I recognised, the distinct sound of an old lady trying to find her purse, house keys, headscarf and handbag all at once. She'd had a cold for the last few days, the first of the winter bugs that settled so fiercely on her lungs. "Gran, listen. Don't you leave the house, okay? I'll go to the station. I'll go now."

The line went dead. If a Beaver's looks could kill, I'd have swiftly followed suit. "Where do you imagine you're going," he rumbled, "in the middle of your none-too-satisfactory performance review?"

I looked at him in disgust. "For God's sake, Cedric. If you can find someone who can touch-type faster than I do, and get from his desk to the bog and back in two minutes flat, hire him. I've got to go."

***

Amazing, the range of possibilities that rushes through your head during a twenty-minute drive. *Kip's car broke down and a friendly bobby gave him a lift to the police station.* That one was fine, and all too likely. I'd buy him a decent car one day. If Mazdas were his pleasure, I'd get him a new one, top of the range, a Love Machine with a vengeance. When I had my job with EON. Because I loved him.

Kip crashed his car and the police need you to identify the body. I trod on the brake too hard, mistimed my biting point and stalled out at the lights. Breathing deeply, I found neutral and started her up again. This was ridiculous. People got called to the morgue for identifications, didn't they? Not the local cop shop. In either case—another broken Mazda or the crowning disaster of my life—why would anyone have called Gran?

I found a parking space in the little tarmac square outside the station. Someone had tried to brighten the place with some planters, but the frost had hit here as well as in Gran's garden, and all the busy lizzies were long dead. I locked up my car, looking around anxiously for Kip's, and then I jogged inside.

The police in our town weren't the natural enemy of students and free spirits everywhere. For one thing most of us knew one another—the coppers, the spirits, the students. For another, even the least ambitious of bobbies would want out from behind a desk here. I felt common cause with Alice Jones, the officer behind the reception counter. I'd been at school with her. She was listlessly tapping at a keyboard, plainly bored to tears.

My arrival didn't cheer her up. "Oh," she said. "It's Oz, isn't it? John Osman. We'd hoped your grandma could come."

"She's not well. I told her to stay at home. Why on earth do you want my gran?"

"Have you spoken to her? Didn't she tell you?"

"The line was bad. Look, is Joe Kipton here? Is he okay?"

"He had a bit of a prang in his car. He's all right. But he damaged the street furniture, so..."

"The what?"

"Street furniture. You know, those plastic bollards they have at junctions."

"You call those things street furniture?"

She frowned and sat up straight. "Does it matter what we call them? Will you be able to drive your friend home?"

My friend? He was my lover, the joy of my life. Small towns had disadvantages as well as the perks, though—plenty of 'em—and I didn't press the point. I just wanted to see him. "Of course. Why do I need to, though? Did he write off the car?"

"Probably, although that's not why..."

She tailed off in relief as the door behind her opened. Kip appeared in the doorway, closely followed by the same brisk young constable who'd come to Gran's house the week before. Kip was white as death. It was more than that—he looked heartsick, ready to sink through the carpet and die.

The police station was old fashioned, built in the days before sheet-glass security screens. The counter top still had a flap you could lift to get through to the other side. I grabbed it and lifted. Nobody made a move to stop me. What the hell had they been doing to him? I strode over to him, tried to take him in my arms.

He made a strange, cringing move back. He'd taught me everything I knew about touch, the fearless sweetness of contact outside the bedroom. He'd held my hand, unconcealed, along some of the roughest streets in town. Not once had he avoided me. "Kip," I said, a rasp of shock in my voice. "What's happened? Has somebody hurt you?"

"No. No, they've been good to me, Oz. They just did what they had to."

"What do you mean?" I couldn't wait for his reply: rounded on the desk officer and the constable, who'd gone to look at the computer screen. "If you think he was driving drunk, you must've got a false reading. He's been on the wagon for..." How long would it be now? "Three months, a week and one day. He's been working really hard. And he never got in the car when he'd been drinking anyway. He just wouldn't."

The constable straightened up. He wasn't much older than I was, and I could tell he was having no fun here today. "You're John Osman, aren't you? We met the other day."

"That's right. Now what's going on?"

"Mr Kipton didn't test positive for alcohol. He..."

"See?" I knew it. Not a single second's doubt. "I told you."

"Mr Osman, please. He failed a drug screen for procodone, an opioid painkiller."

"So he had a headache. So what?"

"There's new guidance on procodone, the amount you can have in your system and still drive."

"If it's new, he can't have known."

"Right. A lot of people don't, so we're just giving warnings and advice when it's a medical dose, the amount you might take for a headache."

"Is that what's happened here? Warnings and advice?"

"No." He turned to Kip. "Mr Kipton, I don't have to speak to your friend if you'd rather I didn't."

Kip made a raw sound of misery. "It's okay. Tell him, please."

"All right. He had a very large dose in his system. Any more and we'd have had to take him to hospital. But he says he's used to taking that much, and—"

"And you *listened* to him?" I wasn't absorbing any of the wider ramifications of this. All I could think of was Kip, running around with a huge dose of procodone—something I'd never heard of, but surely it couldn't be good—in his blood. "He should be in hospital anyway. What are you playing at?"

"Oz, don't. I've declined medical treatment. I'm not worth it."

"Don't say that."

"I'm not about to drop down dead. There's no paracetamol in the stuff I take, nothing to hurt my liver. And this kind of dose is... normal for me."

"What are you talking about?" I reached for him again, and again he recoiled from me with that alien, terrible cringe. "Kip, love. What's *wrong*?"

"Oh, Oz."

"Tell me. Whatever's happened here, we'll fix it. There's nothing we can't put right."

All the time I'd been talking to him, a racket had been going on: a young female voice a couple of rooms away, veering around between sobs, shrieks and babble. I was so used to a certain degree of this at home that I'd tuned it out. In the dead silence that had fallen between me and Kip, the voice became real at last.

The familiarity had made me deaf to it. I folded my arms and began to listen. And finally I understood why they'd called Gran first. "Juliet," said another familiar voice from behind the office door, kindly as ever but beginning to sound a bit fraught. "If you don't calm down, we're going to have to take measures of restraint."

"Oh! Right! Try it, if you think you're hard enough!"

"*Juliet.* That's your brother's car in the car park, isn't it? Come through here right now."

If Kip had come quietly, Jules was putting up a fight. The door swung open again, and Sergeant Claire appeared, the struggling brat in her grip. She half-wrestled Jules past me and Kip and out through the gap in the counter. "You are making a world of trouble for yourself, young lady. Look, there's your brother. There's Oz."

Jules tossed her hair out of her eyes. It took her a moment to register me, and then to my dismay she tore out of Claire's grasp and ran to ball up in a visitor's chair in the corner. "Screw Oz!"

She was way further out along the branch of her crazy tree than after her shoplifting jaunt. Even I'd never seen her this bad. Sergeant Claire began to look concerned. "Are you afraid of your brother, Juliet? Would you like to speak to someone?"

"It's *Jules*, not Juliet! No, I'm not afraid of him. He's just a boring old fart, and now he'll dump Kip and I'll never see him again, and nobody will ever have any fun again as long as they bloody well live." She sprang back out of the chair, stared around her like a hunted fox, and darted out through the reception room door, with Claire—after the shortest pause and eye-roll—in hot pursuit.

Why would I ever dump him? I was stupid with shock: it took me long seconds to see. The trouble was that, even in my darkest moments, my bleakest loss of faith, it would never have occurred to me that Kip would have a skinful of any kind—drink, drugs, anything—then put my sister into his car.

He was watching the penny fall. He didn't try to apologise. Sorry is something you say when you hope or expect to be forgiven. "I had to have something, Oz," he said, his voice flat with despair. "I just had to have something."

***

The officers had made themselves as scarce as the confines of the room allowed. The constable was on the phone to Gran, not a task I envied him, but he was on his own. We all were. Kip had found his way to the door in a series of small retreats. He was good at fading, blending into the woodwork when he didn't want to be seen. I reached past him and seized the door handle. "Don't you dare fucking vanish."

"I'm not. They're done with me, though. The car's scrap, and I've got a year's ban anyway—where would I go?"

The world was wide. Alaska, Canada, Wales. The bottom of the river, if I didn't ease up. I could see what I was doing to him but I couldn't stop. "I don't really care, but you don't get to shuffle off and pretend nothing happened."

"Oz, please. I feel sick."

"I'm taking you to casualty on the way home. There's..." I stopped, my throat in sudden painful spasm. "There's some seats in the corridor outside. The door's open, so you'll get some fresh air. Wait there."

Claire must have chased Jules in a circle. I'd have laughed if I'd had a laugh left in me. As Kip slipped away from me, Jules burst back in through the door behind the counter. "You're all so stupid," she declared, banging her palms down an inch from the desk officer's keyboard. "So stupid and so wrong. Kip saved me, okay? This guy in a fuck-off great four-by-four came tanking down on our side of the road. Kip crashed the car because he swerved to get out of his way."

"It's not the point," Claire said breathlessly, catching her up. "You're an intelligent girl, Jules. I know he's your friend, but you have to see—"

"Actually," Alice Jones interrupted, still tapping absently at her board, "that does fit the traffic constable's remarks about the scene. The tyre marks on the road and the angle of impact with the bollard, I mean."

"See?" Jules demanded, in exactly my own tone of triumph when I'd thought Kip was sober. "He's a hero. He's good. And you're all... persecuting him. If I don't care that he took something then drove me, why should you?" She gave up her unequal battle for justice in a rotten world. "I want to go home now. I want my gran."

I didn't dare touch her. Already I was marked down in Claire's mental files as an abusive elder brother. But Jules had been wrong—I did have to be her mam as well as her dad, and maybe one day her grandma too, though my blood ran slow at the thought. Somehow, despite her cold and the bus ride, I'd thought the old girl might have made it here by now. "I'll take you home. I know what you mean about us not minding if *you* don't, but it's not your decision to make. Not Kip's either. We'll all go back to Gran's, though, and... have a cup of tea or something. Come on."

But of course the row of seats in the corridor was empty. The open doorway too, as if no such man—no such monster, no such cryptid bloody beast—as Joe Kipton had ever existed.

Chapter Six
The Gransformation

Gran's cold had got much worse. I found her that day in the hall, hunched up on the little stool where she sat to pull on her shoes and boots, her headscarf tied tightly in place, her coat buttoned up to her chin, blue in the face with the effort to breathe. Jules and I ran around, united by shared fear. Found her inhalers and nebuliser, helped her upstairs. Jules, with a sudden sweet competence I'd never seen before, undressed her and put her to bed, while I entered into the negotiations it took to get our GP to make a house call.

I spent the rest of the next three days, with breaks for my work shifts and short hours of restless sleep, more or less on the phone. Not within the radiation-proof walls of Beaver's little kingdom, of course—I'd proved to myself once and for all that I needed this job, that chances were like fireflies or anomalous big cats, forever fading back into the dreamscape from which they'd emerged. I'd accepted a reprimand and the loss of my afternoon's wages without a murmur. Who the bloody hell cared? Everything was grey again now: always had been, if I'd had the sense to see.

Still, I phoned and phoned. I had a daily list: the local hospitals, Kip's new flat, his mobile. I sat in the chilly parlour to work through this routine, as far out of Gran's earshot and Jules's as I could get. I added to the list his university department, although my enquiries there were discreet. I didn't want to get him into any hot water there, if he hadn't already jumped.

Water. Jumping. Sick to my soul, I put Alice Jones on my list, and she, with a certain flat kindness and no questions asked, informed me every day that no young men had been hauled out of any local rivers, or found overdosed on booze and pills on or off campus.

To the best of her knowledge, but the world was wide. I stalked Kip's FB timeline, and saw that Yummy Grandmummy had been doing the same. Not subtly, either. Plaintive messages, all in caps, more on the lines of a *wanted, dead or alive* poster from the Wild West. *If anyone knows the whereabouts of Joe Kipton...* No-one did, but some of the comments came from a profile called Cryptid Ken. I joined Ken's group in the guise of an enthusiastic cryptozoologist and lurked, hoping someone there might give the game away.

What was I expecting? *Hey, Kip and I found Sasquatch in British Columbia!* And a photo to prove it, happy lads with frost-chapped faces, grinning for a selfie while the beast waved its arms in the background. And what would I do if ever such a miracle appeared? If, one day, I phoned his flat or his mobile and he simply picked up?

He'd ruined everything. Even if I found him, what did I mean to do about that?

Nothing, of course. I told myself that I just wanted to know he was safe somewhere, as safe as someone like him could ever be. I just wanted to know he was alive.

I wanted this with increasing intensity. Another week passed, and by the end of it I was tight-clenched with fear, twitching every time my phone beeped. I gave up even the pretext of a social life I'd had before my birthday tea. I spent my evenings with Gran, who was now well enough to come downstairs for a few hours each day. She, Jules and I sat in a line on the sofa like three monkeys, staring at the TV.

We wound up watching some strange things. On the second Friday night after Kip's disappearance—fish-and-chips night in our house, eaten on the sofa in deference to Gran's health—a frail, beautiful girl was explaining, with huge charm and intelligence, why she liked to be multiply pierced and then strung up by hooks from the ceiling. I let this wash over me for a while, no longer even concerned that Jules might be getting ideas. Gran too seemed to be taking it all calmly in. Then she said, out of the grease-fragrant blue, "If I were you, Oz, I'd ask Kip's mum where he's gone."

I dropped a handful of chips into Jules's lap, making her yelp and slap my wrist. She and I reacted to stress in different ways. I could barely eat, and she couldn't stop. I'd been sliding my unwanted food onto her plate for days now, guiltily aware I wasn't doing either of us any favours. "Kip's mum? What—Lady Letitia, or whatever she's called?"

"That's right. Lady Letitia."

"She won't know, will she? He hasn't spoken to her in years."

"Still, she might be able to help. She's his mother, after all."

"I don't even know where she lives, Gran."

She had recovered enough to give me a withering look from her end of the sofa. "Kipton Manor, of course."

"I've got no idea where that is. I could look on the internet, I suppose."

"Don't bother. It's in Lower Shilby."

"Lower... No, don't be daft. That's only twenty miles or so away from here, one of those crap little villages where everyone used to work in the mines and now it's all gone."

"Well, there are nice parts too. Anyway, that's where Kip's mum lives. You know that, Oz. He told us."

I was pretty sure he never had. Still, I didn't want to argue. Jules was still mechanically eating her chips, but I could tell she wanted to grab me by the throat and squeeze until I agreed to go to Lower Shilby, or Upper or Lower Anywhere that might by any chance help us find Kip. "All right," I said cautiously. "I'll have a run up there tomorrow, okay? I don't much fancy my chances of busting into Kipton Manor, mind."

"That's a good boy. You don't know until you try."

I returned my attention to the TV. Now the fragile girl was talking to a group of Japanese teenagers dressed as anime characters and rapturously caressing one another. "I don't know," I said grumpily after a while. "If any great fat-arsed president or dictator decided to march us off to World War Three, he'd never be able to raise an army to do it. All the kids would be too busy tattooing each other and tying themselves up."

"You almost sound as if that might be a good thing."

"Well. Look at them. They're doing every nutcase bloody thing in the world except hurt one another, aren't they?"

Jules turned to stare at me, a chip halfway into her mouth. Gran in her turn leaned forward, eyes wide. "Who are you," she said after a moment, "and what have you done with my Oz?"

I was taken aback. Did the pair of them think I'd rather have World War Three? I'd voted Remain, of course, not being lost to all human decency, but since Dad had left I had, I supposed, developed certain views. That young people should pull their socks up and get a job. That responsibility and a sense of duty was no bad thing, and maybe free higher education—a concept held in the highest regard by my mum, Gran and Jules—wasn't a natural right after all.

Christ, where had I gone? Who was I, and what had I done with Oz? I opened my mouth to reply, but somehow in the midst of all these thoughts I'd stumbled my way to the edge of tears. "Jules," said Gran calmly.

"Go into the kitchen and find some occupation. Close the door behind you."

"But, Gran—"

"Now, please, madam."

Resentfully she stalked off. Gran handed me a tissue, though the urge to cry had peaked and passed like an unfinished sneeze. I couldn't remember how it felt to let go and weep. I blew my nose, and sat for a few moments staring at the magnificent phoenix being pricked and inked into someone's skin. I wondered if Kip had ever gone off chasing one of those. "Why did you invite him round for my birthday, Gran?"

She began a new row of stitches. I was starting to suspect that the acid-green monstrosity dangling from her needles was my Christmas sweater. "I've been waiting for you to ask," she said calmly. "Terrible thing to do, wasn't it? I should have respected your life choices."

Despite myself I chuckled. "Have you been at the self-help shelf in Smith's again? You'll have to buy one of those books one day. You can't stand and read them in the aisle."

"Of course not. The assistant brings me a chair. Actually, it was one of my friends in TWAT who gave me the life-choice advice."

Oh, my God. I'd always thought the Angry Teen was Jules. "Gran, I'm in my twenties."

"Not when you first met Kip, you weren't. Nineteen is a young age these days to meet the love of your life, but these things happen."

"They don't. At least... He's not."

She nodded sympathetically, then—as often—carried on as if she hadn't heard me. "So when your birthday came, I asked him. He took a lot of persuading. You must have been very firm."

I'd been savage. I'd ripped him off me like a parasite. "I had to."

"I know you think so. But he was good for you, Oz. Those few days the other week, you looked like a lad your own age again. You forgot all about your dad, and even Jules for a while."

"But he's not. Good, I mean. Look what happened."

"Well, that's something else I learned from my groups. Addicts lie. It's not our fault that they do, and sometimes it's not theirs either. What we've got to choose is what we can live with. We have to draw an emotional line in the sand."

She must have bought one of the books after all, or eaten it. I couldn't cope with these sudden... *gransformations*, my mind supplied, and a silent surge of laughter rocked me. "That's what I did, Gran. I drew my line—after Dad left, and again the other day. It's you who keeps coming in like the sea to wash it out."

She hit the mute button on the remote control. Then she laid down her knitting, took off her glasses and turned to me. I braced. No glib, pre-packaged slice of pop psychology was about to come from her now. With silenced TV, empty hands and bare face had she laid down the law in all the toughest moments of our family life. "Listen to me, Oz. When I was younger, I used to smoke."

69

No need to tell me that. There she was in all the photo albums—in the back garden, at picnics on the beach, standing in front of the tower on Blackpool prom, forever with cigarette in hand. Granddad, too. The house around me was stained and still faintly pungent from all those days, all those burnt-up moments. "Don't try and tell me that's the same as drinking and popping pills. You and my granda worked all your lives. You never let anyone down."

"I want to tell you that the adverts made it look fashionable, and nobody really knew the damage it would do. But by the time your mum was born, that wasn't true anymore. They'd taken the ads off TV and the racing cars. We knew. So I told myself every day I would stop, for Jenny's sake if not my own. But I never did. And Jenny grew up with what we used to call a weak chest, and she started sneaking fags behind the bike shed at school when she was twelve."

"It's harder to stop smoking than almost anything else. Kip said."

"You're trying to forgive me, aren't you? Jenny tried, too. Must be in the genes. But you know what she did the first time she saw me with a fag in my hand near your cot, when she brought you home from hospital? She told me I'd never see her or my grandson again. She meant it, too. So I stopped. Of course it was too late for her."

"She'd stopped too, though."

"The moment she knew she was pregnant. She'd already been diagnosed with COPD."

I leaned forward. I laced my fingers around the back of my skull, as if that would shield me. "Why are you telling me this?"

"Because some people can stop doing bad things, and some can't, not even when other people's lives depend on it. And some can forgive that, and some can't. And there's no way of telling in advance what type you'll fall in love with, and..." She laid a hand on my knee, cautiously, as if no longer sure she had the right. "And what type you are. Oz, I know you don't like talking about your dad. But he did leave some money for you and Jules."

I couldn't keep up with her switches. "I don't need his bloody money."

"No, of course. You have your job. If you needed a week or so off, though, and a bit of a cushion if little Cedric Beaver doesn't take kindly to that... Well. I tell you what I'll do. I'll put some into your account, and then you can have it if you want it, and ignore it if you don't."

I groaned. I put my hand on hers, though, and squeezed it gently tight. "There's no need. And I don't really have time, Gran. Getting down to the high street with you, I mean, and queuing for ages in Lloyds..."

"Oh, don't be ridiculous, Oz. I do have internet banking."

Chapter Seven
Lady Letitia At Home

I drove for miles through the lanes around Lower Shilby. Gran had been right: there were some nice parts, reclaimed scars of opencast now returning to salt flats and seabirds, old pit heaps re-landscaped into dunes. If you stood on the top of the tallest of these—which I did, hoping to catch a glimpse of the towers of Kipton Manor, the observatory dome Kip had described—the views swept northwest all the way to the Cheviots.

But there's nothing less English Heritage than a mined-out seaside town in winter. I gave up my search after two hours and went to park outside the local Spar shop on the outskirts. It occurred to me that I shouldn't arrive empty-handed when visiting Lady Letitia, and although she was probably used to better things than supermarket flowers, there were some nice winter chrysanths in their bucket outside the shop. I picked out a bunch for Gran too, and then, after a reluctant moment, added one for Jules.

When I emerged a few minutes later, a group of lads had taken possession of my car. Of course. Alien vehicle in the parking lot, a natural magnet. Not in the same way as the Mazda, but I did keep my little runabout clean, a pine fragrance tree hanging from the mirror. Jules feigned death-by-boredom whenever she had to get in. Two of the lads were perched on the bonnet. Already my paintwork was marked with rubbery scuff from their heels. Another couple were busy at the back, making the first two laugh by bouncing the car as hard as they could on her springs.

The trouble was that I didn't care. My sister was in meltdown, my gran had most probably killed my ma, and my dad had chosen his fresh new kids in the States over the unsatisfactory pair he'd spawned here. "Hoi," I said tiredly, coming to a halt by the driver's door. "Do any of you know where Kipton Manor is?"

They gawped. I didn't blame them. I'd dressed up for today, thinking I'd stand a better chance of getting in to see Lady Letitia if I wore a smart suit and my charcoal lambswool sweater. My arms were full of flowers. The boys at the back quit testing my suspension. "Kipton Manor?" one of them echoed, as if I'd just stepped out of Downton Abbey. That was a bit steep. My dad had taught me not to trade clarity for local colour in my speech, but I sounded like the northeast coast lad I was. "That's right," I said, patiently as I could manage. "Kipton Manor, where Sir George and Lady Letitia live."

Had I stepped on a wasp's nest here? You could always set your watch back a couple of decades in the pit villages, and when world leaders decide to legitimise hate and xenophobia, the fallout drifts down everywhere, even into unknown, cobwebby corners like this. The lads were still staring. I was used to returning such looks with interest. For years I'd ridden the late bus home after a Friday night clubbing, in skin-tight jeans, spangly T-shirt and just a touch of mascara. I still wasn't scared—felt as if nothing could scare me now, except perhaps a call from Alice Jones. Things could turn awkward, though. It was four to one.

Then, to my bewilderment, one of the boys on the bonnet slid off. Had he taken some kind of fit? He crumpled to his knees on the tarmac and began to whack his palms off the ground. "Kipton Manor!"

The other three broke into howls. I took a step back, frowning. "Lady Letitia!" one of them managed, hanging on to my wing mirror for support. "Sir bloody George!"

If I'd liked them, I'd have dropped an imaginary mic and said I'd be here all week. I was painfully tired, though, gritty with anxiety and loss. Whatever all this was, I couldn't be arsed with it. Stepping over the lad on the ground, I opened the door and got in.

Before I could close up, one of the idiots grabbed the frame of the door. I'd have smacked his hand away, but something in his face—a gleam of intelligence, an inexplicable pity—made me pause. "Kipton Manor!" he choked out again, as if it was the best joke in the world. "You want to try Staines Road, mate. Third *manor* on the left, past the chip shop."

***

I'd noticed Staines Road on my way in. The savoury drift of chips had caught my hungry lunchtime attention as I'd driven past. I wasn't hungry now. I counted doors—it was hard to count houses, so tightly had they been packed in behind their pebbledash—and pulled in by the kerb.

The terrace fronted straight onto the street. I tapped with my knuckles on the door of the third manor, unable to see a knocker or bell. Small scuffling sounds came from behind the door. After a moment it creaked open to reveal a nine or ten-year-old girl, her face on a level with mine.

She was standing on a chair. She must have pulled it into place to unfasten the latch. "Hello," I said uncertainly. "Er... maybe I've got the wrong house."

"Who are you?"

"I'm Oz." I was rapidly losing any sense that I'd found Kipton Manor, but in for a penny. "I've come to see Lady Letitia. Who are you?"

She glanced back over her shoulder. Then she announced, loud enough to be heard by somebody in the next room, "I'm Kip, of course."

My head spun. "Of course."

She offered me a brusque nod. "You look nice. Letty said to let the nice ones in."

Maybe the flowers had done the trick. Taking them delicately from me, she hopped down off her chair and vanished through the only door in the cramped passageway ahead. I lifted the chair out of the way, fastened the latch behind me and followed.

In the centre of the living room, Lady Letitia was holding court from the depths of a chintz armchair. She was dressed in pyjamas and a dressing gown so close in pattern to that of the chair that she almost disappeared. Her thin frame and faded curls added to her air of transience, and I suddenly understood where Kip—my Kip—had picked up his own weird fragility, the sense I'd had even when he should have been most brightly present to me that he had one foot in an otherworld. That he could have melted right out of my arms.

The little girl had laid my flowers across Letitia's lap, where they blazed most horribly against the two sets of chintz. Letitia stroked the petals tenderly. "That was so kind of you, John."

"They're nothing special, I'm afraid. Just from the corner shop." I was distracted by the table against the far wall. Set out on its melamine top was a startling array of pill bottles and little cardboard boxes with prescription labels. "I... I'm sorry to see you're not well."

"I'm as well as I can be. Kip, bring that chair in from the hall, please, so John can sit down. I have the furniture set out like this, you see, so that I'm not always looking at those pills. So I can't just reach out for them. It doesn't help much, but it does keep me under some kind of control. To get to them from here, I'd have to crawl."

"I'm sorry," I said again, helplessly. The little girl came tramping stoically in with the chair—what was I thinking, not to have gone and fetched it myself?—and I sat down in front of her ladyship.

John. The little kid had brought a chair for John. John had been thanked for the flowers. An easy guess, I supposed, for some poor chintz-wrapped nutcase who'd forgotten the age and gender of her only son. "Most people call me Oz," I said uneasily. "But it's fine, if you'd rather—"

"No, no. You're John Osman. If you don't mind my saying so, Kip thinks the sun shines out of your arse."

Not the most ladylike speech. The kid standing patiently by Letitia's armchair didn't seem fazed by it. Suddenly she took pity on me. "Letty calls all of us Kip," she said, looking up for permission and receiving a sweet, spaced-out smile. "Me and my brothers and sisters from next door who look after her, and my mam and dad, too. She couldn't let anyone else but Kip come in and sort her out, you see. Could you, Letty?"

"Oh, no." She shuddered, then leaned forward earnestly in her chair. "The thing is, I'm often aware of it. Who people really are, I mean, and how crazy I must be the rest of the time. This little girl's called April, for example. Go and fetch John a cup of tea, please, April. He looks as if he needs one."

I tried to find a foothold on the cracked sheet-ice of this conversation. "But... out of the people you call Kip, there's only one who knows my name." *Or would have an opinion about the sun and my arse.* "And he hasn't seen you for years."

"Yes, he said he was going to tell you that. To make things simpler."

"Simpler... You *have* seen him, then?"

"My Kip? The real one, my real grown-up boy?"

"Yes." My heart thumped painfully in hope. "Does he come to see you here?"

"Why, yes. Every week. He gets my groceries and hoovers the carpets, even the one on the stairs." Shadows passed over her pale face. "Last week he didn't come. Didn't phone, either. Where is he, John?"

"I was hoping you could tell me."

But she was drifting again. Her forehead was damp, her hands tightening on the arms of the chair. "Why do you call me Lady Letitia? I'm just Letty Kipton."

"Kip said... Well, he made up a story about you. A nice one."

She brightened. "I told him to do that. The very best story he could, to help him get as far away as possible from me."

"I don't think he wants to get away."

"In his mind, I mean. So he could get away from me in his mind. Am I a lady, then, in the story he told you?"

I wanted to pick her up by her ankles, turn her upside down and shake her until clues about Kip's whereabouts fell out. At the same time I was desperately sorry for her, marooned here in her pyjamas. "Yes. Lady Letitia of Kipton Manor."

"Oh, I *like* that. What else am I? What else do I have?"

"He said you were a sculptor, a brilliant one."

"A sculptor! Like Barbara Hepworth, you mean?"

"Very modern, he said, and your pieces fetch thousands of pounds."

"How lovely. Am I shy about my work, shy and modest?"

"You won't let anyone into your studio when you're busy with a new piece."

"And..." She began a tiny rocking movement with her upper body. "And do I have a husband in this manor house of mine? Or am I all alone?"

"No, of course not. You've got a nice husband called George. He's some kind of investment banker, I think, and the two of you travel all over the world. Kipton Manor has an observatory and a maze of little bushes. You and George have a Bentley, and a chauffeur to drive it called Perkins."

"Perkins!" She broke into laughter. "Oh, Kip. Perkins was the name of his first dog. If he's upset, you know, he might have gone to Camp Saucer."

"Is he into UFOs as well?"

"UFOs? No, I don't think so, just his strange beasts and... Oh, I see. Not like flying saucer—*Saorsa*, the Gaelic word for freedom."

"Camp Freedom?"

"That's right. Lots of them go there. Some of them never come back."

I felt as if the weird thread I'd been following had just snapped in my hands, or ended in a tangled knot. Camp Freedom could be anything—at best a Canadian outpost for cryptozoologists on the run, at worst poor Letty's metaphor for suicide or insanity. "Is it... a real place, Letty?"

Before she could reply, a thump shook the front door. She cringed and tucked her feet up on the chair, like a kid avoiding monsters under the bed. "What was that?" I asked. "Someone trying to get in?"

"It's children. They like to knock and run away."

I'd gone through a brief phase of liking the same thing. When Gran had found out what I'd been up to, she'd taken her slipper to the seat of my pants—a punishment often threatened but scarcely ever deployed. The thump came again. I'd learned my lesson well: no game, no joke, could ever excuse the frightening of the old and the frail. I stood up. "They don't seem to get the running-away part."

"They will. Or Kip will chase them. Kip? Kip!"

April shot back into the room as if fired from a gun. "Yes, Letty?"

"Don't call me Letty like that. I'm your mother! Go and get rid of those boys."

The little girl rushed to obey. Gently I got between her and the door and turned her round. "Leave it to me this time, okay?"

"No! She told me to do it."

"That's because she thinks you're a grown-up lad. Go finish making the tea."

She gave me a look of desperation but stood aside. I'd built up a good head of steam by this time, what with my comedy act in the car park and this house with its tantalising traces of the man I wanted to find. I yanked the door wide, and apparently my face was enough: the four or five brats on the kerb leapt skywards, then scattered like shrapnel from a bomb. "That's right," I yelled after them needlessly. "And don't you little sods come back!"

A hand closed in the tail of my jacket. April, towing me away from the door as if her life depended on it... "What's the matter?" I demanded. "They're gone now."

"Don't shout any more. Come inside."

"They're just kids. All they needed was a good fright."

"You don't get it, do you?"

What didn't I get? Before I could ask, the sight of Letty in her chair answered the question. The only pieces of furniture in the room were the armchair and the table. If she'd wanted to be further away from the drugs and the temptations, she could have sat nearer the windows. But if she did that...

A rock hit the glass at high speed, shattering the nearest of the three panes. "Shit," I said helplessly, and made another dive for the door. But this time poor April grabbed my arm and hung off it, a tiny but effective human brake. "Please don't," she whimpered. "Please!"

"Don't be daft. Whoever did that, I've got to catch them."

"Are you coming to live with us? Are you gonna be here every day?"

I let her drag me to a halt. No, I wasn't, but that wasn't the point. "Other people can help you. I'm going to phone the police, and then social services."

She shot up a hand. Her fist closed in the neck of my jumper and her eyes blazed into mine. "No, you are bloody well not. You're gonna go get the hardboard sheet from the cupboard under the stairs. There's a hammer and nails in there too. I'll get the dustpan and brush."

***

And so it was that I spent my afternoon at Kipton Manor doing a range of odd jobs. After I'd brushed up the broken glass and replaced the pane with the hardboard sheet—neatly cut to fit, and edged with several sets of holes from previous use—I unblocked the bathroom sink, fixed a gutter that had been spilling rainwater into the tiny back yard, and put my dusty engineering skills to use in fixing the motor that drained the washing machine. April dogged me suspiciously throughout these tasks, speaking only to direct me to the next. Eventually I understood, took my mobile out of my pocket and left it on the kitchen surface where she could see it. "But it doesn't make any difference," I told her finally, easing back out of the gap between the washing machine and the fridge and sliding down to sit on the floor. "I'll have to tell someone. You can't live like this. Apart from anything else, what would Letty's doctor think of you being in charge of all those drugs?"

She perched on the kitchen's solitary chair. "Doctor!" she echoed scornfully. "Like any doctor would let her have all them. She orders them off the internet."

"Wow. That must cost a fortune."

"That's why she lives here like this. Every penny she's had for years goes to pay for her pills."

"And can't Kip—the real Kip, I mean... Can't he—"

"Don't you say one bloody word against him!"

"Oh, God. I wasn't going to. I just want to find him, that's all."

"Are you surprised he runs away?"

"He wasn't running away from her this time. He was running away from..." I shut up, genuinely scared of the force of her judgement. "He does try to help her, though. He comes here, she said."

"Yeah, but he's not much cop with gutters and washing machines." She wriggled forward and fixed me with a deadly stare. "He knows how to get rid of kids at the door, mind."

"I didn't mean to mess that up for you. What did I do wrong?"

"Their big brothers are way worse than they are. If they see the little ones come screaming up the street like that, they get angry. And then they chuck rocks."

No use telling a nine year old that she couldn't let the local thugs hold her hostage. Hadn't she said that she had brothers of her own? Then light dawned. Groaning inwardly at my own stupidity, I set down the screwdriver she'd found for me and looked her in the face. "You don't have a mum and dad next door, do you? No family at all. It's just you."

"Right. So go ahead and make your little phone calls. Get social services here, and they'll snoop around Letty and put her into a home. They'll take me away too, stick me back into care for my own good. You know what? I've got my own room here, my own stuff, a door I can lock if I want. And she's mad as a box of frogs, but she'd never hurt me. Never."

"Kip! Kip! Kip!"

April and I jumped. The frantic cries from the living room broke our confrontation, and I scrambled up and followed on the kid's heels. Letty was rocking in her chair. She scanned our faces hopelessly. "Get me something, Kip, please. I've got to have something, haven't I?"

April ran over to the table. She dealt swiftly with a couple of childproof caps, shook out some pills and poured a glass of juice from a box. "Kip does get a doctor in to see her sometimes," she said over her shoulder, as if aware that Letty was too far gone to hear her. "When she'll let one near her, I mean. The last one said it was cruel to try and stop her when she's been taking the stuff so long. She'd just... break."

"How can Kip possibly cope with this?"

"He does all right. But she drives him mad sometimes, and he's not like you, with your screwdrivers and your shouting." She put a tender hand to Letty's sweat-tangled hair and helped steady the glass to her mouth. "So he goes off to college and tells his stories, like she wanted him to, and sometimes if something even worse has happened to him—like you—he runs away."

Whatever she'd given Letty was quick to take effect. The spasmodic rocking movements slowed. After a moment she settled back in the chair and looked up with a bright curiosity I'd learned to love on another face. "Still here, then, John?"

"Still here." I crouched in front of her. "I don't know if you remember, or... if you'd be willing to tell me, but we were talking about the place Kip might have gone to if he was upset. A place called Camp..." I didn't even try for the Gaelic pronunciation. "Camp Saucer."

"Of course I remember."

"Where is it, Letty? Where's Kip gone?"

"It's on the shore of Loch Ness, John. He's gone to look for the monster."

Chapter Eight
Wheels Over Lid

I stopped off at Gran's long enough to pack a bag. The old woman put the chrysanthemums I'd bought her into a vase, then came wheezing up the stairs with a pile of clean underwear for me. I'd have stopped her, helped her back down, settled her with her cough medicine and tissues, but I just didn't have time. I'd given thought to heading straight north as I was, in my smart casuals and business shoes.

I met her on the landing. She was staring at the carpet, where the flowers I'd bought for Jules had been upended and dumped. We exchanged a glance, then we both looked at Jules's bedroom door, which was tightly and eloquently shut.

Jules was a brat, I decided. I'd spent the afternoon with a kid four years her junior who took the weight of the world on her shoulders every day, ran a household, somehow kept a drug addict in equilibrium between overdose and cold-turkey death. I picked up the flowers, took the pile of freshly laundered undies from Gran and went back into my room.

Then it hit me—and it did come like a blow, a weird sharp sting out of nowhere—why having an older male relative disappear from home might feel like a catastrophe to Jules. I hadn't said where I was going or when I intended to be back.

Why? Neither was a secret. I hadn't told Gran either. I turned, opening my mouth, but she was placidly folding jumpers and my Black Sabbath T-shirt into my rucksack. "You don't have to pack for me, Gran."

"Oh, let an old woman feel useful. I've been in bed all week."

"You should probably be there now."

"You can be useful too if you want, Oz. Just not in this room."

I rolled my eyes and went back onto the landing. Was the silence radiating from behind Jules's door worse than the protest drums? I reached for the handle, then felt another sharp sting and knocked instead. "Jules? Can I come in?"

The silence deepened, but that wasn't the same as a refusal. I pushed the door open. Oh boy, this was a bad one—past the point of percussion and dino suits, tantrums or self-care shoplifting. She was nothing but a lump beneath the duvet. I sat down gingerly on the edge of the bed, making sure not to touch her, and was rewarded by a squeezed, half-suffocated sob. "For God's sake. Can you listen?"

Just about. She was quiet, at any rate, and I dived for the window of opportunity. "I'm going to a place in Scotland near Loch Ness, okay? It's three hundred miles away, six hours' drive. I'll be back in..." Why did I have to tell her when I'd be back? Wasn't it enough that Cedric Beaver would be timing every second of my AWOL from behind his little desk? The prickle came again, sharp enough to make me wince this time. *All right, all right*, I told the new inner voice, or presence, or avenging bloody hedgehog or whatever it was. *I get why she needs a return date. I do.* "Three days. I'll be home in three days."

Not enough. I sighed. What was April doing in Kipton Manor right now—changing underwear? Defending Letitia from vandals? But she had her own set of problems, and Jules had hers. "The reason why I'm going there is because I want to find Kip."

The bump beneath the duvet jerked as if tasered. Jules's head popped out. "Kip?"

"That's right. Your hero, even if he did try to kill you."

"Kip might be at this place?" She yanked her phone out from beneath the pillow. "What's the number for Loch Ness? Has it got a website? I can phone them. I..."

"Jules." Like I hadn't tried all that myself—not phoning the loch but the sane equivalent, trying to trace Camp Saorsa online the moment I was back in my car. "There aren't any numbers. It's just a tiny little place called..." This was no good. If I called it Camp Saucer I'd never live it down. Jules would shriek with laughter every time the place got mentioned for the rest of both our lives. To make matters worse, Gran had appeared in the doorway, beaming in expectation. It wasn't that difficult, surely. Letty had put a little shush on the second S of the word. *Come on, Oz. Think how Sean Connery might say it.* "Camp Saorsa. I think it means *freedom.*"

Jules's mouth twitched. But, having gained so much, she was willing to let it slide. "All right. If you're not back when you said you'd be, though—*exactly* when—I'm running away from home."

Looking at her, I could almost believe it was me she wanted back again, not just Kip. "Well," said Gran, breaking the moment, "that'll be nice for you, Oz. A little taste of Saucer is just what you need."

***

I didn't take a map book for my journey. Day trips to Scotland were regular holiday fare for kids growing up in the northeast, and I was familiar with the roads. When the skies began to darken around half past three, I switched on the satnav just in case.

I was way off course. I pulled into the next layby. With lorries thundering by so closely on my right that the whole car shook, I stared at the satnav's screen and slowly accepted that I'd mixed up the route to Loch Lomond with Loch Ness.

For God's sake. How many times had my mam and dad rented a log cabin by Loch Lomond? The garden of Scotland, everything in a kind of jewelled miniature, its deeply indented shoreline a playground for kids and dogs... Jules had been quite a lot of fun then, clutching my hand as she toddled amongst the pools. Game for anything, as you would be with two smiling parents sitting on their picnic blanket, applauding your every move. I supposed the roads had looked a lot different to a carefree kid in the back seat of the car.

I needed to get eastbound, then, and as fast as I could. I didn't know what kind of apocalyptic weather was waiting in the heaped-up clouds, but I didn't want to find out in a Glasgow-bound traffic jam on the M74. The satnav was suggesting Inverness, and by this time I was open to suggestions. As well as packing my underwear, Gran had sneaked a flask of tea into the car. I took time for a cuppa, sent her a Facebook message to say thanks— the quickest way of getting her attention, it seemed—and set off again, reminding myself with every gear change that Kip might not be at Camp Saorsa at all, and killing myself in my rush to find out would benefit no-one.

It was just that he should've called by now, no matter what sorrows had overtaken our second try at love. Memories began to fly in with the splash of raindrops on my screen. What had I said to him at the police station? Nothing, I told myself fiercely, switching on the wipers. Nothing to make him run. I'd pushed benefit of the doubt all the way into self-delusion before I'd given up and believed the cops. By rights he should be chasing me about the country, not the other way round.

Saorsa was my last hope. On the outskirts of Inverness, the satnav tried to send me round the north side of Loch Ness via the A82, but I'd seen the signs for a rat's nest of roadworks up ahead, and I couldn't wait. I veered off the main road and onto a dark, narrow lane. Now I had to get westbound again, and that was easy because night and the rising storm were both coming at me out of that direction. What I planned to do when I reached the loch, I had no idea. Ness was huge, a grand diagonal trench that ran for twenty three miles across the country.

Well, to hell with it: I'd just drive all the way around, and round again if I had to. Up in the hills near a place with the dream-like name of Flichity marked on a signpost and not much else, the wind dropped. Neither storm nor oncoming dark had been a useful landmark after all: night ate the road in one gulp, and the rain began a dead-drop perpendicular fall. My driver's side windscreen wiper chose that moment to squeal and grind to a halt, and I pulled into a gap by the roadside, blind and directionless, suddenly worn out.

For half an hour now the satnav had been nagging me to make a U-turn. How was I meant to do that on a ribbon-thin single-track with ditches on either side? I switched the engine off. I'd get out and fix the wiper in a moment. I just wanted to close my eyes.

Leaning my head back, I let the million-footed percussion of water on the roof engulf me. At least my car *had* a roof. We'd have been bailing for our lives in Kip's Mazda by now, duct-taping the worst of the holes in the rotting canvas. What had happened to the latest long-nose, I wondered, after she'd fought the street furniture and lost? Insurance companies wrote cars off for nothing these days, and none of Kip's love machines had ever been worth much more than their weight in scrap. Yearning seized me. I'd have given everything I had to be parked up by the prom on Friday night, the scent of fish and chips mingling with damp drop-top, Kip athletically smoking a fag by sticking his head and shoulders out into the rain. Eating half a box of mints before he made a move to kiss me. Those were our early days, before he'd begun to tackle his addictions.

I pushed away the Friday-night scene, sweeter than life though it had been to me at the time, vividly though I could still taste that gentle, searching, warm-skinned minty kiss. What was I doing out here? If I found him, what would I do—open my arms and take him back? I'd always known he was a danger to himself. I'd never, ever have believed he'd have put anyone else at risk, especially not Jules, whom he'd loved with a comradely power, as if the pair of them had shared a battlefield in some previous life. It just wasn't in his nature, I'd have sworn.

I'd been wrong. If he wasn't at Saorsa, that would be a blessing, not a disaster. I'd have exhausted all the possibilities of searching for him, discharged my obligations. I could file a missing-persons report, Alice Jones had said, but the police would be slow to act on it: Kip was a wanderer anyway, prone to absences much longer than this. If only I could lose the image of tangled curls adrift in the current of a river. Of the hand that had clasped mine along our rough city streets, unclenching in water, opening, letting everything go...

Somebody knocked on the window. I jumped so hard that I whacked one thigh off the steering wheel and gave the horn an accidental blast. "Shit," I said, reaching for the button that would wind the window down, getting nothing but a click for my pains and remembering I'd have to turn the key in the ignition. Everything was electronic in here, new and sensible, and bloody useless the minute the power was off. I lowered the window an inch. No need to make things easy for whatever had just caught up with me. "Yes? Can I help?"

"Ye cannae park here."

Oh, great. Already the locals had found me out. My headlights had come on along with the ignition. By the glare reflecting from the passing-place sign just ahead of me, I made out a burly, Barbour-clad figure standing beside the car, peering in through the cracked-down window.

For once in my life, I lost my temper. Various fears and furies met inside me: a head-on collision, a fire in an otherwise cold and lonely world. I opened the car door and lurched out. "What?" I demanded, looking a disconcertingly long way up into the bearded face of this new arrival. "Am I blocking you or one of your four-by-four-driving mates from tanking up and down this godforsaken track chasing pheasants, or whatever it is that you do? My windscreen wiper's broken. I just needed to pull in for a minute. One minute!"

He reached inside his coat. Wow, did they go in for handgun executions here, instead of pretending to shoot you by accident with a rifle on the moors? Before my blood had time to chill, he produced—to my utter bewilderment—a compact black umbrella. "Put that up," he advised, "before ye get soaked through. When I say ye cannae park here, it's because this road flash-floods in weather like this. We saw your lights from the window. Do ye want to pull the car up onto our drive, and have a cup of tea until it passes?"

I was a bad judge of character. The real villains lived beneath my nose for years, and I ended up yelling at people who wanted to save me. "Right," I managed, trying to back down. Undoing the strap and velcro on the brolly was beyond me at this minute, and I handed it back to him. "Thanks. Sorry. I've got to get back on the road. I'll just carry on."

My new friend picked the wiper off my screen, dislodged a twig from under it and set it back. "That ought to solve your problem there. Where are you headed for? All the hill roads on this side of the loch will be bad tonight."

"It's a place called Camp..." Oh, I couldn't go through this again, not with a Scot so deeply dyed in the wool that I could practically hear bagpipes. "Well, it's a place where people go to hunt for the Loch Ness monster."

Which of course sounded far worse. He only nodded, though. "That'll be Saorsa. Camp Freedom." He looked me over. "Ye dinnae seem the type, if ye don't mind my saying so. Are ye sure about that tea?"

Outlined in the brightly-lit doorway of a croft a few yards up the hill, a woman was anxiously watching. That was the life to aspire to, I'd come to think. Solid walls,

somebody to love you, Saturday nights in front of the
telly, not buggering about in the dark after someone who
might not even be...

Alive anymore, my mind supplied, finishing the thought
I'd been dodging all week. "Yes! I mean... I've got to go."

"Take the next right, then, and follow the singletrack
down towards the loch. The camp's off in the woods to
the left. A damned eyesore, if you ask me—ought to be
pulled down. There's no sign, but ye'll know when you've
got there. If you reach Rowanburn village, you've gone
too far."

I thanked him awkwardly. We nodded at each other,
curt British strangers in the storm, and then he turned
away. My clothes gave an unhappy squelch as I sat down
in the driver's seat. I was wet to the skin. Ahead of me lay
who knew how many miles of flash-flooding singletrack
darkness, and what Barbour Guy had meant by *you'll know
when you've got there*, I had no idea. But none of this
mattered. I'd tanked up outside Inverness and could go all
night if I had to. I'd even checked the pressure on my
tyres. Priding myself rather on all this foresight, I put the
car into gear.

***

Camp Saorsa lay less than two miles from my passing
place. The road down to the loch was a rain-glimmered
tunnel of bare hawthorns and overhanging birch. And I
did know when I'd got there, yes: a giant model of the
monster loomed up suddenly from the verge.

If I'd expected green plastic, tam o'shanter and an idiotic grin, I couldn't have been more wrong. This monster was made from a single huge log, slender neck rising from a half-uprooted bole in the heather and ferns. She'd been polished and carved. Her great head looked down at me patiently. Someone had given her green glass bottle bottoms for eyes, and she was marked all over with rusted nail-head scales. Was she garlanded, wearing a crown? She was wonderful. Involuntarily I tramped the gas. The tunnel rushed up at me. Kip had to be here, I was certain. He had to be alive.

The flash floods had taken out one huge bite of tarmac ahead. My front tyres dropped into it. The road was cambered off to the left and my back end slewed round. I had time for one strangled yelp before gravity grabbed me—a jerk like a loch-swimming fish might feel, snatched from below by whatever was meant to lurk at the bottom of Ness—and the car flipped wheels-over-lid off the road.

Chapter Nine
Sam the Psychonaut

One flip only. In later days, when I came back to stare in wonder at the near-sheer pitch of the slope from roadside to loch, I knew how lucky I'd been. Maybe my car was too boring to bounce. She landed on her chassis with a bone-jarring crunch. I grabbed the wheel, but I couldn't bring either of us out of this dive: all I could do was brace as she plunged downhill. Rocks, undergrowth. Branches whipping the window. Ahead of me, stark in my lights, the trunk of the biggest fucking pine tree I'd ever seen, the one that had been waiting for me at the end of the road all my life.

No. No, not yet. I hauled the wheel down to the right. At the same time I yanked up the handbrake, and these two tiny denials of fate gave me just enough traction to shoot past the tree by an inch. My wing mirror smashed off the trunk. The car ploughed into a deep bramble patch and ground to a shuddering halt.

A time went by. I measured it in the thud of my heart, the rasp of air in and out of my lungs. Anything beyond that was cosmetic. Was extras, was cherry on top. I was somehow still alive. Beyond the brambles, water rippled in the furthest reach of my headlights. Above me there were stars.

Something passed across my beam. The movement might have scared me, if I'd had one drop of adrenaline left to spare. I listened to the crunch of footsteps in the undergrowth, and then for the second time that night someone tapped on the passenger window.

A full contrast to Barbour Guy. This was... *Mr Blazer*, my rattled brain decided, and I opened the door to get a better look at him.

He was lovely, I decided. If I'd got it wrong about being alive, and this was the welcoming committee for whatever happened next, we were off to a good start. Nothing like him had ever crossed my path before. He was slim, with glossy dark hair and a pair of glasses that looked as if they'd cost more than my car. His blazer and pale fawn slacks were immaculately cut. *Preppy*, the Americans might have called the whole effect. Elegant, and wholly unsuited to the night, although the rain had stopped at last. Already the nice trousers were torn and stained with mud. "Hi," I said, for want of any better opening gambit. "Are you all right?"

He broke into a wide, engaging grin. "Me?"

"Well, yeah. Did I bring you out of a business meeting, or... or a party?"

"No, not at all. I was just out for a walk. Then your car fell out of the sky at me, and I saw you roll down the hill and into this bush. So I should be asking if *you're* okay, right?"

He was Canadian. We'd had a big enough contingent from the States and Canada in the Engineering school for me to distinguish the accent. Somehow that added to his charms, like finding Justin Trudeau in the lochside woods at midnight. "I think I am. I don't know how, but..." I paused, ran a hand over my head and patted myself down. "Yeah. I'm fine."

"Your car doesn't look too bad either. We'll get it out of the bushes for you in the morning. Where were you heading?"

"Here, if this Camp Saorsa." There! All it had taken was a car crash to knock the name off my tongue. I'd said it with proper Gaelic verve. I put out a hand. "My name's John Osman. Everyone calls me Oz."

"I'm Sam. Sam..." He frowned, as if in an effort of recall. "Well, Sam will do. You'd better come on out of there. The angelic brethren will be looking for you by now."

"The angelic who?"

"Oh, I know I'm not meant to know. It's all okay, though—you can trust me. We'll just go down to the shore so they can see you when they next pass. I won't even look when they pick you up, I promise."

I'd let him help me a little way from the car. I needed to go back and switch off the headlights—no chance of getting out of here if my battery went flat—but now I took advantage of their unforgiving light. Yes, he was smart as a new coat of paint, ready for the cover of *Esquire* magazine. He was also outrageously high. Whatever his poison, it had shrunk his pupils to odd-sized pinpricks, lost in a wild iris sea.

Well, it all figured. This was where Kip came for his *saorsa*, his freedom and escape. When Barbour Guy had said I didn't look the type, he hadn't meant monsters. He'd meant junkies. The hot pain of this realisation carried me past a question I'd thought I'd struggle to ask, with so much hanging on the answer. "Do you know someone called Joe Kipton? Kip?"

"Oh, my God. Is he one of you?"

No. He's one of you. "He's a friend of mine. I came to try and find him. Is he here?"

"I should've known. That kind of gentleness, and no barricades, you know? Just this beautiful open soul. He had to be an angel. Yes, he's here."

"And he's okay? He's alive?"

"I can still experience him, yes."

I swallowed hard. My hands fell open, as if letting go of the weight of fear I'd been hauling around. This much established, nothing else mattered: I could turn my practical mind to immediate problems. "Right. That's good. Listen, Sam—I don't know about Kip, but I didn't come down in a chariot from the stars, and nor did you. It's a really cold night. Do you have a house or something around here, some place I can take you back to?"

"No house, no."

"Okay. A cabin, or—well, you look a bit smart for someone who came from a tent, but..."

"I have a tree." He swayed on his feet. "I do understand, you know. Why you can't tell me the truth."

"Er, okay. Hang on till I switch off my lights. Then... why don't you show me your tree?"

He led me out through the last of the undergrowth and onto the shore of the loch. My town-bred gaze cracked wide open: east to west, there was nothing but water, limitless, delicately gleaming. The storm had passed on to wash other feckless travellers off the road and down the rabbit hole, and here at Loch Ness a perfect winter calm prevailed. As I watched—helplessly clutching Sam's wrist for balance—the last of the clouds turned to cobwebs and revealed a dazzling full moon. "Oh, dude," said Sam. "That's your ride. They're on their way."

"They can wait a few minutes. Come on."

Twenty yards or so downshore, a conifer had extended one huge branch in an archway over the sand. I wasn't great on natural history but could pick this one out as a larch, just ending its yearly dump of millions of needles, cinnamon-silver in the moonlight. They hushed our footsteps to a slithery whisper as we approached, and I began to make out lights among the twisted knuckles of roots. Not fairy lights, either: a high-end laptop, an LED lantern and what looked like a body-mounted camera in its harness, hooked onto a smaller branch and trained on a pile of cushions where I guessed Sam had been at work before he came to my rescue. For God's sake, was he *actually* living in a tree?

My eyes adjusted, and I struggled not to laugh. On a flat stretch of the beach beyond the larch stood the biggest mobile home I'd ever seen. One of the newest, too—fresh off the production line, to judge from her plates. "Wow. Is that yours?"

"I can experience it, yes." He gestured to his cushions. "This is where the reality's at, though. The interface. I'm making a documentary about the connection between psychoactive substances and places of power, places like this where human consciousness interacts with cryptids and other strange phenomena. I found some fantastic mushrooms under the pines up there. *Amanita* of some kind, but not muscaria. Not phalloides either, or I'd be dead by now."

Shit. I didn't know whether to call the police or an ambulance. A glance at my mobile told me I couldn't do either: there wasn't so much as a flicker of signal. "You've been... eating these mushrooms?"

"Well, normally I'd make a tincture or dry them out and smoke them. They tasted good, though, and I thought I'd just give them a try." He banged the heel of one hand off his brow. "Hey! I *can* experience the van. I gave the crew a night off so I could get some peace for this experiment. There's loads of room, if you need a place to crash."

"That's really kind of you. I've got to find Kip, though. Is he... experiencing a van here, too?"

Sam gave a snort of laughter. "Don't do that, man. It's cute, but it doesn't suit you. Yeah, he's upshore from here, tucked back in the woods at the far east end. If you know him, you'll know the van."

"Okay. Thank you. In that case, I'd better be—"

"Oh, I understand. You're trying to find a way of ending this encounter without hurting my feelings or revealing what you are. I have to say, for one of the angelic presences, you're very polite. And whatever this amanita is, I'm experiencing you deeply. It's as if you're really here."

"I *am* really here. Look, you seem like a nice guy, even if you are unhinged. These experiments you do—you use your own body as a test tube, right?"

Finally I'd managed to affront him. I usually did find a way, even with sweetest, least uptight natures on earth. "Of course," he said indignantly. "I wouldn't have the right to use anyone else."

"Okay. I'm just trying to find out if you need help."

There was that beaming smile again. He suddenly folded down onto his cushions and leaned his back against the larch. "No, man. Look how bright the moon is! They're putting out the silver carpet for you, Oz, all the way to the shore. I'll hide my eyes while you go."

I opened my mouth to protest. But he'd raised both hands to cover his face, like a little kid determined not to cheat at hide-and-seek. I backed away quietly over the needle-covered roots.

He was so thin, though. His wounds were self-inflicted, just like Kip's, but I was suddenly painfully sorry for him, with his expensive gear and his imaginary crew. Some poor little rich kid, I reckoned, who'd taken a wrong turn on the road to nirvana and been hopelessly lost ever since. I noticed that one of the doors of the fantastic RUV was standing open. Cautiously I approached. The inside was just as immaculate as the exterior. I didn't venture further than the entrance to the living room. From there I could see into a bedroom, twice as big as my gran's. A whole array of preppy, stylish blazers, shirts and slacks was hanging on a rail along one wall.

All I needed was the blanket neatly folded on the nearest chair. I grabbed it, distractedly admiring the softness and design. I closed the outer door and eased back down the steps.

Sam was still leaning against the tree, apparently blissfully asleep. His face was pale in the light from his laptop screen, and dozens of tiny words were reflected in his expensive specs. When I draped the blanket over his shoulders he leaned forward, eyes still closed, and gave a deep shudder of delight. "Oh, man," he said. "The brush of an angel's wing!"

***

I went back to my car. I took my rucksack out of the boot and locked up. She had some scrapes and dents, but looked as if she'd still drive. If not, I was insured. She belonged to the finance company, not me. I remembered Kip watching his last-but-one Mazda being towed away. He'd been grief-stricken, as if he'd had to sell his favourite horse.

We were different people. How different, I had yet to find out. Kip was here and alive, so the urgency of my journey was gone. All I had to do was find his van, and I could take my time about that, enjoy a moonlit stroll along the loch into whatever drug-soaked la-la land he'd chosen for his refuge.

I started down the beach at a jog. I had some dents and scrapes myself, and the rucksack thumped painfully off my back, but when I tried to slow down, some demon nipped at my arse and I stumbled on. This stretch of the shore was vacant apart from Sam's weird domain. Up ahead, a cluster of lights glowed through the pines. I began to pass tumbledown cabins on my right. No dogs barked, and no-one came out to investigate the irregular crunch of my feet on the shingle. Maybe everyone was at the pub in Rowanburn. Cabin, trailer, caravan, and then at last the road I should have come in on, a patchy strip of tarmac ending in weeds just shy of the loch shore. A rotting wooden sign declared the place to be Saorsa.

Barbour Guy had been right. The place was an eyesore. I just wasn't sure whose eyes were meant to be pained by it. *Not in my back yard* was clearly in force here, just like everywhere else, and because I felt possessive of my own yard—well, Gran's garden anyway, with its wind-battered apple tree and plastic chairs—I tried not to be a hypocrite. I wouldn't have wanted to look out of my expensive holiday lodge onto this mess of trailers, tarps and rusting caravans either.

Still, as far as I could make out through the moon-silvered dark, Camp Saorsa stood alone. No cottages or crofts overlooked it, and the hush was extraordinary for a hippy encampment on a Saturday night. I was the noisiest thing there, gasping for breath as I stopped to get my bearings, pebbles scattering out from under my feet. What had Sam said—that Kip's van was tucked away at the far eastern end of the site? Only one track led in that direction. More of a deer trail, really, a gap in the undergrowth leading away through the trees. I tightened the straps of my ruckie and set off.

Sam turned out to be right. I did recognise Kip's van, and for the same reason as I'd known which stretch of this desolate forest was Saorsa. Halfway up the crag, half-buried in bracken and rocks, another monster reigned. This one was smaller, but just as neatly reinvented from the main trunk of a still-living tree. Glass eyes and mirror shards gave back the moonlight in an eerie spangle. Between the creature's wooden fangs, someone had inserted a placard. I slowed up to read the elegant, weather-faded script.

AoE ≠ EoA. Only someone who knew him, who'd lain with him under his glowing green ceiling, would know what it meant. This monster was a guardian. Its neck was protectively arched across the doorway to the most horrendous caravan I'd ever seen.

Seriously. The mobile equivalent of the cabin in *Night Of The Living Dead*, except more cramped. A two-man tourer at best, although how it had ever got towed in here, I couldn't imagine. Moss had ooze-grown halfway up its sides. I could smell the damp from here, that unique bargain-holiday stink of fabric and foam rubber falling to bits in a wet climate. Net curtains hung sadly in the dark windows. A foul thought hit me, turning the last of Gran's tea to acid in my gut. What did Sam know, about Kip and his struggles with life? If ever there was a place where a worn-out human animal might choose to crawl off and die...

So I threw off my rucksack, and with it my lesson from Jules about privacy, warnings and doors. I hit the slime-covered steps at a run and duly almost broke my leg. "Fuck," I said to the starlight and the pines, staggering back to my feet. "Oh, Kip, no. Not this. No."

The handle turned easily, but the door stuck in its frame. I shoved it hard and I half-fell inside.

Jesus, you couldn't swing a cat. The place was sunk in a clammy, bone-cold dark. I grabbed my phone. Still no signal, but I used it as a torch, swinging it from left to right in the one unsteady sweep it took to tell me that no-one was home.

Did fear or relief hit me hardest? If he wasn't here—Schrödinger's Kip!—he was still as much alive as dead to me. Finding his body in the woods behind the van would collapse the probability wave soon enough, and take me down with it, but that hadn't happened yet. I'd have to go and look. I'd have to let go my death-grip on the edge of the caravan door, pull myself the fuck together, turn around, get out of here, and...

"Oz?"

"Shit!" I said, and it came out in a pure soprano. On the far side of the tiny fold-down table, something I'd taken for a heap of blankets had moved. "Kip! Jesus Christ. Is that you?"

A tangled head appeared over the edge of the table. Oh, he'd found something worse than booze and pills out here, hadn't he? His eyes were sunk back into his skull. A week's growth of stubble marked his hollow cheeks. He grabbed the table and used it to help him sit up. "For fuck's sake, Oz. Don't you ever knock?"

Chapter Ten
Into The Woods

There was one decent bit of kit in the place: a portable heater with a supply line to the outside. Kneeling beside it, I recognised it for the one that had gone missing from the engineering department two years previously. "It's freezing in here. Did you run out of gas?"

"No. It just stopped working."

"Can you remember when?"

"Just after I'd switched to a new bottle."

"Your OPSO's probably tripped, then."

"Fascinating. How the bloody hell did you find me, Oz?"

Of course I'd expected the question. I'd even thought up an answer on the long road north. "I took a tip from Gran and stalked you on Facebook. I talked to Cryptid Kenny and the guys in your other groups. One of them said you might have come here."

"I've never told anyone about Saorsa. Cryptid hunters come to Loch Ness all the time, but nobody here talks about this campsite. It's special."

I shrugged uneasily. "Kip, it's four acres of mud."

"Still."

He could pack a lot of meaning into one word. *It is special, Oz, in ways you're too thick to suspect, but that's not the point. Who the fuck told you I was here?* I sighed and gave up the game. "I saw your mum."

He flinched as if I'd hit him. "Right," he said aridly. "I'd ask how you found *her*, but I don't think I care anymore."

I didn't blame him. I was furious with myself for not building a better story, or at least for not holding on tighter to the one I had. Out of the two of us he was the storyteller, I supposed, on a scale I'd only discovered in Letty Kipton's manor. "Give me five minutes, okay? I'm just gonna check your connections."

I always carried a good Swiss Army knife. More of a mechanic's habit than an engineer's, born of a lifelong curiosity about how the gadgets and machines around me worked. I'd always liked to fix things. Shivering in the mud behind Kip's van, I propped my phone where it would shed a bit of light. Sure enough, the over-pressure shut-off valve had tripped. The valve cover was missing and had probably been damaged or lost by whoever had fitted the gas cylinders.

I'd ask how you found her. If he had asked, it would've been a bloody good question. A simple answer on the surface of things: *my gran told me where she was.* I'd swallowed that in the busy heat of my departure. No miracle if Gran, in the course of a long and unpredictable life, had found out where Kipton Manor was, a local stately home. No such manor existed, though, and still she'd known enough to send me to that godforsaken village.

No time to think about it now. My knife didn't run to an adjustable spanner, but by pressing its sturdiest blade against the side of the bolt, I managed to disconnect the outlet pipe. A faint hissing sound rewarded me. That would clear the system of its overload. I waited until the hissing stopped and the weird, hollow tang of Calor had faded on the breeze, then reconnected the cylinders and the pipe.

Inside the van, Kip remained exactly where I'd left him. He looked like a patient in a dentist's waiting room, listening resignedly to the drill. I cranked the ignition on the heater and it straight away popped into orange-blue life. "This one's designed to heat a space the size of a basketball court," I said. "We used it for ambient tests on new alloys."

"I used it to heat up a communal yurt in Wales for an ABC group. Is that why you're here? To collect?"

My mouth dried out. "I just meant it'll warm this place through fast. Kip, I—"

"Why have you come? If you've met Letty, you know how big of a liar I am. Everything's over."

I tried a step towards him. He twisted out from behind the table and dodged past me. I thought he was heading for the door, but before I could reach to stop him he folded down onto a canvas stool by the gas stove, curled up and started rubbing his shoulders as if he hadn't been warm for weeks. I reached over the table into his nest of blankets and pulled out the top one. Unlike Sam, he didn't mistake me for any kind of angel as I wrapped it round him: recoiled from me as far as he could. "Thanks for that. But you can go."

"Will you come with me?"

"What?"

"Come away from here. Does the pub in Rowanburn have accommodation?"

"Yes. I can't leave Saorsa, though. It's the only place where I'm functional."

I perched uncomfortably on the edge of the table. "You don't look functional. You're ill."

"It's only a cold."

I'd seen enough gritty TV to know that colds—red eyes, runny nose—could mask all kinds of drug use. "You need to get out of this van. It's damp, and..." An idea struck me. "Do you know the guy at the far end of the site, the Canadian with the huge RV?"

"Sam? You've met him?"

"I've... experienced him, yeah. If you don't want to leave the camp, he could maybe put you up for a night, until I can..." I fell silent. Like a lot of my ideas, this one was tarnishing fast. What was I thinking, sending Kip off to Chemical City? "On second thoughts, no. He's nuts."

"He's one of the sanest people I've met."

"Right, with his mushroom experiments and his imaginary film crew."

Kip chuckled. "You don't watch many YouTube channels, do you?"

Channel 4 was more like it for me these days, Tuesday nights with Gran and *Bake Off*. It hadn't always been that way. A handful of guys had set up a kind of experimental, bare-knuckle engineering camp in the woods near Kielder, testing out designs for EON. I'd devoured their YouTube offerings as a student. "No," I said shortly. "Why?"

"He's Sam Bouchard, the investigative journalist." Kip huddled closer to the stove. "Huge in Canada, although they keep trying to shut him down. He wants to disprove the myth that all psychoactive drugs are bad. To remind people that some of them used to be sacred."

If I opened my mouth, my gran would come out. *I'm sure there's a crying need for that.* But I didn't want to bait Kip or snipe at his friends. "Okay. He seemed nice. He was way off with the fairies when I saw him, though. And then that mansion of a van—you could sleep ten in there, although all I saw was his collection of blazers... No, don't go there. I'll work something else out. I'll..."

"Oz, wait a second." He looked wearier than ever. I wanted to shake him, get him to tell me what he'd taken. I wanted to fix him up, just like the gas pipe for the stove. He rubbed his eyes. "That's the Psychonaut company van. It does sleep ten—a dozen, actually, when everyone's home. The crew is real. They're in Rowanburn tonight, having a drink. As for the clothes, it's Sam's signature look for TV—you know, smart and clean, not a fucked-up hippy like me. It's usually muddy where they're filming, so he needs a lot of spares."

For a fucked-up hippy, he was crystal clear. Then, he always had been. No matter how far off his wagon he'd tumbled, he'd always made sense: more than I did, in my sane, sober skin. A huge sneeze rattled him. I pulled a tissue out of the box on the table and knelt to hand it to him. "Bless you."

"Thanks. Look, Sam would make room for me, but I don't want to disturb him while he's journeying."

"While he's doing what?"

A faint grin flickered. "Tripping, you'd call it. That's why his company's called Psychonaut—like astronaut, only he travels through inner space. I'll be fine here. Thanks for coming out, but go get back in your car now and try and find a place to sleep in the village. If not the pub, there's a few B&Bs you could try."

"I can't. My car broke down."

If he was a perfect liar, he had a perfect gift for picking up a lie from someone else. An alert stillness came over him. He focused on me properly for the first time. "Broke down? Where—on the access road?"

"Er, no. Further up the shore."

"There's no other road." His attention was like velvet-wrapped forceps. "What happened?"

"The rain washed a bit of the tarmac away on the top of the crags. I... Well, the car's in a bramble bush down at the bottom. I'm okay."

"You came off the road? All the way down that cliff?"

"Yeah, but—"

"The car must've rolled."

"Only once. Then she kind of went down like... Did you ever go sledging on a bin bag?"

"Oh my God, Oz. You've been in a car crash."

I remembered a kid at my school who'd come back after getting run down by a car. He was a nice lad, and we'd clustered round him with this exact same mix of alarm and admiration. *Oh, shit! But... wow.* "Yeah," I said, letting myself feel the truth of it. "I suppose so."

"A proper one." The childish interest dropped away and Kip lurched to his feet, eyes suddenly wide in the light from the gas stove. "Christ. What if you're hurt?"

"I'm not. I don't know how I got away with it, but there's not a mark on me."

"Have you looked?"

"No, but..."

He touched a button on the camping lantern hanging from a hook in the ceiling. Harsh white light filled the van. He took hold of my jaw and gently turned my head, first to the right and then the left. He ran a hand over my hair, looking perhaps for blood or shards of glass. Then he pushed my jacket off my shoulders.

I stopped him and finished the job myself. If I too was childishly impressed that I'd survived my life's biggest adventure, I was freaked out as well. I'd been so fucking scared, and the roll of the car and the onrush of the pine trunk had taken up little eternities. I was longing to jump into somebody's arms for comfort, and the only person I'd ever done that with in my adult life was Kip. Clenching my teeth to stay in control—to stop the wave of shock that would have made them chatter—I stripped off my jumper as well, and stood with downcast eyes for his inspection. "I can't see anything," he said, "but you still might have a concussion or whiplash. I should call an ambulance."

"Good luck with that. I haven't had a signal for the last hour and a half." I glanced up at him. "Maybe one of Sam's mates could take me in his spaceship."

"Who was visiting tonight?"

"The angelic brethren, he said. He thought I was one of them."

Kip pushed me to arm's length. He blew out his cheeks and surveyed me. "Boy. He really *must* be off his tits."

"Oh, ta."

"I think you're all right. But wake me up in the night if you feel rough, okay? I'll get somebody to run you into Fort William."

"Wake you up?" The lantern was picking out with cruel detail every corner of the van, including the tiny bench where Kip had been sleeping. "We can't both stay here. There's no room."

"Yeah, there is." He let me go. The table had criss-cross legs, like a foldaway clothes drier, and I watched with interest while he unhitched the top dowel from its notch and lowered the surface until it was level with the bench. Then he took hold of the back of the narrow seat opposite and tugged it so that the cushions unfolded into a mattress. "There you go."

The bed looked tempting as hell. The pattern of pink and orange flowers had a luminosity of their own, and reminded me painfully of Letty's pyjamas, but the damp and the dirt of the rest of the van hadn't made their way here. I could smell the freshness of the linen. "Are you sure, though? I mean, we're not—"

"Oz, shut up. I don't know about you, but I feel like crap and I just want to go to sleep. We have a bed, and we're warm, thanks to you and that thermonuclear stove."

"Maybe I'd better switch it off overnight. Have you had it checked for carbon monoxide? Do you have a meter, or—"

"*Oz.* Come to bed."

I swallowed a wail of pain. Oh, what nights that invitation had once heralded! All that was over now. We'd lie on Kip's bed like a pair of twigs washed by the river onto the same bank. "Is there..." I cleared my throat and tried again. "Is there a shower block or something? I need to wash up."

"It's not that kind of campsite. There's water bottles and a towel over there, and other than that it's the great outdoors." He pulled a plastic bag out of the cupboard under the sink. "Loo roll in here, and biodegradable bags. Anything more than a pee, use this shovel."

I looked into the bag, then up at him. "You are kidding."

"Nope. Get over it, Oz. The rain's stopped, and there's no wolves or bears. You can do whatever you need to under the starriest sky in the world."

***

So I laid my weary bones down beside him. Gran had packed a pair of warm pyjamas for me: her favourites, not mine, in a blazing tartan surely visible from space. After a short tussle I'd persuaded Kip to wear them, and had been looking for a T-shirt instead when I'd discovered the second set, as if the old woman had predicted my every decision and need. I thought I could hear the clash of our colours as we lay there, each of us neatly stretched out on our own side of the bed.

There was certainly nothing else to hear. My ears gaped nervously at the silence. When I swallowed, the sound of it scraped and popped. I'd lived all my life within the whisper of traffic. I'd been on my share of country holidays, but the hush here was deep as the earth, interrupted only by...

I listened carefully. The sound was tiny, high-pitched, rhythmic. Shit, it was Kip's chest. That noise had accompanied every visit I'd made to my mum in hospital, before they'd stopped letting me visit her at all. She'd always set aside her oxygen mask so as not to scare me, and so I'd learned the meaning of that laboured, compromised squeak.

Something hit the top of the van—a pine cone, or a bolt dropping off one of Sam's passing spaceships—and I jumped hard. "Oh, fuck. Sorry."

"It's okay. You'll get used to the quiet."

"I'm hoping not to have to. We'll be in a Travelodge this time tomorrow night if I can get my car fixed."

"We?"

"Yep. You and me. Away from the cold, the damp and whatever else it is that's making you sick."

"I told you, it's just a cold. Why are you still making plans for us, Oz? You know about my mum now. You know what I am."

I wanted to say something comforting, like *it makes no difference to me*. Both parts were true. The subtraction of a fantasy mum from the whole fantasy world in which he lived could make little difference to the way I saw him, and I loved him so hard that my toes ached and my guts coiled up into spasms. But he was impossible. He'd crossed my line in the sand so many times that I barely had a line left. "What has that got to do with anything?" I said, sounding grumpy without meaning to. "I've found you, and I'm not about to leave you here to catch your death. I wish you'd told me about Letty. I could've helped you out with her, and she seems nice, if—"

"Oz?"

"Yeah?"

"I know I raised the subject, but can we not talk about my mum?"

I shut up promptly. Another silence fell, punctuated by that rhythmic squeak. Kip turned on his side and coughed harshly. How had I ended up in bed with him, too awkward to reach out and rub his back? After almost a minute, when I hoped he'd fallen asleep, he said, sounding utterly lost, "How's Jules?"

"She's okay. Listen, though, Kip—"

"We can't talk about her, can we? Like my mum."

This was ridiculous. I ought to get out of bed, tuck Kip up as best I could and go and sleep in my car. But a wave of exhaustion hit me out of the blue, and the van and the pinewoods and all the troubles and beauty they held began to recede from me. I rolled over, suddenly too wiped to care that the movement brought me within his arms' reach.

Something prodded me in the back. I fumbled at the tangle of blankets. "What's that?"

"What? Oh. It's just my clock."

He too must have been on the edge of sleep. His voice was hoarse, muffled by his pillow. "Oh," I managed unsteadily. "Your clock. Right." I pulled it out. I hadn't seen one like this for years. It was pre-digital, about the size and shape of a brick, with big luminous numbers that flipped over as the seconds and minutes passed. "What's this for?"

I heard his pause. If I'd learned to recognise it before, that heartbeat while he reached for his next lie, I'd have saved myself and him a world of pain. This time he must have come up empty. When he spoke, his voice was raw and real. "I put it on the table in front of me when I'm in bed, or reading or eating or whatever. Time seems to stop here sometimes. The clock helps to make it go away."

Oh, Kip. The words died in my throat. What could I say? Why would a beautiful, bright lad be wishing away his every minute in a dump like this? I hated the reason that occurred to me. How time must crawl, in the trenches between hits of whatever he was on! I hated that thought. I hated the van. I hated the ceiling of the van for not being painted with luminous, wonderful words that had cracked open my stuffy little world and let my soul briefly fly, and what I hated most of all was being back in the car again, thundering down the tunnel to the place where the Loch Ness monster had taken a bite out of the road.

I'd have sworn I was wide awake while I was hating all these things. My body jerked in one of the huge, heart-stopping spasms of early sleep. This time I hit the pine trunk dead-on. The screen smashed and the steering wheel slammed into my chest.

"Oz, it's all right. Oz!"

His arms were around me. His grasp was a safety belt I hadn't known existed. He lifted me back and up out of the wreckage of my car. I let the cry of terror I'd been sitting on all night rip up and out of my throat, and his hold on me tightened. "Ssh, Oz. I've got you. You're all right."

Chapter Eleven
Jesus Christ!

Kip's van looked worse still by daylight. So did Kip. The skin around his nose was red and raw, his hair matted with sweat. He was still sound asleep, so I tiptoed over to my rucksack—allowing my bare feet as little contact as possible with the floor—and got dressed.

There was always the possibility that he really did just have a cold. *Fix the obvious first*, Professor Leighton-Smythe had said to us engineering undergrads. *No good tinkering with the engine if the wheels are falling off.* I paid my visit to the great outdoors, plastic bucket and water bottle in hand, and then I returned to the van and grabbed my wallet and coat. I thought about writing him a note, but decided the presence of my ruckie perched by the sink would tell him I hadn't run off.

If that was important to him. Well, it was tough. I put his clock on the tiny window ledge so he'd see it when he woke up and time wouldn't stand still for him, and I set off down the deer track to the site.

Camp Saorsa was astir. In the morning sunlight, the mess of tarps had separated out into a little village. Cook fires were kindling in neatly built pits of stone, their woodsmoke reminding me that I was hungry. Beside them, a few of the residents of the tents and vans were gathering, blinking sleepily and clutching tin mugs. Parkas, afghans, one or two surprisingly posh anoraks... Everyone looked at me as I passed, and I wished I had some credentials to show, a placard to hold. *Just visiting Kip. Not in any way a plainclothes cop.* Instead I tried for a smile and a friendly wave, and they let me pass by as if that was enough.

To my surprise, someone on the far side of the access-road clearing was waving back. I tried to remember where I'd met a girl with a rainbow-dyed crewcut and pierced eyebrows. At uni? No, I didn't think so, and I probably would have noticed her among the filing cabinets and the howling wasteland of desks in my council office. She jogged across the turning circle to meet me. Wow, the tiny studs in her eyebrows made little rainbows too. I tried and failed not to gawp, and she grinned at me, clearly used to it. "Hi. Are you Oz?"

"Er... yes."

"John Osman, crashed your car here last night, tremendously polite to our Sam even though he was off his face and kept calling you an angel."

"I'm not sure I was that polite, but yes. Is he okay this morning?"

"Fine. Thrilled to bits with his new mushroom. I'm Holly, his production assistant. We managed to chop away most of the brambles from around your car, so he sent me to find you. And to ask you and Kip to breakfast, if you'd like."

I tried to take all this in. Even after Kip's lucid explanation last night, I still hadn't quite believed in Sam's team. "Kip's not well. I was going to walk into the village and get him something for his cold."

"It's a long walk. Do you want to come and see if you can get your car out? One of us will give you a lift to the village if not."

"Okay. Thanks."

"Or you can raid our medicine cabinet. Colds are an occupational hazard for cryptid hunters in winter, and there's some kind of bug going round. Everyone's had it. Come on."

My car keys were in my coat pocket. I followed Holly back along the shoreline where I'd run and stumbled the night before. What was wrong with me, that I couldn't appreciate the differences? A perfect morning had dawned over the loch. Larch-needle orange was singing to cold clear blue along the water's edge. I felt five miles out from the beauty of it all, even from the clarity of the air in my lungs.

Quite a long way from my manners, as well. A bunch of strangers had spent hours hacking my car out of the undergrowth. I must have left the handbrake off: I could see her now, battered but mostly intact on the sand. I was about to improve on my grunt of thanks when something else occurred to me. "Sam seems really nice, Holly."

"Oh, seriously. You won't meet a sweeter guy, unless it's Kip."

"You seem nice too. And all your friends who dug my car out."

"We do our best." She flashed me a perceptive grin. "But?"

"Kip's been here for a week. His van's a mess, and he's ill. So..."

"Why didn't we dig him out too?" She grabbed my arm as I tripped on a piece of driftwood. "It's one of the rules of the camp. Well, not a rule, exactly—more like a policy. We only help people who ask to be helped."

"I didn't ask."

"Nor did you tell us—politely but very clearly—to leave your car the fuck alone in the bushes."

"And... Kip did tell you that? The equivalent, anyway?"

"Pretty much."

We'd reached Sam's larch tree. I came to a halt. The cushions were still in place, but the stretch of beach I could see through the branches had been transformed into what looked like a busy, very professional film set. The dozen or so crewmembers Kip had told me about were dashing about between the RV and their various bits of gear, poring over camera screens, adjusting a lamp over a plate of lovingly arranged red mushrooms. Fly agaric, I knew those ones were called. They had little white warts, and were on a list drummed into me by my mum of things not to be eaten or touched. I had in due course drummed this information into Jules. "I think it's bollocks," I said.

Jules looked at me with interest. "Which part? The psychotropics, or the idea that they might have more powerful effects in areas where there's lots of cryptid sightings? Because, you know, Sam loves different views. He'd probably like a talking-heads piece with you explaining your opinion. You're very handsome. We should try and do it before you have a shave."

"No. God, no."

"No to what?"

"Everything. I mean—none of that. What I think is bollocks is the idea that you'd wait for someone like Kip to ask for help, or listen to him when he turns it down."

"Oh, right. We should force help on him?"

"In certain circumstances, yes."

"And is that what you're gonna do?"

"I'm gonna force some Beecham's Powders on him if I can find any. And then—yeah, if I think he's really sick, I'm taking him out of here. Slung over my shoulder like a piece of meat if I have to."

I couldn't read her gaze. The glimmering jewels in her eyebrows were a distraction. "I think you're missing the point of Saorsa, Oz," she said seriously. "It means—"

"Yes, I know. Freedom."

***

Five husky cameramen pushed, rocked and shoved my car from the beach to the access road. There were some flat patches of wet sand where I could put her in gear and drive, and they all ran along with me, yelling and laughing. When we hit the shingle and stones again, they fell into their places: two on either side and one at the back, while I sat behind the wheel feeling like an idiot and steering when told. In a basket on the passenger seat I had a bottle of cough medicine, Beecham's Powders as requested, medicated tissues and a tub of Vick. All of these items were new and sealed, as if Sam or Holly had read my unworthy thoughts. Sam, already resplendent in fresh blazer and slacks, had waved at me distractedly from across the set, and Holly had brought out the medical supplies. Like Sam, she didn't seem to resent my different views. She'd smiled and invited me and Kip to the shared Sunday barbecue on the beach, if Kip was well enough.

Once I was safely installed on the tarmac, I said goodbye to the camera guys. We shook hands all round. They waved away my efforts to thank them, as if all this was normal routine, and I remembered with a sudden ache that I had once been that kind of guy, running around the engineering department, helping out as needed between study sessions. Time had become so tight behind desk six that I'd resented having to pause to pick up so much as a paperclip. I watched them striding off back towards Camp Mushroom, and then I set off for the van.

Those *had* been some unworthy thoughts. As if these nice people, who even in their darkest hours would hurt no-one but themselves, would spike Kip's cough syrup! The trouble was that I couldn't stop thinking this way. What if I got back to the van and he was more cheerful, if he'd brightened up the way he used to do between the main course and dessert at a restaurant, after he'd excused himself and come back from the loo?

Why not just wonder if his dealer came to call, Oz? I shook my head. Then, as if the demons inside me had found an outward form, a shape reared up in front of me on the path.

A man with horns. Shit. I dropped the basket. The guy was huge, his antlered head brushing the lower branches of the pines. A little way behind him on the track was another man, this one ordinary, although surely exotic in a place like this, with dark skin and black eyes flashing in debate. The two were locked in argument, and didn't slow up until the horned one almost knocked me down. "Oh," he said. "Sorry, man. Didn't see you there." He paused, long enough to lower then raise the antlers in the most thorough onceover I'd ever received. "Wow. What an oversight. Look at *you*."

"This is what I *mean*," said his companion, pushing in front of him. "You just run into someone—almost literally. And straight away you're either locking horns or butting your big randy head at them—boys, girls, everything. You don't give people a chance, Herne. Exercise some restraint."

"That might work for you, mate, but it's not the wildwood way." Still, he backed up a step. "Sorry, handsome young stranger I'd love to fuck if convenient. And appropriate, of course. My name's Herne, and this chap is my ancient enemy, Jesus."

I couldn't have heard him right. I was too busy processing his offer to think about anything else. Did Camp Saorsa contain nothing but hot guys? I blinked, and he was suddenly ordinary, apart from the weird headdress—tall and broad-shouldered, but not the princely creature I'd thought I was seeing a moment ago. It was just that he smelled so nice—like earth and trees, with a tang of some rutty thing else that sent heat beating down towards my groin. Quickly I picked up my basket and held it in front of me. "Hi," I said. I didn't bother with my *John Osman* this time. John Osman was getting left behind in the dust, or maybe beneath desk six. "I'm Oz. Um, it's not convenient, I'm afraid, and... not appropriate, either." He did have lovely eyes, and I was ridiculously sorry to see them fill with sadness. "It's nothing personal. I'm here to see Kip."

"Oh. *Oh!*" The sorrow vanished, replaced by an unholy gleam. "Let the forces of life flow on! Flax, flag, fodder and frig!"

"*Herne.*" Once more his friend—his ancient enemy—intervened. "Leave him alone. Have you got enough stuff in your basket there, Oz?"

"Er, yes. I think so. It's just some things for Kip's cold."

"Right. Tell him we hope he feels better." His voice was softly accented. Spanish, maybe? He smiled, and it was for some reason pure sunlight. I relaxed a little in its bone-melting warmth, which was always a mistake around here. "Don't worry about your erection," he went on. "Herne gives everybody one of those. Even the girls."

They continued on their route. Herne squeezed past me, ducking his horns, waggling his eyebrows. "*Especially* the girls."

***

I needn't have worried about Kip feeling better or more cheerful. He'd been trying to get up and dressed, and had given up on this process halfway. I found him shivering on the end of the bed, naked but for his jeans. I was warm as toast from my adventures, so I shrugged out of my jacket and pulled my jumper off over my head. Quickly, before it could lose body warmth, I shook it the right way out and sat down beside him. "Here. Let's get you into this."

He dived in obediently. He tried to push my hands away when I helped him with the sleeves, but he'd lost ground overnight and his movements were unconvincing. "Kip," I said hoarsely. "I really want you to come away with me and get checked out by a doctor. Please. I'll bring you back here afterwards if that's what you want."

He reappeared through the neck hole, flushed and tangled and as ever more interested in my affairs than his own. "Oh, did you get your car sorted out?"

"I did. Some of Sam's friends helped me, and she's just down the track there, waiting."

"Okay. I tell you what—if I'm not any better by tomorrow, I'll do whatever you want. It's difficult to get a doctor around here on a Sunday, and..."

A fit of coughing seized him. At least I had something to offer him now. I reached into the basket for the tub of Vick, and without thinking uncapped it. For years I'd helped Jules on and off with her little garments, especially after my mum had got too weak and sick to do it. She'd watched me in a mixture of pride and sadness, and I hadn't understood about the sorrow, because it was Osman family legend back then that she would be fine. The only person who hadn't bought into it had been Mum herself. I lifted the hem of the jumper and pressed a good dollop of the Vick to Kip's chest. "Gran swears by this stuff, you know. If you rub it on the soles of your feet, it stops you from coughing at night."

"And will you let me do that part for myself?"

"What?"

"The foot thing."

I froze. We really weren't on the kind of terms where I ought to be tenderly massaging his chest. But before I could withdraw my hand, he took a sudden hold of my wrist, and once more I tried and failed to read a human face. If I did it for him, I'd be sure to find the place beneath his collar bones where the dry ache had collected. I'd be sure to seek out each little bump where his ribs connected to his sternum, and when I'd done that, I'd know whereabouts on his back to rub some more and ease out the itch from his lungs. "I'll leave the foot part to you," I said. "But let me do this bit. Okay?"

He nodded mutely. He stared out through the window while I worked on his chest, studiously avoiding so much as a brush with a nipple, but he was very tired: when I reached up under his sweater at the back he gave a defeated moan, leaned forward and hid his face against my shoulder.

I didn't know what to do. I was as stupidly shy with him as when we'd first met. I was running out of Vick, so I reached out and fumbled among the blankets. "Hang on a sec while I find the tub. It must've gone down the side of the bed."

He raised his head a little. "It's here. In your basket."

"That's just the box. I've already..."

There were two boxes, though. One was empty, the other still sealed. And that would have been fine, would just have been part of the mad generosity I kept running into here, just Holly or Sam popping me in an extra. I could cope with that.

But I had two of everything. Two bottles of cough mixture, two lots of powders. No, wait. I only had one loaf, a massive crusty cobbler. I only had one neatly packaged slab of what smelled deliciously like smoked fish.

Kip peered in past my shoulder. "Oh," he said. "You managed to rustle up some breakfast. Who did you meet?"

Absently I wiped my fingers on the edge of my T-shirt. Only then did I notice I was wearing my Black Sabbath one, which Gran must have packed for me carefully. First thing that morning I'd just made a grab for it in the dark, but nothing here seemed random. Nothing here made any bloody sense. "I met," I said carefully, "a girl with rainbow studs instead of eyebrows. I met a guy with horns."

"Sounds like Holly and Herne. Did Herne have his friend with him?"

"There was another guy, yeah. Who was he?"

"You'll find out this afternoon, if the Sunday barbecue's on."

"It is. We're invited, if you're well enough."

Kip sneezed violently. Experimentally I grabbed both boxes of Kleenex. Neither evaporated in my grasp, so I opened one and handed him a tissue. "I'll try to be," he said ruefully, blowing his nose. "These smell nice."

"Yeah. They're medicated."

I honestly couldn't think of anything else to say. I handed him a bottle of cough mixture, and I took the basket and the rest of its contents over to the sink. I emptied out bread, fish and boxes onto the draining board and stared at them.

Jesus Christ!

Chapter Twelve
The Mexican, or: My Foot In It

"You're wearing your T-shirt."

I'd probably stated the obvious a few times that morning myself. "Yes. Why not?"

"I dunno, Oz. I think in your place, I might've put everything to do with me into a bin bag and dumped it."

"I did that with all your other stuff. Thought I'd hang on to this, though. Might be worth a bob or two one day."

We were sitting in the sun. It was warmer out here than in the van. I'd tried lighting the heater, but the fumes had made Kip's cough worse, so I'd added two blankets to the sweater he was already wearing and helped him outdoors, so bundled up that he'd barely fit through the door. He'd directed me to a storage hut behind the van, and there I'd found two deckchairs and a foldaway table. We were quite deluxe. I glanced across, and found myself on the receiving end of the first real smile he'd given me since my arrival. "Bastard," he said, and the scrape of affection in his voice made my mug shake in my grasp. The van and the outdoor cupboard were better stocked than I could have predicted, and so we had coffee, juice, bread and smoked herring for breakfast.

I understood now. Holly had brought out supplies for me in a basket, and I'd barely glanced into it before the camera lads had come to rock and roll my car off Mushroom Beach. She'd been more generous than I'd had any right to expect, that was all. She liked Kip, so she'd doubled up on the medicines and slipped some food in there too. When I thought about the mechanics of this—the size of the loaf, and the capacity of the basket to hide it—my engineer's brain did begin to object, so I gave it something else to think about. Something other than Kip's smile. "This is quite a decent little touring van," I said, shielding my eyes to get a better look at the shape of it against the trees. "Under the rust and the muck, anyway. You really have let it get into a mess."

He took another cautious bite of his bread. "It's good stuff, that Vick. I'm feeling a bit better."

"That's great, but..."

"I feel like I want to defend myself, and last night I didn't care enough to bother. It's not all my mess. Anyone who needs a place to stay can live here when I'm not around, and the last lot left it like this."

"Serves you right for being such a..." Oh, my God. How had that sentence been about to end—a *socialist*? I had nothing whatever against socialists. I'd been one myself in my teens for a couple of weeks, until I'd worked out the commitment and sacrifice involved. "A softie," I finished lamely. "Your last lot wrecked the place."

"Yes, they did, and the ones before left it spotless, with a bunch of flowers on the table. You can't tell, Oz. You just can't tell."

I got up and walked to the edge of the little clearing where the van sat. When Kip spoke to me that way, it made me feel as though he had a grip on the world while I was just flailing around. That was nonsense: I wasn't the one hiding out in a dirty caravan on the edge of Loch Ness. I took hold of a slender birch trunk to ground myself in reality, but of course no trees could be relied upon here—this one dipped its crown, a few gold leaves still attached, and revealed to me a fairytale castle on the far side of the loch.

I knew this one, though. Tissue-paper cut-out though it might be this morning, layers of blue on grey in the mist, this castle was a solid piece of Scottish tourism real estate. Everyone visited there. I could pronounce it, too. "That's Urquhart, isn't it?" I said to Kip, who'd come to stand beside me, blankets clutched around him. "I've been there a couple of times. Never seen it from this side of the loch."

I must have done a good job of transforming the Q to a K and dropping the H—*Urkart!*—because he nodded and let his shoulder bump off mine. "Was that when you were a kid?"

"Yeah. With my mum and dad and Jules."

I hadn't meant to mention any of them. Parents and sisters were a minefield for me and Kip, weren't they? I was instantly sorry when he let go a faint sigh and said, "Yeah, it's a beautiful place. And you and I have got to talk."

"I thought neither of us wanted to."

"Just one thing, then. I do need to know how you found Letitia. I've tried to look after her, though I've made a right pig's ear of it, and if she's taken to telling people where she lives, then..."

"Right." I wanted to tell him that, as pig's ears went, he'd created the best silk purse he could, but he didn't need my judgement. "I understand. I know this is gonna sound weird, but my Gran told me where she was. Not her address, don't worry—just that Kipton Manor was in Lower Shilby. She said you'd told *her*."

"Pretty sure I never did."

"Anyway, I went there and asked for directions, and nobody knew about the manor, of course. It was just a couple of local lads, and they knew your mum's name."

"Lady Letitia. I bet they gave you some stick."

"They thought they were funny. I dealt with it."

He pulled the blanket more tightly around him. "One thing I always meant to say to you, Oz. When your dad left, and you dumped me, it... broke my bloody heart. But I knew why you were doing it. You even gave me a weird kind of hope."

"Christ. How?"

"By showing me that good kids can come from bad parents. I hated what you did—leaving uni, taking that arsehole's armpit of a job. I could still see that you meant it all to be good."

I couldn't bear this. I wanted to deny it, even though those same words had been my mantra while I tore myself away from everything in my life that I'd loved. I backed away, out of the circle of warmth Kip was emitting from inside his layers. "Speaking of Gran, I'd better phone her, although..." I checked my phone, just barely stopped myself from throwing it into the bushes. "Shit. That's great, Kip—catch your death of cold and maroon yourself somewhere with no phone signal."

"I wouldn't worry about Gran," he said, then added dryly, "I'm sure she's got us in clear view in her crystal ball."

"She's the least mystical person I know. She is bloody cunning, though, and she must have been up to something. She's always up to something."

I pushed my hands into my pockets and glared off towards Urquhart. Anger was such a warm and comfortable thing to feel instead of pain. I could stoke my fires by standing here listing everyone who'd annoyed me: Gran, Jules, Cedric. My dad for leaving, mum for dying. Anyone else? Sunil Patwardhan, perhaps, for parking his bike outside Gran's house and staring at Jules's window. As for Kip...

Out in the middle of the loch, just where the last of the mist was dissolving in sunlight, something broke the surface. If the pine tree I'd almost hit last night had come alive, grown a smooth skin and flexible spine and taken to the water... Blindly I caught the edge of Kip's blanket and dragged him over. "Kip. Look."

As soon as I pointed, the vision was gone. Kip was staring eagerly, and just at that moment I'd have given anything to bring it back for him. That was nonsense, though. There was probably a very good reason why my brain had come up with a pine log to make sense of what I'd seen. "Sorry. It's nothing."

"Did you see something?"

"No. Just a tree trunk."

He glanced down at my fist, still clenched tight in his blanket. "You were pretty excited, though."

"I was not. I just..."

"People often see her near Urquhart. Was she swimming east or west?"

"No, she... Oh, for God's sake, Kip. There is no *she*. It was a log, and people see things like that near Urquhart because the castle's on a headland and they're looking out at the water anyway. Or they're on this side of the loch, looking at Urquhart."

"We totally accept that. That's why we check all the sightings near the castle as carefully as we can. Why are you so upset about it, Oz?"

I wasn't. I just needed to blow my nose. I took the tissue he handed me and surreptitiously swiped at my eyes as well. "I swear, if you're giving me your cold... Look, what the hell do you think this thing in the loch really is? You call it *she*, and it's like you're talking about—I dunno, a goddess of some kind. Did you make those carvings, the one up by the road and that one over the caravan door?"

"Not really. They're pine logs. I just carved out their natural shape a bit, and everyone here brings things they find—bottle tops, bits of mirror glass, old pottery from the beach—to add to them."

"They're beautiful. But I still don't understand."

"I know you're trying to keep an open mind."

"It's not easy. Everyone I meet here seems bonkers."

"I can hear your hinges creaking. But just hold on. Somebody usually gives a talk at the Sunday barbecues, and that might help."

"Do you reckon I'm letting you go any further than that deckchair?" I looked into the pale face raised to mine. His features were as finely turned as the rest of him, but his beard came in with piratical vigour, as if his inner world was always ready to overwhelm him. "Sit down before you drop. Finish your tea, and I'll fix you another Beecham's."

***

In some ways I was well suited to a place like this, even if everyone I'd met so far did seem clinically insane. My threshold for credulity was high, and my brain would automatically throw out cobwebs and monsters in favour of practical tasks to hand.

No shortage of those around here. Once I'd got Kip installed in his deckchair, I went to work. First I took out the few bits of moveable furniture from the van. Then I hauled out the carpets, three bits of orange shag pile with decaying rubber underlay, and enjoyed banging these off the trunk of a tree until every breadcrumb and unidentifiable lump had been dislodged. By the time this was done I was warm enough to strip off my jacket, so Ozzy and his band, the devil and the angel strode indoors with me to grab the bedlinen and shake it briskly in the sunlight. Kip watched these proceedings over the top of his mug. "You don't have to do all this, Oz."

"I do. I'd be the bloke who lived in your van for a week, built an extension and installed a septic tank."

"But would you leave me flowers?"

"No. You don't need flowers. You need..." I gave the sleeping bag one last violent snap. "You need somewhere hygienic to eat and sleep. Have you got any cleaning stuff?"

"Try the hut round the back. I've never seen you like this. You're a machine."

A machine that liked building machines. I liked this image of myself—painless, professional, back at work in the engineering department. Well, I'd take what I could get. I headed for the hut, and to my surprise found there not only a tub of Dettol but a bucket and a foldaway mop. Whatever microbes had been lurking in Kip's van— real ones, or the tiny daily build-up of spiritual dross that brought people down, blinded them, left them open to sickness and addiction—they had better look out. I boiled up a kettle on the hob, sloshed Dettol into the bucket and started to ply the mop across the floor.

Three boilings and two buckets later, the van was clean. I squeezed out one last sponge and came to lean in the doorway, feeling like the little psychic lady out of *Poltergeist*. "This van is clean. Do you want to go back to bed now? Your quilt's no longer a biohazard."

He pushed stiffly out of the deckchair. "Wow," he said, making his way up the steps. He edged past me, and I edged away, feeling sick that even such normal contact between us had to be curtailed. "Looks like the *Country Living* scrapyard edition." He sobered, and cast me a marrow-melting smile over his shoulder. "Seriously. It's great. I don't want to live in a pigsty. I've just been... Well. This is much nicer."

"Come on, then. Roll yourself back into bed."

I would, if you'd roll with me. That was the Kip thing to say. He looked as if he'd have liked to, but then his expression altered. "Uh-oh. Watch out, Oz. Stag attack."

Something prodded me in the back. I jumped and whipped round, almost upsetting my bucket. There at the foot of the caravan steps stood Herne. Either his antlers had sprouted or he'd changed his headdress—and it had to be the second thing, hadn't it?—because the horns were now long enough to poke me from nearly a yard's range. "What are you playing at?" I asked uncomfortably. "That hurt."

"Sorry, Oz-man. I just dropped in to say that lunch is ready, if you two aren't stuffed with loaves and fishes." He raised his head and sniffed the air. "That smells good! No relative of mine, I'm glad to say. Whoa, Kip! Having company suits you. I could just eat the two of you up."

***

"Is it a pheromone thing of some kind?"
"What?"

"Herne. Does he wear some kind of perfume or oil?"

I thought it was safe enough to ask. Herne was on the far side of the fire, chatting animatedly to Holly, who was practically melting with longing for him. The wide circumference of the firepit was busy with conversation and laughter. The whole population of Saorsa must have turned out: kids, hippies, incongruous tourist types in brand-new outdoor gear. Every one of them had greeted Kip with the greatest kindness and pleasure at seeing him up and about again, which still didn't let them off the hook, I reckoned, for leaving him to live or die up there in his van. If I was still missing the point of freedom, then so be it.

But he did look better. "I don't think so," he said, settling more comfortably onto the rock we were sharing. "He's just one of those... really attractive guys."

Something ached in my chest. On the day when Kip found someone else seriously attractive, my world would darken. But why shouldn't he? "I don't get it," I said. "Nobody's *that* attractive. You had to hand me a cushion while we were talking to him back at the van."

"I keep that cushion there for when he visits. I had to stand behind the chair. He's a menace."

Our eyes met. I loved his sexy innocence. Growing up where I had, I'd arrived at uni still a bit afraid that the things I desired were dirty or wrong. He'd blown all that away like sand in a sweet sea breeze. "Oh, man," said a richly accented voice behind me. "Love on the shores of the loch. We'll definitely use that."

I twisted round. Sam and a cameraman were beaming down at me. I really wasn't in the mood for my five minutes of fame. "Hoi," I began, but Kip laid a hand on my arm. "Bugger off, Sam," he said kindly. "You and I both know you won't use a thing without permission, but Oz doesn't know that yet. Go film Holly and Herne, if you want a romantic backdrop."

"Yeah. I think I'd better go break that up, or I'll lose a good assistant to the charms of the wildwood." He put down a hand to me. "Sorry, Oz. Didn't mean to ruin your moment."

I'd scarcely been having one. All my moments were safe in the past, if *safe* meant the same thing as *forever lost*. I gave Sam's hand a brief shake, and watched him and the camera guy pick their way through the crowd to their next victim. "I thought he was supposed to be filming mushrooms out here. Or monsters, or... monsters who eat mushrooms or whatever. Not me."

"He's interested in people more than anything—how they mix with the monsters and mushrooms. You'll often see him wandering about, just filming stuff at random. Then he'll sit up all night with Holly, picking out the bits he wants to use."

I could see that the group around the fire would catch a filmmaker's eye. For me, half of the faces were distorted by heat-shimmer. Clouds of rich smoke were on the rise, and not just from the burning logs. A furry tang of dope came and went on the air. As I watched, another member of Sam's crew reached into the circle to lift an outrageously massive joint from Holly's fingers. He took a big hit, whistled in admiration, then came to join the half-dozen or so of his colleagues sitting on rocks or blankets on the sand. Two of the tourist types, full of surprises, were passing around what looked like a handcrafted, *Homes and Gardens*-style bong.

I had to get Kip out of here. I was pleased that he'd felt well enough to make it down to the shore, and I'd make sure he got a good share of the mutton legs finishing their roast on the spit over the fire, but after that we were gone. This place would corrupt a priest. At the very least, the smoke was making him cough. "How long does this beanfeast tend to last? I don't think sitting around here in the cold is gonna do you any good at all."

"Not long now. Look, there's Jesus. If he's walking up and down the beach like that, it means he's nearly worked out what he's going to say."

I frowned and squinted through the smoke. There was the stocky, dark-haired guy I'd met in the woods with Herne. He seemed a general favourite: every time his energetic pacing brought him past the group, two or three people raised an encouraging cheer. *Jesus! Yeah, come on, man! Jesus!*

I felt a penny drop inside my brain. A sense of revelation filled me, and perhaps because I was inhaling so much second-hand dope, I didn't stop to think twice. I was proud of myself. And this lot of hippies round the fire were so bloody right-on and PC, I was sure they'd be happy to get the chance to fix the error of their ways. "Kip, that guy..."

"Who, Jesus?"

"Well—yeah, I know everybody's saying his name like that. When I first met him, I thought he must be Spanish. But now I come to think about it, I think he might be Mexican. So you'd say his name..." I paused to get it just right, as I had with *Saorsa*. "Hey-soos."

It was one of those moments when, for no particular reason, everyone in a social group stops talking at once. I'd raised my voice so Kip could hear me above the background buzz, and so my theory about the ethnicity of Herne's friend, and the right way to say his name, carried loud and clear across the fire. "*Hey-soos?*" echoed one of the camera guys, wonderingly. "He's not Mexican, you chump. He's Palestinian. He's a doctor called Zadi from Fort William, comes here for his weekends." He shook his head, grinning. "Hey-soos!"

On the far side of the fire, Holly let go a helpless snort. She clapped a hand to her mouth, but the damage was done, the cork out. A few moments of silence elapsed, and then the whole group exploded into laughter.

Chapter Thirteen
What Goes In Loch Ness

All except Kip. To my dismay—I just wanted to sink into the sand and disappear—he clambered to his feet. "Shut up," he said, sounding as near to angry as I'd ever heard him. "Shut up, the lot of you. Oz only just got here. He doesn't know all the stuff that goes on in this free-range nuthouse. Leave him alone."

The laughter died. Small, shocked glances darted across the fire, as if a cross word from Kip was as unexpected to the free-range nuts as it had been to me. The weird group dynamic settled upon Holly as spokesperson, and she ran her hands in embarrassment over her rainbow crop. "Hey, Oz. We didn't mean to upset you."

Maybe I didn't want to vanish after all. Placid Kip, who should've been born with a CND symbol tattooed onto his brow, was ready to knock heads together on my behalf. I put up a hand and drew him back down to sit beside me. "I'm not upset," I said. "I must've sounded like a right chump, just like..."

"Charlie," said the camera guy agreeably, holding up two peaceful fingers.

"Just like Charlie said. All right, I give in. Why do you call him Jesus?"

Holly jerked a thumb back over her shoulder. Like everyone else here, Zadi must have a few tricks up his sleeve, or at least a pile of clothes behind a tree. I could've sworn I'd watched his whole progress up and down the beach, but there he was, settling comfortably on the bole of a tree just outside the circle, dressed from head to toe in a kind of long white robe. He'd unclipped his hair, which now fell around his shoulders in a rich tangle. I blinked and rubbed my eyes. The lunacy was notching up a point or two. Had the guy crowned himself with some kind of glowstick from a concert? The air above his head was weirdly radiant... Then the wind shifted and the effect disappeared, probably born of my second-hand high in the first place. I leaned in close to Kip and spoke under the chatter and ripple of applause, carefully this time. "Have you seriously brought me to the shores of Loch Galilee to listen to Jesus?"

He glanced at me in amusement. "Looks like it, doesn't it? On a Sunday, too."

"Is this guy—Zadi—the one who's going to give the talk?"

"That's right. And you're not the only one who has doubts. Here comes Herne."

A few whoops and cries went up like fireworks from the group. Herne, who'd torn himself away from Holly and gone jogging off into the undergrowth a minute ago, had suddenly emerged onto the beach. He was still dressed in jeans and a sweater, but these were the only ordinary things about him. He stood tall and forbidding, casting a strange shadow in the low midday sun, and his horns were longer than ever. "By what right," he cried, setting his hands on his hips, "do you seduce the children of Earth with thy words?"

The crowd broke into cheers, as if this was a regular performance. Zadi waited until the noise had died down. "By what right do you prevent me?" he asked mildly. "Do you think they're idiots who can't choose for themselves? And, to be fair, am I the one who goes in for seduction around here?"

Herne frowned. A cloud passed over the sun, and I half-expected a lightning bolt. Then he shrugged. "Okay. Fair enough."

"What—is that it?"

"For today, yeah."

A chorus of groans went up. Sam, who'd been eagerly following the action with a hand-held camera of his own, gave a disgusted laugh. "Are you kidding? You guys got into a fistfight last Sunday."

"That was then. This is a busy time of year for both of us. I think I'll just sit and listen today."

He came and settled in the circle opposite Zadi, apologising here and there as his horns caught in dreadlocks and woolly hats. Why didn't he just take them off? "They seriously got into a fight?" I asked Kip softly. "Jesus and the guy with horns, rolling around on the beach?"

"Pretty much. They used to be together, I heard."

"What—boyfriends?"

"Yeah. Then something went terribly wrong and they split up. But they can't leave it alone, and so they wander around this place at the weekends, arguing about everything under the sun. Anyway, Zadi's ready. We should listen."

I could do that. The anxious impulse that had brought me up here, the need to fix and change things that had kept me busy ever since—these painful, restless feelings were at last easing off. Maybe I'd just run out of steam, or inhaled too much dope. Pushy Christians had always found short shrift on the doorstep of my secular family home, though Gran occasionally frightened Jehovah's Witnesses by asking them in for tea. Well, whatever Zadi's agenda, I could sit here and indulge Kip by putting up with it for half an hour. I composed my face into a polite and neutral mask, all ready for a sermon. "First of all," said Zadi, with the greatest solemnity, "dogs."

Silence fell. There was a strange, guilty edge to it. For me, this was the final surreal cherry on the cake, and I had to bite down hard on a giggle. Dogs? Finally it was Holly who spoke once more for the group. "It's one of the rules, isn't it? Not that there's many of them, but... no dogs at Saorsa."

"Right. Anyone want to tell me why? Oz?"

Oh, for God's sake. Hands were shooting up all around me, giving me flashbacks to junior school, another place where, if the question didn't have to do with physics, nuts or bolts, I seldom had a clue. "Well, it's a beautiful place. The beach and the woods, and the water stretching out as far as you can see in both directions... Dogs can be messy, I suppose. People need to clean up after them."

I'd said more than I'd meant to. I wasn't much given to observation about the natural world. Zadi was nodding vigorously, though. "That's right. Let's take a moment, everyone, to look at the beauty Oz has conjured up for us. The beach and the woods, and the water stretching out as far as you can see in both directions. Blessed be."

"Hoi," interjected Herne from across the fire. "That's my line."

"What?"

"You say *amen*. I say *blessed be*."

Zadi's eyes filled with sadness. "True enough. A lot of my stuff got mixed up with yours, didn't it? Well, can I get an amen for the beauty of the water and the woods?"

"A-men!" said the crowd in brisk chorus, with a practised double clap.

"And, since the subject came up, a blessed be?"

The *blessed be* came back more softly, with an odd, deep vibration. I closed my lips firmly against an impulse to join in. Just crowd mentality, and I knew how changeable and dangerous that could be. "Okay," Zadi went on. "Oz is right about the clean-up angle, though I hope that would happen anywhere. What about here?

Why do we ask our visitors to Saorsa to leave their noble companions behind, to forego their sacred protection and love?"

Now all of the hands were staying down. I was fairly sure everyone knew, but attention was gathering upon one of the tourist types, a short lady with a very long waterproof coat. Timidly, glancing around her in a kind of wry surrender, she raised a hand. "Because of the noise," she said. "Because any kind of rustling or barking might frighten Her Ladyship away."

"That's right, Eleanor. And why does that matter to us? Is it just because we want to see Her Ladyship, fulfil our dreams and confirm our beliefs?"

"No, no. It's because she deserves a quiet shore, a place in this last wilderness where she can exist the way she used to before humans came along. But Maggie's so quiet, Jesus. She hardly makes any sounds at all."

In direct contradiction, something beneath the skirts of Eleanor's long coat unleashed a storm of barking. The fabric heaved, and a muscular little body shot forth. Holly made a grab for the creature and missed. Charlie did better, but the tiny dog he'd captured gave such a heartrending yelp that he let it go. "All right, all right," said Zadi resignedly. "Suffer the little bulldog to come unto me."

Maggie—a compact French bulldog pup with eyes and ears almost bigger than herself—headed for his robes like a furry missile. He reached down to help her onto his knee, where she sat down, instantly calm, surveying the group round the fire. "Honestly, Eleanor. You know better than this."

"I do. But I just got her, and I couldn't bear to leave her at home."

"Rules are rules. Not my rules, either—the rules we all drew up together as a group, when Saorsa stopped being a campsite and became a community. You were there."

"Yes, I know. If I couldn't bear to leave her, I should've stayed with her at home." Eleanor ducked her head. "Do you want me to go?"

"You were planning to stay till midweek, weren't you?"

"Wednesday, yes. It's my last visit before next summer, and I just miss the people here so much."

Zadi took hold of the little dog's ears. Gently he extended them until she looked like a bright-eyed bat. "No, don't go. Keep her away from the shoreline, that's all. Unless anyone in the group objects?"

No-one did. There must've been a bit of a conspiracy of silence going on about Maggie anyway, I reckoned, unless Eleanor had been smuggling her about all the time beneath her long coat. "All right," Zadi said. "Let's move on to our affirmations. Why do we speak as we do of the creature of Loch Ness? Why *Her Ladyship*?"

"Because of her royalty," Eleanor responded eagerly, keen to redeem herself. "Her sovereignty over these waters. Blessed be Her Ladyship."

Again came the fervent response. This time Kip didn't join in, and I remembered Her Ladyship of Staines Road, far more lost in the waters of the world than any imaginary cryptid. Unthinkingly I put an arm around his waist. He stiffened for a second as if in surprise, then leaned against me. "That's right," Zadi said, still caressing the bulldog pup, which had curled up on his lap and fallen asleep. "Her Ladyship. And why do we never join in with the crowds who come to the far side of the loch to stare? Why don't we call her the monster?"

Kip raised his head. He said, not quite steadily, "No creature is monstrous in its own environment."

"Exactly. And beautifully put."

"Not me. Star Trek, original series. The episode about the Horta."

"What, *The Devil In The Dark*? I don't remember that line."

"It was in the James Blish book adaptation, not the script." He grinned. "Hey, I'm a bigger geek than you are."

"By a long Scottish mile, it looks like. So—ladies, gentlemen, wee illicit dogs—here we are gathered at Saorsa, to camp out under the stars, enjoy the peace of our far-flung stretch of this loch, and to hope, all of us, one day to have a sighting of Her Ladyship. Why is it possible, even in these days of sonar, when every inch of the great Ness has been sounded and mapped? George, will you tell us, if speech is still at your command?"

A dreadlocked guy in his thirties had captured the bong on its circuit and not let go. He was draped across a rock, his eyes wide and vacant. "Loch Ness lies in the Great Glen Fault," he said dreamily. "The Fault is a rift valley formed seven hundred million years ago, and it runs from Loch Linnhe to the Black Isle. The loch was carved out at the end of the last glacial period, and everybody knew how deep it was—seven hundred and fifty four feet—until the 1990s, when a new sonar scan added eighty two feet to that. Then they found a layer of sediment to add eighty two feet more, and below that, clay, depth unknown, all the way down to the bedrock. So you see, everyone knows everything about Her Ladyship's waters, except that they don't."

"Thank you, George."

"Wait a bit, Jesus. Not finished. Loch Oiche lies in the same fault, Lochs Lochy and Dochfour. Loch Linnhe takes you to the open sea. Are the lochs connected by some subterranean system of faults? Could a creature come and go? Who the fuck knows? George only knows the bong is good."

"Holly, he's started to talk about himself in the third person. Take that off him, please." Zadi nodded pleasantly at the gathered crowd. "Professor George Kingsley of Glasgow University, everyone. I should add that he's on his holidays. The upshot is, my friends, that no-one truly understands the loch. And, as we all say here at Saorsa, absence of evidence is not the same as..."

"Evidence of absence!" the group roared back at him joyously.

"And, if ever we saw Her Ladyship, who would we tell?"

"No-one! We swear! No-one!"

"Oz, it's tough on you to ask this when you've just arrived, but will you keep our vow of secrecy too?"

"How does that work with Sam and the film crew?"

"They take their vow every Sunday along with the rest of us. I'd hate to put them to the test if they got any actual footage, but we trust them. We're ready to trust you."

They were serious about this. Even George the geologist had sat up and was watching me with a trace of anxiety. I couldn't begin to tell him how little cause he had for alarm. "I swear," I said solemnly, "that if ever I see any kind of monst-... er, *creature* in the loch around here, I will never tell anyone. Count on me."

They took my declaration in good part, which was more than I deserved. Charlie gave the mutton legs on the spit a last spin, and a couple of kids began to pat out a beat on brightly painted hand drums. This was where the affirmations ended and the music, lunch and partying began, I guessed. I didn't want to piss on anyone's chips, but I had to get something straight. "Hang on," I said, to no-one in particular, and again the buzz of voices dropped fatally away to make room for mine. This time I ploughed boldly into the gap. "Hang on. Are you saying that... none of you have ever *seen* this creature?"

Holly paused, bong in hand. Zadi—I was starting to think of him as Jesus myself, and I made a scrabbling inner effort to hold on to reality—gazed benignly down at me, the baby bulldog now upside down in his lap, pink belly rippling with snores. Sam the psychonaut reared up through the smoke outside the circle, camera lens gleaming, making the most of the new dramatic silence.

"What," Holly said doubtingly at last. "A real, undeniable sighting? No, of course not."

"Then..." I paused, making a gesture that was meant to take in the tents and caravans, the loch and the carved, bejewelled pine trunks at the top of the road and outside Kip's van. "What's the point of it all, then? All this?"

"I don't know. It just doesn't matter, that's all."

I had everyone's attention. I wished I could let it go. I wished Sam would stop filming, and that Kip hadn't sat up and straightened away from me, but this was ridiculous. "Wouldn't it, though? If you really saw her? You're not gonna tell me that wouldn't mean something to you all."

Maggie's owner cleared her throat. "It would mean quite a bit to me, actually." She turned to meet Holly's astonished gaze. "Well, it would! Just imagine. If that was true—really, truly true, I mean, not just our Camp Saorsa philosophy—anything could be true. Couldn't it? The yeti, or spacemen, or even something outright bonkers like the afterlife or God." She blushed. "Sorry, Jesus. No offence intended."

"None taken." Frowning slightly, Zadi looked around the group. "What about the rest of you? Oz asked a fair question, didn't he? *Is* a philosophy enough? What would it mean to you all, if we got a clear sighting and had to stop loving just the *idea* of her? What would we do?"

Nobody answered. Everyone was looking at Kip, who'd scrambled upright and was staring down at me. All the colour he'd gained from the fireside and the company had faded away. "You bloody idiot, Oz. You just don't get it, do you?"

"Kip, don't." Zadi glanced at Herne, who lowered his big head sadly. "Don't let there be any more strife between those who love each other."

"He has to know it would mean everything for us to see her. Sorry—I shouldn't speak for the group. It would just mean the bloody world to me."

***

Jesus caught up with me in the car park. He was carrying three slices of mutton in a big white bun, and the tiny French bulldog was dancing at his heels. "No more loaves and fishes?" I demanded, backing up against my car like a cornered rat. "Take that to Kip. I don't want any."

"Herne's gone after Kip. He'll see that he eats, don't worry."

"Why didn't someone see to it before? He was half-starved when I got here."

"He wasn't asking then."

"And he is now?"

"Yes, if you can listen."

I wasn't taking that, not even from a guy in white robes and a halo. "You've got no idea what I've listened to from Kip. You don't know anything about us. If you want to fix a relationship up, you can make a start on your own."

"Ouch," he said, and rubbed his cheek as if I'd struck him. "I guess that means I have to turn the other one."

"What?"

"Nothing. Just... don't leave."

But I had to. I hadn't been at Saorsa for twenty four hours, and already I'd upset the mad, delicate balance that prevailed along the shore. How many Sunday afternoons had been passed around the fire, no-one really giving a shit if they saw the monster or not? How had I managed to make Kip look at me that way? "Tell him I'll pick my gear up from him sometime. I've got my wallet and keys."

"Where are you going?"

Home, I wanted to say. When I thought about that word, though, I saw first of all in my mind's eye Kip's university digs. Then I saw my own, and then I flashed back to the nice kid's bedroom I'd had in my parents' house, and it hit me for the first time that, right up until the time when he'd ditched out on us, I'd had a pretty good dad. I flinched away. One of the few things holding me together was my conviction that he'd been a prick and I therefore had to do better. *Home* was the box room in my gran's house, the place she'd cleared out for me so I'd have a place to lay my head when I gave up my dreams and took up my shitty new job. "I'm going back to my gran's house. I don't belong here," I said, and then added in desperation, because his gaze was so piercingly kind, "I don't belong anywhere, okay? Just let me go."

Chapter Fourteen
The Cryptid and the Canary

I couldn't even storm off with conviction. My car might have looked okay, and had driven all right on the flat, but by the time we reached the top of the hill she was complaining loudly, losing power no matter how hard I revved. I jockeyed her into a layby on the far side of the road, so at least I was off Saorsa property. No more freedom for me. Clearly I couldn't handle it.

I did know how to fix a car, though. I carried a full set of spanners, plastic ties and jubilee clips. I'd got Kip a corresponding set, but he preferred his cars beyond repair when he bought them. Ridiculous. Scrambling out, I took deep breaths of the resin-scented air. Noise and power-loss like that usually meant exhaust, so I popped the boot, grabbed my kit and lay down on the damp tarmac and gravel.

For a while I was content. I set aside the events of the day so far. A broken machine above me, wet ground below: these were real things, and sandwiched between them I did have a place where I belonged. I'd been panicky and unimaginative when I'd jumped behind my desk at the Civic Centre. I didn't want to think too much about the money my dad had left me, but I could've taken a few months out, surely, trained as a garage mechanic or an RAC engineer. I liked that last idea, the image of myself as a knight in a shining repair van. Wriggling further under the car, I found the place where my crash had dislodged the exhaust pipe. Really I needed a welding torch, but for now a couple of the larger clips would do.

Right. I had a working car. No reason now for me not to blaze on out of here. Instead I got back inside and sat staring blankly at the shifting gleam of sunlight through the pines. I didn't remember taking the sandwich from Zadi, but there it was on the dashboard, aromatic and still warm, to judge by the butterfly wings of steam it was painting on the glass. I didn't think I could be hungry, not after the debacle by the loch, but when I tried a bite of the meat it was delicious, tender and rich with woodsmoke. Shamefaced, wiping my fingers on the bread, I ate the lot. Then, instead of planting my foot on the gas and heading south, I fell asleep.

In my dream, the wooden monster on the far side of the road came to life. *No, Oz-Man,* she corrected me, steaming up my windscreen in butterfly wings with the breath from her nostrils. *I've been alive all along. Not everyone needs fixing.* She turned her head so she could peer at me from one mirror-shard, bottle-top eye and then the other. *Some things are just fine as they are.*

"Oz. Oz!"

Someone was looking through my far-side window, anxiously knocking. I flipped the central lock, unsure of when I'd decided to seal myself in. The passenger door flew open, and Kip tumbled into the seat. "Oz! Thank God."

The dash clock said I'd slept for half an hour. I was woolly, spaced out and numb, and fairly sure that the monster had pulled me out of the car and started licking me. "Where... Where did you come from?"

"It was Herne. At first he said you'd gone off with Holly and Sam, but he just wants everyone to be happy, so... he lies. Eventually he admitted you'd left, so I..." He doubled up coughing, and I grabbed his shoulder before he could bang his head off the dashboard. "I ran after the car. Like a lost dog."

Neither of us could cope with that image. He was smiling wanly, but his eyes filled with tears, and I let him go and turned to glare out over the loch. "You couldn't have known you'd catch me."

"Yeah, I could. The road's still out."

Of course it was. What had I been planning to do— tear off at ninety and repeat last night's performance? "I was gonna find another way out. Through the village or something."

"There isn't another way. Look, will you talk to me for five minutes? Then you can go down into Rowanburn and find somewhere to stay, or whatever you want to do, but..."

Coughing interrupted him again. I leaned past him to dig into the glove box. I tried to keep it tidy, but Jules fought me back with half-finished packets of humbugs. Grateful for once for her liking for menthol Tunes, I pulled one out of the pack and unwrapped it, and was painfully touched when Kip let me pop it straight into his mouth. "Ta," he managed around it. "Just ran up the hill. 'M okay."

"Why wouldn't I talk to you?"

"Well, because of... You know. Down there."

"What, because you told me off in front of your mates?" Our eyes met: we both knew full well that he'd started by defending me. "Talk. I'm listening."

"Why did you come out here to find me, after what I did to Jules?"

I lost a breath. I'd been expecting monster-talk. A reproof, maybe, for turning my bullying headlights of science on a group of harmless loonies who just wanted to believe. Here he was, though—alone with me, face to face with the thing that had broken us down.

So I had to face it too. I reached down past my layers of bullshit and evasion. "When I think about that," I said, hardly knowing what was about to come out of my mouth, "it makes me so fucking angry that I want to punch out the windscreen. But... not with you."

"That's stupid, Oz. Why not with me?"

"Because..." Shit, this was hard! I gave the wheel a push, hit the horn by accident and startled a grazing deer into the woods. "Because who am I to judge you, all right? There's nothing I could possibly say or do that's worse than what you've been doing to yourself."

The larch trees were still dropping needles. From time to time a shift in the wind would send a cascade of them whispering down across the road and the roof of the car. "But you know who I am," Kip said eventually. "You know what my demons are too, though calling them that feels like a copout."

"I met them at the same time I met you. You never hid anything from me."

"I did. I did, Oz. I honestly thought the pills were so much better than everything else I'd been taking, so much cleaner, more..."

He was struggling for a word. I'd always wanted to help him, so I struggled too. "Legit?"

"Exactly. Like if it came in a little white box, it was okay. I fucking knew it wasn't, and I didn't tell you. I still drove."

This time when I looked for words, none came. Only the whisper of larch needles, and after a moment he picked up the wrong end of my silence. "Sorry," he said, and started to get out of the car.

I grabbed his wrist. "Don't go."

He subsided back into his seat. "I'm glad you came out," he said, a touch of raw desperation in his voice. "But I don't think I can do this anymore—sitting here being sorry, saying sorry, while you look at me like that and I can't work out if you'll ever really forgive me or not."

I couldn't work it out either. All I could do was let him off the hook by turning away. He pulled his arm free, but only far enough to break my grip, and then he dropped his hand into mine and held tight. We both sat staring out of our respective windows. I could feel the feverish heat of his palm. "I don't understand."

"I know. I can't explain, though, not any better than I already—"

"Not about that. About this place and why people come here."

"What? It's a campsite, that's all."

"No, it's not. I've been charging around like a raging bull, but even I can see there's something about it that draws people, and..." I gave his hand a squeeze and let it go. "I want to understand that. I want to understand how tales about monsters and yetis can make smart, nice people drop everything and follow them around the world."

"You want me to teach you about cryptids?"

"I guess so. I don't have to sleep in your van. I could—"

"Oh, Oz."

I dared a glance. He still looked like shit, but he'd started to smile, and it suddenly felt like sunrise here in my dented car. I smiled back helplessly. "What?"

"Mi van es su van, Oz-man."

***

The beach party was in full swing when Kip and I parked up and made our way back along the shore. Zadi had tucked his feet up under his robes and was happily shouting at the crowd across the beat of the drums. His voice reached me in fragments, vibrant and strange. "Do we hunt Her Ladyship?" he cried. "Do we set traps, or go out with the sonar boats to bombard her with alien sounds?" A chorus of denial came back at him. Holly had her hand up in the air like a schoolgirl. "Tell us, then, Holly. Why?"

"We don't hunt her. We set up our cameras and we hope, but only to honour her."

"That's right. Why?"

Geology George, thoroughly awake now, almost pushed her off her rock in his eagerness to reply. "Because what's different to ourselves is sacred. Amen and blessed be!"

How stupid of me, to have worried that my little splash of cold water could put out fires like these! Zadi caught sight of us and waved, and Herne poked his horns in an unmistakeable gesture and gave us a lascivious thumbs-up. A chant arose out of the drumming, a wildly beautiful song to the lady of the lake, combined voices spiralling up with the woodsmoke to the clouds.

The singing followed us through the woods. By the time we reached Kip's clearing, the words were hard to distinguish from the rush of wind in the pines. I opened the caravan door and followed him inside.

A nicer place to come back to now. The tang of disinfectant had subsided and the air smelled clean. I left the door open and cracked a window before crouching to light the gas stove, thinking it better to warm everything through with good ventilation than to sit in a lung-catching fug. I hated the sound of distressed breathing.

I'd given Kip my arm on our way back up from the shore, but it had taken him all his time, and now he was leaning against the sink unit, shivering and trying not to cough, the tiny squeaking rasp I'd come to dread all too obvious in our sudden awkward silence.

What was he on? I'd turned the contents of the van upside down in my cleaning efforts, and hadn't caught so much as a trace in the air of dope. No empty bottles, or full ones for that matter. No sign of gear. Pills were easier to conceal, I supposed. It was none of my business, except that I could've taken better care of him if I knew the whole picture. If I had some idea of what I was trying to patch up with my Vick and my Beecham's powders. I gestured to the bench and table, still flattened down with the sleeping bag and quilt neatly laid on top. "You should probably go to bed."

"Probably. I was there all week before you arrived, though. Here, I'll fold it back."

"I'll do it."

"Right. I'll make us a cuppa, then."

I had to stop my twitchy reflex to keep him still and quiet. Conceding him the kettle and mugs, I gathered up the bedlinen and put it in the cupboard over the door. The table and two long bench seats unfolded nicely once I'd worked out the stowaway design. Solid and clever. I liked it. I patted the seat cushions back into place and caught him watching me with an affection I'd missed so much that my own lungs gave a faint squeak of pain. "There you go," I said unsteadily. "Sit down and introduce me to the wonderful world of cryptozoology."

"Hang on until the kettle boils. You'll definitely need a cup of tea."

Once we were both armed with steaming mugs, he squeezed in beside me at the melamine table. Trusting he might be, but the table still boasted a neat hidden drawer on its underside: I looked away deliberately when he popped it open, determined not to check it for his stash. He pulled out an e-reader familiar to me from many nights of study in his university flat. "Okay, you asked for it," he said, tapping the screen. "Here's the paper I've been working on so far."

"A paper? For a journal, or..."

"No. The university."

"I thought Wilson was ready to kick you off the PhD programme for this stuff."

"She was." He flipped the reader upright in its case and propped it. "When we got back together—after your gran set us up, I mean, during that glorious... What was it? Six days?"

"Five and a half."

"Everything looked different to me. So I went back to Wilson and I told her why I think the study of cryptids has a place in conservation biology."

"Just like you're about to tell me."

"If you can stand it."

I grabbed the table edge and made a pantomime of bracing. "I'll try. And... Wilson bought this?"

"She said she'd put my proposal to the funding board herself. And when I came out here... Well, I didn't care at first. But Herne came sniffing and snooping like he always does, and I told him a bit about it just to get rid of him, and before I knew it I had half a dozen people in here telling me I had to carry on."

"Are these the same half dozen who left you to cough your lungs up in the cold?"

He went still. Then he pushed the reader to arm's length and eased round on the bench to look at me. "Oz, you're one of the brightest lads I ever met. But you don't take stuff in properly sometimes, do you?"

I was a bit affronted. Taking stuff in was my forte. I was the first member of my family to attend university or get any higher education at all, and I'd learned what I needed to know in order to function behind desk six. "What do you mean?"

"I'm sure Sam's told you. He and Holly and pretty much everyone else around here made regular deputations to find out if they could help me. I told them to back off, and I said I would leave if they didn't. I was happy to talk about anything else."

"Sam did tell me, yeah. Holly, too. She said I was... missing the point of freedom."

Kip chuckled. "Really? Couldn't have put it better myself."

"But I don't *get* it, Kip."

"I know you don't *want* to get it. But that's a different thing."

I sat back. I hated the thought that he might be right, and promptly my mind skidded off in the hope of finding other explanations. "Okay," I said grumpily when I failed. "Fair enough. So you went back to work?"

"Yeah. Only thing keeping me sane."

"That's a debatable point. Come on, then. Convince me the way you convinced Prof Wilson."

"Throat's a bit sore. I'll have to let my work do most of the talking."

"I can read this?"

"Course." He pushed the reader in my direction. "Just don't poke your big engineer's thumb on the screen every time you think something's wrong."

I reached for his cold medicines and lined them up in front of him on the table. That damned clock of his was also on the window ledge. When I thought about him curled up in damp blankets here, staring at the numbers rolling grudgingly by... "Do you still want to look at that?"

"Nope. I'm not sure I'm having a good time, but you're certainly making it fly."

He was right. Already the light was shifting outside, the beginnings of afternoon dusk. Soon I would close up the van and curtains and secure us against a winter night. Meanwhile, I'd try to crank open my mind far enough to understand why Kip, Herne, Holly, Sam, Zadi and all the others were here. Why I was. I turned the clock face-down.

***

Like all good stories, Kip's grabbed me from the beginning. His heading—the opening gambit with which he hoped to charm the hard-headed funding panel—made me smile. "*The Cryptid and the Canary,* Kip?"

"Yeah. That's my overall thesis. As long as people are seeing these things, it means we've enough resources left—enough forests, clean waterways, wilderness—to sustain biodiversity across the whole planet. It's when the sightings drop that we're reaching danger levels of habitat destruction."

"The cryptids have nowhere to hide."

"Right. So they're like the canaries the coal miners used to take down the shafts with them to warn about gas. When the bird keels over, or the monsters disappear, it's a red flag. A kind of thermometer."

"But there's so many factors. People's ability to travel and find these things, for one."

Already my thumb was hovering. "I know," he said, and to my surprise pulled my hand away and brushed a kiss to my knuckles. "That's the beauty of it. Think about the upsurge of sightings during the sixties and seventies. Does that tie into my thesis, or was it all part of the countercultural hippie movement where going off and seeing normal, capitalist stuff like lions on safari wasn't enough anymore? Maybe there was a feeling that the cryptids were only going to show themselves to special people, spiritual ones. Sightings no money could buy. Or you could take the view that hippies and other subculture groups are seizing on the idea of cryptids because the reality of what we're doing to tangible animals in our rainforests and our oceans is too much to bear. And then there's the whole question mark over whether these things exist at all."

"Not for you."

"Yes, for me. I've been chasing them for years. I've seen evidence, but I've never experienced anything I could truthfully say was a sighting of a cryptid animal."

"Seriously?"

"Seriously. Track marks, unidentifiable scat, hoots and growls in the night. I've been just about frightened to death a few times, and something invisible once chased me for half a mile through the woods in Snowdonia National Park, but that's just the point—I didn't *see* it."

"I thought you must be on first-name terms with half these monsters. What keeps you going, if you've never really..."

"Just what I painted on the ceiling in my flat. Lack of evidence from my one tiny point of view means nothing on a global scale. And these questions too, the ones you're asking me now and the ones I've always asked myself. Some bits of the planet are so overrun by humans they're at crisis point for space and resources, and other bits—sometimes within a couple of hundred miles—are wilderness. The Arctic, the Russian taiga, deep-sea trenches like the Marianas... We know next to nothing about those places. Absence of evidence is no good at all."

His voice rasped to silence. I hadn't thought to bring a spoon over, but he took the bottle of cough mixture out of my hand, uncapped it and knocked back an absentminded swig. The label was familiar, a recipe based on Gran's favourite principle that the nastier it tasted, the more good it would do. I handed him a tissue to wipe the reactive tears from his eyes. "Okay, you've got me."

"I have? Is that good?"

"If you were teaching a course on this stuff, I'd be first through the door for your lectures." I resisted the brightening of his face: the funding committee would give him a harder time than this. "The only trouble is, I'm not sure if I should be turning up at the biology department or philosophical studies."

"Absolutely." He gave me the reader back. "That's why the rest of this sets out all the hard data I could compile about cryptid sighting areas and their geopolitical contexts—the attitudes of the societies around them to conservation, their infrastructure and resources, what portion of their economy they're willing and able to dedicate to habitat preservation and wildlife protection. Have you heard of Cuddly Animal Syndrome?"

I pushed aside the image that had sprung into my mind: biologists in bunny suits, indulging an off-duty kink. "No," I said cautiously. "I don't think so."

"I bet you've seen it in action. Jules has it. She was so pissed off when I told her. You know she gives half her pocket money to the Labrador guide-dog puppy appeal?"

"What, the one permanently set up in the Eldon centre? She does not."

"She does too. She's in love with the furry little faces. Wet noses, big eyes. So I asked her, if she knew for certain that some really ugly jungle bug was going to help cure cancer in five years' time, would she change her donation to a rainforest charity?"

"Wow. You like to put your head in the lion's mouth. What did she say?"

"Nothing. She sat and thought about it with steam coming out of her ears for nearly ten minutes, then she gave me the finger and walked off."

I snorted with laughter. "The little shit. She hasn't had pocket money for months, what with paying off one misdemeanour and another. Gran's housekeeping cash has been going missing, though."

"Really?"

"Yeah. Robbing your gran to pay for puppies—where does that fit in with your ecological world view?"

"Oh, God. I don't know—somewhere between the gutter and the stars, like everyone else." He grinned at me, and there we were, just as we had been back when the world still made sense, discussing Jules and her crimes. Any minute now he'd come up with a plan to help me and the old lady strategise around her. Then his face shadowed. "Anyway. People do this, especially in the UK. If a thing's cute and furry it gets the money, and that attitude has some serious ramifications for funding. I've tried to analyse it all down in this document here, but you can read it for yourself. You're right—I am a bit tired."

"Want me to put the bed up?"

"No, no. I'll just stretch out on the other bench."

"Okay." I watched while he pulled himself out from behind the table and took a blanket and pillow from the cupboard. "If you wake up and I'm not here, I'll just have gone down to the village to get us some supplies, all right? I'll be back soon."

Chapter Fifteen
Snap

Next day the weather broke at Camp Saorsa. Cracked, I should say: there was an abyss between Sunday's chilly sunlight and the sideways sleet that hit me as I stepped outside for my morning ablutions. Swearing, I dived back in for a hat and coat. Kip regarded me from over the top of the quilt beneath which we'd spent the night, sharing body warmth but nothing else.

The store in Rowanburn had turned out to be well stocked. I'd picked up not only our groceries but a carbon-monoxide detector from the camping section, and after fixing us some breakfast I tried to settle to tinker with it. The stove had caused it to give off the faintest beep, as if Kip's stolen equipment might have liked to poison us, but couldn't quite be bothered to finish the job.

It was that kind of day. Kip had barely eaten or spoken, huddled up on the far side of the melamine table over his tea and toast while the sleet battered the windows and the wind rocked our tiny refuge on its frame. The smells of damp I'd exorcised yesterday were creeping back out from the carpet and the walls. I wondered if he wanted his clock set upright again—if, despite his assurance that his van was my van, I'd overstayed my welcome.

Well, it was time to start making decisions. By rights I should be three hundred miles south of here today. I set the monitor down. "I don't think you've got a leak. That stove was never built to be dragged around the place, though."

"Right."

"You should leave this gadget switched on anyway. And check the connections regularly. The pipes aren't a good fit for here."

"All right, so I nicked the damn stove. Stop fucking nagging me, Oz."

My eyebrows nearly hit the mould-splotched ceiling. Before I could get breath to speak, Kip buried his face in his hands. "Sorry. I'm sorry. I could hardly sleep last night for coughing."

That makes two of us. I kept that to myself. He looked awful this morning, almost transparent in the grey light. "Should've let me rub Vick on your feet," I said, stirring my tea with as much patience as I could muster. "I just don't want you to die of carbon monoxide."

"I can think of worse ways. You just go to sleep, don't you?"

"Yep, and you leave a lovely cherry-red corpse for whichever poor bastard happens to find you. It's the all-round perfect way of offing yourself. Want a refill on your tea?"

"No. I've got to go and make a phone call."

"Me too." I glanced at my watch. Monday morning, time ticking up towards nine o'clock. "There's no signal here. What do we have to do, go stand in the kiosk in Rowanburn?"

"No. There's a clear patch at the top of the hill behind the van."

"I wish you'd told me that the other night when I thought you were dying of pneumonia."

"Missing the point of *saorsa*, Oz."

"I'll saorsa your arse for you in a minute."

So together we wrapped up in waterproofs, woolly hats and scarves. Together we tramped up the hill, and then tramped discreetly away from one another far enough to let each other make our phone calls in privacy. Five minutes later we met up again. I thought my call had been bad. Cedric Beaver had, as it turned out, been watching my empty seat behind desk six since half past eight. He'd taken my absence, and my stated determination to extend it, just exactly as I might have expected. I doubted I'd have a job to go back to, no matter how many strings Gran could pull out of Cedric's past on my behalf.

But Kip's call had been worse. He came to stand in front of me, icy drops spilling off the edge of his hood. "I'm gonna have to go home."

"Was that your mum?"

177

"Yeah. Well, April, anyway—the little girl who looks after her."

"I met April."

"Did you?"

"Yes. She was there when I visited." Suddenly I wanted to tell him how I'd helped her, how I'd fixed up the washing machine and the window, but then I'd have had to tell him how I'd provoked the neighbour kids into breaking it in the first place. "Is something wrong with your mum?"

"There'll never be anything right with her. She did a Jules, but on a grand scale."

"Pinched the grocery money?"

"And not for Labrador pups, either. She must've been watching April to see where I hid the cash."

"I didn't think she ever left the house."

"She doesn't. She usually buys off the internet, but the local dealers know what she wants. One of them must've come knocking on the door while April was out."

"Oh, shit, Kip. I'm so fucking sorry."

I wished something more helpful or constructive had come out of my mouth. He didn't seem to mind, though: looked a shade less miserable through the veil of sleet. "Don't worry. I'm pretty used to it. I'll have to go back and sort her out, though. She'll be skint."

"Does she have PayPal?"

"What?"

"PayPal. What's her address?"

"Well—yeah, she does, but I changed her password and swore April to secrecy."

"So the kid runs it for her? All the better." My phone signal had disappeared. I turned around and jumped onto the nearest rock. "C'mon, Kip, just tell me. I don't want to go home yet, and... neither do you, although what the bloody hell we're doing up here, I don't know. We can call it a loan if you want."

"What loan? What are you doing?"

"Sending her some money. I can spare it, okay? My dad left me some dosh when he buggered off, and I want to help." The signal came back. "PayPal addie. Now!"

He jumped at my shout, and gave up the address as if I'd fished it out of him with a hook. I wrapped my arm around an overhanging branch for balance and stood on my toes long enough to key in my info and make the transfer. "There. Sorted."

He was wide-eyed when I got back down to him. "You didn't have to do that, Oz."

"It wasn't much. Just enough to cover a grocery bill or two."

"I'll text April and tell her."

"She's got control of the mobile phone, too?"

"This is the third. Letty sold the others. I'm gonna have to cut her internet off one day, but it's the only contact with the outside world she's got."

"Jesus." I put an arm around him. "Listen to me. I know you do your best for her, but... there's no way she should be living the way she is."

"The alternatives are a care home or the loony wing of a hospital. She's forty two years old."

179

"I wasn't thinking about her. I was thinking about you, dealing with her year in, year out."

For a moment I thought he'd pull away. He'd gone to incredible lengths to ensure no-one ever found out what he'd done. Maybe despite everything he didn't want me to know. "It's okay," he said indistinctly through the fastenings of his hood. "Don't think of me as good, though, Oz. Not as a good son. She wanted to talk to me today, and... I hung up before April could put her on. There's whole weeks when I can't stand to see her."

Could he possibly think I'd blame him? Letty was charming, sweet, and dangerous as a box of snakes. "Come on," I said roughly, tightening my grip. "If you stay out here much longer, I won't have to worry about carbon monoxide knocking you off."

"Hypothermia's not a bad death either, is it? Another one where you just—"

"Kip, do me a favour and shut up."

We trudged in silence back down the slope. We were almost at the van before he stopped me, slithering round in front of me in the leaf mould to plant his hands on my chest. "Oz."

"What now?"

"I'm skint until I get my next grant payment through. I've been writing for some conservation journals, but..."

But Letty's a bottomless pit. "Don't worry. I mean, it's good about the journals. I didn't know about those."

"I've been doing them for a while, under a different name so they wouldn't brush me off as that nutter who chases monsters. Joni Petko."

I gaped. The Petko articles had featured regularly in the university magazine, the dean and faculty understandably proud of their contributing student. "You're Joni Petko?"

"I thought you'd work it out. It's a direct anagram of..."

"Joe Kipton." I stopped myself from slapping my brow. "No, I didn't work it out. I thought you were a girl from Latvia. Those are some serious publications you've been getting into."

"I know. I'm pleased. And they pay, which is good, because I've had to support all my own bad habits as well as Letty's." He offered me a wan grin. "What I'm saying is, I can pay you back. And I will."

"For God's sake. It really doesn't matter. I just—"

"Oz, do *me* a favour. I'm trying to say thank you for the loan."

***

Neither of us wanted to go home. Over the course of that day, though, it became increasingly hard for me to work out what good would be served by either of us staying.

Staying together, at any rate. Bundling Kip back into the van, rediscovering its warmth, I'd felt a matching heat inside: he was talking to me, letting a bit of light and air in at last on the stifling world he'd shared with his mum.

But what were we meant to do with ourselves all day cooped up in a one-room van? Once upon a time the answer to that would have been obvious. *If the van's a-rockin'...* Now its only movements were the small, unhappy shifts on its chassis as Kip paced back and forth. Five steps from end to end: a brief, fraught pause, never quite the same length as any of the others. Five steps back. I'd pulled a paperback out of my rucksack in an effort to read. He wasn't annoying me, I told myself, and even if he was, he had a right to pace in his own van. "Hoi, you," I said, as gently as I could. "Caged beast. Your tea's getting cold."

"You're a lot like your gran in some ways. A cup of tea for all occasions."

That hadn't felt like a compliment. "Right. Okay, yeah. Probably."

"Do you remember when Mr Patwardhan got run over in the street outside her house, and Mrs P got left behind by the ambulance crew in all the chaos? *Go and put the kettle on, Kip.*" He shook his head. "Come rain, come shine, disaster or tragedy. Let's just have a nice cuppa."

Not annoying me at all. I set the book down. "Your point being?"

Saner lights came into his eyes. He flopped down onto the bench opposite me, put his elbows on the table and ran his hands through his hair. "The point being, I guess, that Mrs P got a hot drink when she needed one most, with sugar for the shock. That she had a neighbour who'd take her in and comfort her, and phone and pay for a taxi to take her into hospital. Those eternal cuppas—your Gran's and yours—are a symbol for all the resources in the house, all the food and drink and shelter. The person you're helping can't use them all at once, but at least they know they're there. That *you* are. That's the point."

I sat back. "You do make nice apologies. Fancy a game of snap?"

"Of what?"

"Snap. You flip a card, I flip a card. If one of us—"

"I know what snap is, you dork. I haven't got any cards."

"I don't believe it. Countless poor lost souls have been stuck here on rainy days, haven't they?"

"Yeah, but…"

"I bet one of them left us a legacy. Can't be in here, because I've checked every inch, but I'll go and have a look in your storage hut." I gave him my best comic effort at a wink. "You sit and finish your tea."

He rolled his eyes at me. "Yes, Grandma."

I was right about the legacy. In fact I hit pay dirt: not only a deck of cards but a miniature Scrabble set and Monopoly. Let the games begin! If Kip thought I was tiresome now, wait till he'd seen me at the end of a long, bitter property battle on the streets of London. I gathered up these treasures and began to squeeze back out of the hut.

And there, wedged into the furthest corner of the top shelf, was his stash. I froze, clutching my stupid little boxes to my chest. He wasn't a man to do anything by halves, my Kip. Half a dozen white cardboard cartons, neatly labelled and bagged in plastic. Procodone: his fallback crack when booze had failed and everything else had proved too expensive, unwieldy or obvious.

I wanted to throw them into the woods. But you didn't do that on a pristine loch shore, didn't throw away your toxic crap and leave it to poison the badgers and birds. I didn't even have a toilet to flush the things down, the way junkies do in the movies when they've decided to reform.

And I wasn't the junkie. Kip's pills weren't my business. The only business I had was to decide—what had Gran said?—where to draw my line in the sand. Tugging my hood up, I made my way back through the sleet to the van's front door.

***

I beat him hollow at Monopoly. Clearly he hadn't wasted as much of his youth as I had, and I couldn't imagine Letty at the kind of family table where I'd grown up, battling my boring, dying, treacherous, beloved mam and dad for possession of a row of plastic houses and hotels. Snap, too: he lacked the competitive edge. When it came to Scrabble, though, he blew me away like a handful of dust. Before I could sort out my consonants from my vowels he had *quixotic* lined up and ready to go, *quartz* and *trapeze* and—joining up to the tail of my pitiful *dare*— *zoophobe*, which turned out to be a fear of animals, not of Whipsnade or Regent's Park.

He was so bloody bright. Left to himself, he'd have turned the board into a story, Kip as Don Quixote with quartz-tipped sword, flying in on his trapeze to fight zoophobe Oz, who didn't dare do anything. I wanted to point out to him that I wasn't scared of animals in general, just very doubtful of cryptids. But it was just a game. He walloped me by several hundred points, then sat staring past me out into the unrelenting rain. "Oz," he said eventually. "I want to ask you for something, and it seems so bloody unfair."

Shit. What? What would I do if the loan to Letty hadn't been enough? What if he asked me for money to score? I laced my fingers together and wondered once more if we both shouldn't have got into our cars and cleared out of Camp Saorsa at dawn, gone back to what passed for our ordinary lives. On which subject, Kip didn't even have a car anymore, as far as I knew. How had he got here? Did he need another Love Machine, a rusted-out Mazda to drive into the ground?

I took a deep breath. I set aside my zoophobia, xenophobia, sheer ingrained cowardice or whatever else it was that had brought me to this point in my life with more fears than hopes, more grit in my eyes than dreams. "Anything. What do you need?"

"You know when I was pacing before, and it was driving you nuts?"

"Not really."

"It was, and I don't blame you. But I need to do some more of that. I... I need to bounce off the walls. And I don't want you to see me that way."

He was asking me to go. No, not even that—just to let him alone for a while. Why was such a simple, reasonable request harder to grant than the cash-for-dope would have been, or buying him a car? This was it, I supposed. This was the point where I had to walk out and let him choose, and if that meant procodone or whatever else he had hidden about the place, it wasn't my business but his.

Except that I loved him. Why couldn't I say it? The time wasn't right—he wanted solitude, not professions of undying devotion from me—but still the words were burning on the root of my tongue. "Right," I said, half-choking on them, upsetting the Scrabble box onto the floor as I got to my feet. "I'll go for a walk, then. Do you want me to pick those bits up?"

"No. It'll give me something useful to do while I'm tearing up the carpets. I'm sorry, Oz. Must be the weather, or Mercury retrograde or a bunged-up ley line or something. Go and hang out with Sam's crew if the weather stays as horrible as this, but... I have to be on my own for a while. I just feel like shit."

I looked at him miserably. *Snap.*

Chapter Sixteen
Angelic Brethren

Sam was on the beach when I got down there, smartly kitted out in waterproofs, busily filming. His camera had its own snug little jacket and a hood to shield the lens. He waved and beckoned as if he'd been expecting me. "Hey, Oz! Just in time for the greatest show on earth."

I looked up and down the beach, then out across the loch's rain-pitted surface to see if I was missing anything. "What's going on? Is the monster—er, is Her Ladyship putting in an appearance?"

"It's okay. You can call her the monster when you're with me. I respect the camp rules when I'm around the others, but I don't belong here. Just passing through."

I went to stand beside him. I tried to see through his eyes, or his lens at any rate. The only living souls on the beach were Zadi and Herne. Zadi had reverted to an anorak and jeans, but Herne was still wearing his headdress. "Are you filming those two? Doesn't Herne ever take off his horns?"

"That, my friend…" He paused to adjust the lens hood. "That is a question for the angelic brethren. I will ask them for you, if you like."

I stole a sideways glance at him, trying to see behind the anti-glare coating of his spectacles. He was fantastically elegant. You could've taken him to church or a garden party or back home to meet your mum, but somewhere behind all that branding and waterproofing, he was high as a kite.

This was something I was going to have to get used to. If I meant to help Kip—on his terms, not mine—I had to learn about the places behind the looking glass, down the rabbit hole. People took drugs for a reason. No good me denying that, the way I might deny the existence of the loch monster or Bigfoot. Sam seemed like a reasonable, good-natured guy even when tripping. He might be a good place to start. "So," I began experimentally, "when you say you don't belong here, do you mean you belong with them?"

"With who?"

"With the brethren. The angels. Is that where you come from?"

He rocked with laughter, not letting the movement reach his lens. "No, man. I come from Port Hope in Ontario. Nice place. Great downtown, lots of antiques. Two sisters, one brother. Come to think of it, I guess Paul would be my next of kin now that our parents are dead." Balancing the camera, he reached into an inner pocket with his free hand. "Here, take his card. Why were you asking me about the angels? Am I obviously smashed?"

"No. Well. Not in any bad way."

"Something about the eyes, though, right? Usually I'm on the other end of this camera so I can see. You busted me, Oz-man. I'm trialling a brand new mix of the psilocybins and amanitas we've found around here."

Fuck me, that sounded dangerous. Still, I had to try to respect him—his *saorsa*, his experience, the fact that he knew what he was doing. "And... do you smoke that, or..."

"Injected extractions. I cooked 'em right up in my lab in the trailer. The thing is, I don't feel high at all. Everything's just incredibly detailed and beautiful. Hey, look—Zadi's going for it."

For a paddle, from what I could see. Why this was worthy of Sam's documentary time, I wasn't sure, unless he wanted to record Britain's Most Eccentric at their finest. Here on this freezing loch shore, temperatures dropping by the minute as the northeast wind got up, Zadi was taking off his boots and socks. Herne didn't look too impressed by this procedure either: was watching his former other half with lowered brow, arms folded over his chest. Absently I pushed the card Sam had given me into my pocket. "What's he up to?"

"Hush. I'm gonna open my mic up to full. They tend not to notice I'm here once they get going on one of these bouts, but I don't want to disturb them, and the audio will be worth having. Try not to let the stones crunch under your feet."

I stood tensely still. Because he'd asked me to, it now seemed perilously difficult not to crunch the stones. I felt

189

perverse temptations to jump around, fall over, run noisily back up the shore and burst in on whatever the hell I'd left Kip alone to do in his van. Letting go of a breath, I tried to focus on Zadi and Herne. Zadi, now barefoot, was gingerly making his way to the water's edge. The stones must have been slippery—he flailed one arm in Herne's direction and almost fell. His voice flew at me on the wind, filled with pain. "You could at least help."

Herne didn't budge, except to point downwards. "Are you kidding? Have you seen these?"

Zadi got his balance and had a look, interested despite himself. "Oh, wow. Did you just get those?"

"This morning. I woke up and they were there."

From somewhere—from God only knew what bizarre online fancy-dress store, perhaps—he'd acquired a pair of hooves. He must be on tiptoe inside them, because they'd pushed his heels off the ground and he was taller still, a great burly half-beast in the rain. Zadi gave a shout of laughter. "Those are great. Cloven, are they?"

"Right up the middle. That's why I don't want to get them wet."

"According to our standardised cultural mythology, that makes you the devil, I believe."

"What—not wanting to get wet feet?"

"No, you idiot. Cloven hooves."

Herne roared back at him. Laughter or a threat, I couldn't tell: his voice was like a trumpet blast. "Don't you quote standardised mythology at me. Is that the same culture that shows me rampaging through every other horror movie, eating babies for breakfast and puppies for dessert? I'm the lord of the ancient wildwood, and it's not my fault if your lot hijacked my horns."

"My lot?"

"Well, I suppose that's not fair. It's amazing how many people still believe in the devil who don't believe in you."

"That's modern times for you, I suppose." Zadi set out over the rocks again. "Come on, your lordship. Give me your hand."

"No chance. Listen to me. The water's the water. Air's air, fire's fire, earth is gorgeous, smelly, mossy earth. Let them be what they are, can't you? Enjoy them that way."

I gave Sam an uneasy nudge. "Are those two all right down there?"

"As good as they ever are."

"They're not about to drown each other or anything?" I remembered I wasn't supposed to be making a noise. "Oh. Sorry."

"Don't worry. I'll edit you out."

"What are they trying to do?"

"Herne? Nothing but enjoy life, I think. Zadi's trying to walk on the water."

I was just far enough gone to ask. "And... does he ever succeed?"

He gave a snorting chuckle. "Of course not."

"But this is a regular performance? He keeps trying?"

"Yeah, and all he ever gets is soaked. Which is a shame, because if he came to me, I could give him something to make him fly."

"Surely he's had enough already."

"Who, our Jesus? Clean as a whistle. Doesn't even drink."

"Then he's just..." I was trying to be more open to this place and the people who took refuge here, so I searched for a kindly word and failed. "He's just nuts. Why do you keep filming him?"

"Well, in part because it's interesting how people with delusions—if he is deluded—act out their madness. The societal backdrop to that, I mean. Who would he pretend to be if he lived in a pre-Christian era, or on a different planet?" He grinned. "I bet you're hoping that's rhetorical, Oz-Man. Who would a guy who thinks he's Jesus pretend to be if he was an alien? Anyway, I want to record it. And you never know—maybe one day..."

His drop into silence startled me. He'd gone absolutely still. I'd given up on watching Zadi—no fun for me in witnessing some poor nutter in his fight against reality—but now I looked again.

He was two yards out from the shore. And he must have found some flat-topped rock to stand on, a rock whose surface coincided exactly with that of the loch, because his feet were poised among the raindrops. Very carefully, not wanting to disturb Sam's focus, I took hold of his arm. "Sam, look."

The spell broke. I felt a kind of weird pop at the back of my throat, and I briefly smelled salt and copper. Zadi gave a yelp and dropped through the surface like a stone, sending up an explosion of spray.

Herne waded out for him, new hooves and all. "I told you," he bellowed, taking hold of him by both armpits and hoisting him upright. "I bloody told you. Let the water be water. Let local laws of physics apply!"

"But there must be more..." Zadi struggled in his grip, then submitted to being hauled ashore. "There must be more to life than that. There must."

"Why? We've got this whole beautiful Earth. Ah, man, if you'd settled for me as I was, and stopped pulling both of us to shreds..."

Abruptly Sam lowered the camera. "That'll do for today."

"Did you see that? Did it record?"

"I don't know. I'll look in a minute. We should get out of here—they're arguing."

"Don't they argue all the time?"

"Yes, about religion and cosmology and the ultimate fate of the universe. Not about why they broke up." He shook his head. "Not my kind of reality TV. Come on."

"But... can I watch the recording?"

"I tell you what. I just want to go and think about what *I* saw, not what the camera did. And you're a great guy, and I'm really glad you came rolling down that hill to find Kip, but I think I want to do it on my own." Turning the camera upside down, he flipped open a tiny drive drawer and took out the media card. "So I'm gonna give this to you. For safekeeping, and to watch whenever you want. It should play on anything with an SD slot. Catch you later, Oz-Man."

He set out along the beach. I watched his skinny figure fade into the rain. Everyone wanted to be alone today. Herne and Zadi had gone off in their separate directions. Trying to convince myself that I too preferred my own company, I crunched my way down to the water's edge. There was enough sand here to display a pattern of boot prints and deeply cloven hooves. I thought about wading out to find Zadi's rock. Or maybe I wanted to dash back to the car and see if I'd remembered to sling my laptop into the boot before leaving Gran's. The laptop had an SD drive. I could watch Sam's film for myself. I could see what there was to be seen.

Instead I sat down on a flat rock of my own, suddenly lonelier than I'd ever been in my life. The sensation was like gravel passing through my insides. I listened without much interest to the slither and scrape of feet on the shingle behind me. I didn't want Zadi back, or Herne. Not even Sam, nice guy though he was. I only wanted...

"Oz."

I twisted round. There in the downpour, almost unrecognisable under his layers of woollies and waterproofs, stood Kip. I tried to stand up, but the algae-slick stones rolled out from under my boots. He saved me the trouble, dropping down to sit beside me on my rock. "Oz," he said again, as if he wasn't quite sure, and I unzipped his hood far enough to expose his sweet mouth. He tasted of menthol Tunes and good times, a world I'd loved and lost. He closed his eyes: the rain had stuck his eyelashes together, and he looked wildly beautiful, something freshly tossed out of a place even Zadi and Herne could agree might be heaven. To my relief, after a heartstopping pause, he kissed me back. "Shouldn't be doing this," he said, voice muffled against my cheek. "I'll give you my cold."

"I'll take it." I was so bloody happy to see him. I wanted him—the root of my cock, stiffening at the brush of his mouth across my ear, was the only warm part of me—but I also didn't care if we never fucked again, if he would only stay here with me, alive and real, on this rock in the rain. I threw my arms around him. "Oh, Kip."

"It's okay. I've got you." He returned my embrace, his fists closing tight in my jacket, and I lost all sense of needing to correct him, tell him it was the other way around and I had *him*, in the power of his hold. He was always so much stronger than he looked. "Everything's gonna be okay, but I've got to talk to you, Oz."

Reluctantly I let him go. "Did you get some good pacing done?"

"Not bad. I didn't claw up the carpets, though. You made the place too nice."

"You could've ripped it apart for all I care. Anything that would help."

"That's what I want to talk to you about. Things that help."

Oh, I didn't want to have this conversation. At last it was sinking in with me, though, that when it came to Kip and the way he dealt with or failed to deal with his problems, what I wanted didn't matter. I took his hand, chilly in its wet fingerless glove, and put both of mine around it. "Talk."

"I want to ask you something. Will you try to tell me the truth?"

"I feel like I'm losing my grip on the truth, after a couple of days here. But I will try, yeah."

He edged closer to me so that his hip was pressing mine. "Okay. What would you... What would you do, Oz, if any time you felt rough—not just a bit, but week-long, belly-flop shit—you could pop two little pills and make it go away?"

Obediently I tried to think. All I could come up with was an objection. "It comes back, though, doesn't it?"

"Yeah, of course. But imagine if you could get a *break* from it—not some uncertain, endorphin-rush bollocks like going for a jog or doing bloody Zumba for an hour. A definite, right-now time of feeling better, delivered in two little pills, any time you need it. What would you do?"

"But it's not real. It's... false euphoria, brain chemistry. Isn't it?"

His hand clenched into a fist. "Oh, for fuck's sake, Oz. It's *all* just brain chemistry. Brain squirts out a juice, you have a feeling. And a feeling's just a feeling—if you're having it, it's real." He stared out grimly over the loch. "I don't even get why anyone would *want* to be clean. I don't see the charms of the lifestyle. The whole world turns into one of those stupid little stools people have, the ones you bark your shins off, and everything you hit when you fall over has a razor's edge."

At last I understood what he was asking me. Not what I thought, not for an argument or one of my endless supply of opinions. A wave of sorrow went through me, that Kip had had to live among the shin-barking stools and the razors. "I'm sorry," I said, hardly sounding it with the ragged-edged rasp of my words. "I'm sorry, then. You're asking me what I would do."

"If you can tell me. If I've got any right to ask."

"Okay. If my world was like that, I'd probably turn to pills or drink myself."

"Seriously?"

"Seriously. I get it, all right? And I love you. I want you as you are, even if you've got a fight on your hands. It's my fight, too. Even if... Even if you've lost."

He laid his head on my shoulder. For the best part of a minute, the soaking wet, razor-edged world was fine with me—beautiful in a way I'd never dreamt, alive and real. Then he shifted a bit and looked downshore, towards an outcrop of larches on a small rocky promontory a hundred yards or so to the east. "Oz, is that Sam down there?"

He'd wandered off in that direction. "Could be. I was just talking to him a few minutes ago."

"He's not moving."

"Well, you know him. He's probably communing with his inner spaceman."

"I don't think so. He's lying down."

I turned to look. Kip's eyes were sharper than mine, but when he pointed, I too could see the lanky shape sprawled beneath the trees. His head and shoulders seemed to be propped on an exposed root. He'd chosen a perfect vantage point: the loch laid out before him so he could watch for monsters, above him a sky full of angels. Under his hand, if he wished, the rich rare earth which yielded the mushrooms and marvels he loved.

And there was something wrong. I lurched to my feet, pulling Kip up with me, and we stood holding on to each other. Then, without need for another word, we both set off at a run.

***

For a bunch of feckless hippies, the people of Saorsa came together well in an emergency. Herne dashed out of the woods and caught up with me and Kip on the beach. He could move like the wind in his ridiculous hooves, and like the wind he swept past us when he saw our goal. He made short work of the promontory rocks and knelt at Sam's side.

Then he put back his head and let loose a shout, a full-blooded version of the sound I'd heard before. It shook the air like a trumpet blast and brought Zadi out onto the beach at full pelt: I guessed that, no matter how hard they fought, the two were never far apart. Someone had told me that Zadi was a doctor, when not messing about in robes and halo by Loch Ness. Kip and I converged with him, and we helped one another clamber up through the trees and tumbled stones to where Sam lay. Kip grabbed hold of me and held me still once we were there: in silence I obeyed him. *Give the doctor room to do his work.* I was breathless, and the run had almost done for poor Kip. I drew him in to lean against me.

The rain had stopped at last. Pallid winter sunlight began to make its way through the clouds. Herne's cry had roused the whole camp, and soon the promontory was alive with good neighbours bearing blankets, flasks, discreet offers to help. Holly and half the film crew came barrelling down the beach: I guessed that they were under strict orders from Sam to get to the scene of any unusual activity as fast as possible. Herne went down to intercept them. He didn't say a word, but he put out his arms, and Holly ran blindly into them.

And none of it did any good. Zadi got to his feet. He took out his mobile, dialled and began to speak, his voice low and businesslike. I could see Sam's face now. His eyes were wide open. I could see the sky in them. He'd taken off his glasses, as if to study something beyond their range. Whatever it was—whatever vision had come to him from the inside or the outside of his strange world—it had left him with a look of pure, blissed-out wonder.

My head spun. I'd never seen a dead body before. Gran might have left Granddad in his coffin on the parlour table, but the lid had been firmly clamped down. And no-one had let me anywhere near my mum, not in the days after her death or even in the week or so before. The only person who knew anything about all this was Kip. Kip knew. He put an arm around me. "Come down here, sweetheart. Come away."

He could *sweetheart* me all he wanted. He sat me down on the sloping bank to the loch, but when he tried to push my head between my knees to stop me from fainting, I recoiled. The dazzle was clearing from my eyes. I could hear again through the buzz of insects in my ears, and, most importantly, I could speak. I sucked in a breath. "You see? You see?"

"Yes, I saw." He held out a shaking hand to me. "Sam's dead. I saw."

He thought I was in shock. He didn't know that I was clearer, more lucid, than ever in my life before. I didn't need his comfort. I needed to sort something out. "Do you fucking well *see*?"

"I don't... I don't know. See what?"

"I tried, Kip. God help me, I tried to understand. I know I've been a stuffed-up little prig, and I came out here, and I thought about things, like maybe all addictions aren't bad, and maybe some people can handle it, and..." I dug my hands into the loamy earth and grappled my way upright. "I dunno—I must've forgotten I've been watching people die of their addictions since I was fourteen. I liked Sam. I was talking to him half an hour ago. Do you *see*?!"

He sat sprawled, staring up at me. "You think I'm gonna end up like that."

"Why the fuck would I think anything else? One day, one night..." I had to stop: somewhere during my tirade I'd started to cry, and tears and snot were running down the back of my throat. "One drink, one cigarette, one pill, one bloody... mushroom too many, and that's it. You're gone. I'll look into *your* eyes and see nothing but sky."

"If I was doing any of that stuff anymore."

"I'll be talking to you, and I'll be thinking what a fucking incredible guy you are. How in all the history of all guys everywhere, there's never been one like you, like my Kip, and there can't ever be one again. And half an hour later, I'll..." I swayed and grabbed at a tree branch. "What?"

"If I was drinking any more. Or taking pills, or shooting up, or even fucking smoking. I'm clean."

My heart lurched. "Don't."

"Don't what?"

"Don't mess with me about this. You sat in my gran's kitchen and told me you were clean before."

"No. I told you I'd stopped drinking. And I let you think there was more to it than that, because I was a lying arsehole, like... not like *all* addicts, but like my kind. Then I crashed the car with Jules in it, and I understood. I finally fucking understood what I'd done. So I came here, and I shut myself up with nothing. Nothing at all."

"Why didn't you say?"

He rolled up onto his knees. He put out his hands like a suppliant, and I'd have died rather than fail to make the catch. "Would you have believed me?" he asked, letting me lift him to stand in front of me. "I didn't believe myself. I didn't want to tell you until I could be sure."

He was sure now. He caressed my knuckles with his thumbs. His eyes did have the sky in them, but there was a blaze of life between the clouds. I leaned towards him until our brows touched, and as if we'd both been made of glass I saw again—from his point of view this time— the bed in the caravan, the miserable pile of blankets, the clock for forcing time to go by. "Jesus, Kip. You've had nothing?"

"For a week and three days now. Not that I'm counting."

"It must've been so hard."

"Still is. I think it always will be. It was fucking horrendous today, which is why I threw you out. But once you were gone, I remembered how much worse it was without you. So I set off to bring you back home."

"Seriously? What help have I been?"

"You've been Oz." He made a sound between a chuckle and a sob, and his breath came and went warmly against my cheek. "You looked after me. You talked to me, told me off, just like you always used to. Made me feel like there was some kind of... normality in the world, good normality, and I could be part of it through you."

Mi world es su world, I wanted to tell him. But I couldn't make such vast promises. "If there's any tiny thing I can do," I told him instead, "to make normality any tiny bloody bit more bearable for you, I'll do it."

"You already did. You tidied up and you fixed things. I put our games away so the place wouldn't look like shit again when you came back, and when I went into the hut outside, I realised you must've seen all the dope I brought with me. Did you check the packets?"

"Course not. I wasn't gonna touch your stuff."

"I haven't either. They're all still sealed up."

"Okay. I'm glad about that, but... what I said to you before, back on the beach there—it's not conditional."

His grip on me became more powerful. "Careful. I'd never ask you—"

"I know. I'm offering. I'm sorry I yelled at you about..." I paused, listening to a distant drift of sirens, and the anguished babble of voices upslope. "About poor

Sam, but I do bloody mean it. I do forgive you about Jules, and I do love you. Whether or not you're clean."

A desperate wail cut through the hush between us. At the top of the bank, Holly was striding back and forth. The sun was catching her rainbow gems, but it was a firework display over a bomb site: she could barely speak. "I can't remember," she managed between sobs. "He did tell me. It was Port somewhere or other in Canada. Can we get his phone out of his pocket and have a look?"

"No. We mustn't touch him or disturb anything until the police get here." That was Zadi, trying and failing to stop her and hold her still. "Who's his next of kin?"

"His parents are dead. His brother's name is... Oh, fuck, I don't *know*!"

I knew. I planted a kiss on Kip's brow then let him go. "Holly," I said, and she whipped round to face me as if she'd forgotten my existence. I climbed back up onto the promontory rocks where Sam lay, surrounded by the people of Saorsa. Some were crying. Herne was kneeling at Sam's feet, silent, not touching, the shadow of his horns embracing the body. Others were staring, as I had, into the face of an absolute unknown. "His brother's name is Paul," I said, pulling the business card from my pocket. "Look. He gave me this."

She stumbled towards me. "He did? When?"

"Just half an hour ago, before he..." The weird conversation we'd shared came rushing back to hit me, and I pulled out the card from my pocket. "Shit. He gave me this, and he said his next of kin was Paul. Oh, God. Do you think he knew?"

Zadi strode over. "No," he said, with the same unexpected authority I'd heard in his call to the police. "He might've been feeling pretty strange, but he couldn't have known. I'd guess that whatever took him out did it straight away, and painlessly from the look of it. There was nothing you could've done."

I wasn't so sure. I was learning, as Kip had done, that no-one could get you off the hook. Maybe I could help now, though. Holly had fumbled out her phone. She took the card from me and began to dial. Sobs were still racking her. "It's okay," I said, handing her a tissue from my pocket and at the same time abstracting the phone from her shaky grasp. "I'll do that."

"He doesn't know you."

"He doesn't know any of us, does he?"

"No, I guess he doesn't." Fresh tears of relief spilled down her face. "Oh, God, Oz. *Would* you?"

Offering was one thing. Now I had to deliver. I gave her as cheerful a nod as I could produce, turned away and took a few steps back down the promontory. I was about to call a man I'd never met—wake him up in the middle of the night, haul him out of his dreams and tell him that his brother was dead. I sat down on a fallen larch trunk. Holly had managed to key in the number. All I had to do was press dial.

A warm hand soft-landed on my head. Another reached over my shoulder and lifted the phone away. "Here," Kip said, sitting down beside me on the trunk. "Let me."

Chapter Seventeen
Hungry Bones

Winter dusk had almost consumed Saorsa. The officers who'd responded to Zadi's 999 call, and the others who'd arrived later with the coroner, had all been kind enough. They'd focused intently on Sam, though, on the hours before and possible reasons for his death. I'd told my story as clearly as I could. So had the shell-shocked film crew. Zadi had stayed in the background for all these conversations: quiet, professional, a foot in both camps. Eventually the coroner's team had lifted Sam and carried him to the black van waiting upshore. The officers had taken contact details from everyone, and then they'd left us alone.

Us. Alone. There was nothing anymore to separate me from these people. I was alone with them in the oncoming wilderness night, part of the huddle we'd formed on the beach. I had one arm around Kip. Eleanor, clutching the bulldog pup for comfort, was huddled against me. Holly was hanging on to as many of her colleagues as she could. Herne and Zadi had gathered some of the others, each on his opposite edge of the circle. At length Holly found her voice. "Bless you for talking to Paul, Kip. Was it very awful?"

Kip straightened up. "He was really calm. I don't know if they... maybe weren't close, or if he's been expecting something like this to happen. He says we're not to do anything until he gets here."

"What could we do?"

"I think he meant by way of any kind of ceremony. He sounded pretty stern."

"Oh, God. Do you think he's some kind of horrendous fundie Christian? No offence, Zadi."

Zadi shook his head. "None taken. Those aren't really fundamentalists, though, Holly. No-one who pays real attention to their holy texts could act as they do. They're extremists, which is different."

Apparently no time was the wrong time for a spiritual debate. Murmurs of interest went around the circle. "I don't know what he is," Kip said wearily, "but I think we've got to respect his wishes as far as we can while still respecting Sam's. Does anybody know what those were? Holly?"

"Not a clue. He knew he was living on the edge, but he never told me what he wanted us to do if he... if he ever slipped off. He just said his family would deal with it."

"In that case, we've definitely got to wait for Paul. He's in London on a business trip. He said he could be up here by tomorrow afternoon. I know everybody wants to do something—build a fire or have a ritual or just—I dunno, rewrite today so this never bloody happened. But sometimes all you can do is hold out and let bad nights pass." He shrugged, tried for a smile. "All of you know that, or you'd never have come here. It's a good place for those kinds of night."

They listened to him carefully. I found myself thinking about all the times when he must have visited before, when he hadn't been ill and beaten down. How well some of them must know him, aspects of him I'd never dared discover for myself. Whatever they'd seen of him during those times, it made them attend his words now, accept his guidance. The circle began to break up. Each one of the dispersing group had a glance for him, a touch to his shoulder, a reflection of his shadowed smile. At last it was only the two of us, hand-in-hand on the empty beach.

And so I took my lad home. The van in the woods felt more like a home than I ever could have believed, but I supposed that depended on what had happened to you in the outside world. On who you were with. I'd have settled for a cave with him tonight. I steered him to the camping stool in front of the stove, lit the gas and parted him from his wet waterproofs, which I hung with mine on a rack over the door. I'd laid down a towel for the dual purpose of blocking out draughts and catching drips. Bearing in mind what he'd said about the symbolic power of tea, I put the kettle on, then began preparations for supper. I had no home to offer, and little by way of resources, but whatever I did have was his.

He caught my wrist as I passed him, as if he'd read the thought. "Oz."

"What is it? Are you all right?"

"Yeah. Come here, though."

I crouched beside him. The hollow look in his eyes had a new dimension for me now. "Oh, mate. Of all the places in the world to try and get clean..."

"I know. You've seen more booze and joints flying about here than you ever have in your life before."

"It's like the Union bar with tents. What were you thinking?"

"That's just it, though. It's out in the open here. No-one's nipping vodka out of a thermos in the bogs before they get dragged in to see the boss. No middle-aged ladies politely hitting the Valium in their middle-class, middle-England bedrooms, all on their own. People here wave joints around like banners. They sit by the fire at night and pour home-brewed cider down their throats. If anyone's got anything, they'll try to share it with you before you get halfway to your caravan door."

"And does that *help*?"

"Yes. I can say no to that, for some reason. It's secrets and silences that break me."

I settled on my knees in front of him. He was shivering, so I snagged a blanket from off one bench and tucked it over his lap. "Okay. In some weird way that does make sense. Is the withdrawal making you sick?"

"No. I just caught the grot from hell when I came out here, on top of everything else." He chuckled hoarsely. "No wonder I ended up lying there watching the clock.

To be honest, procodone isn't bad in terms of physical withdrawal."

"Bad in other ways, though."

"I don't know if I can even tell you."

I swallowed hard. I didn't even really want to know. But I had to, if my promises were going to be more than empty words. "Can you try?"

"The psychological dependence... It goes on forever. It feels like all your bones have got their own stomach, and all those stomachs are always empty and nagging for food. Always aching. It doesn't stop. Jesus, I don't want to hurt you. I've tried to keep this to myself."

"I know. But I'm asking."

"When I saw Sam today—that last glimpse we had of him, with the sky in his eyes and that smile on his face—I envied him. I don't want to be dead, Oz, but... fuck, I'm not sure if I want to be alive either. Not feeling like this."

He half-fell off the stool into my arms. He was feverish and lithe, and when I thought about losing him, I too wanted to follow Sam into the cloud-swept unknown. I put a hand into the hair at the back of his neck, reached down and grabbed his skinny arse. I hadn't meant for the move to be sexy, but he gave a startled moan and instead of burrowing against my shoulder, suddenly sat up and kissed me. "Don't," I said, muffled against his warm mouth. "I wasn't even thinking about... I just want to feed your hungry bones."

"*I'm* thinking. It's the only good thing I thought about at all while I was alone. I haven't thought about much else since you found me."

I aided his scramble upright. I glanced at the benches and table, and he gave me a fraught little nod that sent me shivering to work on their transformation. Such a neat system, and sturdy, too, ready to take a good pounding... I wasn't so sure about Kip. He was leaning where I'd propped him, and he was hard under his jeans but otherwise looked ready to crash. I took out the blankets from their cupboard, tossed them over the mattress and held out the quilt enticingly. "Come here."

"You sexy thing, with your bedlinen, you."

"Come on. You know you want it."

He half-crawled, half-fell into the nest I'd made for him. I kicked off my boots, helped him to get rid of his, and then I followed him in, pulling the quilt over both of us. He wasn't up for much, but I could make him feel better, rub the sharp-toothed edges off his cravings for a while. He'd taught me—by tender, repeated example—how to give a good blow job. Diving down, I found my way under enough of his layers to kiss his belly. "Poor Sam," he said, and sucked in a breath on a sob. "Jesus, poor Sam!"

"I know. He was good to me when I first got here."

"He thought you were an angel."

"Well, like you said..." I undid his top button and unzipped him. "...he *was* off his tits at the time."

"I'm not so sure."

"About him, or—"

"No. About you."

***

"Kip! Oz! Oz! Kip!"

The door shook under a flurry of blows from outside. Dreams exploded to starry shreds inside my skull and I bolted upright, convinced that Jules was about to burst into my bedroom and find me naked with Kip. But she'd love that, wouldn't she? Kip and Oz, sitting in a tree... That would mean car rides, fish and chips, endless indulgence of all her bratty tantrums, life back to her idea of normal.

I would love it too. Why shouldn't she be indulged? Kip sat up beside me. If we'd been sitting in a tree, at some point he must have fallen out and landed in a pool of morning glory. His mouth was reddened with whisker-rash, his erection unmistakeable beneath the quilt. He was perfect. "Bloody hell," he said. "Who's that?"

Not Jules, of course. My sleep-drenched brain checked its files for female voices. "Holly. What does she want?"

"I can think of a great way of finding out."

"What?"

"Open the door and ask her, you dope. You'll have to do it, or she'll think the Loch Ness monster moved into our van overnight."

I gave the beast a yearning caress on top of the quilt. The door had no lock. I'd just thrown back the blankets to do Kip's bidding when Holly worked this out for herself and tumbled inside. She was carrying a camera, which I sincerely hoped was turned off. "Oh," she said, barely pausing to take in the scene. "You two are back together. That's good. But you both have to come with me, right now."

Kip bunched up the quilt in his lap. "What's wrong? Sam's brother isn't here already, is he?"

"No. No. It's *her*."

"Shit. His mum? A sister?"

"For God's sake. Her Ladyship! This is it. Come *on*."

She spun round in the doorway, leapt the steps and dashed away, leaving the door wide open to the frosty breeze. I was still processing. Not Jules, not Sam's mum or his sister. My scalp prickled at the thought that Letty might have somehow made it out here. She'd be like a fox in the henhouse, wouldn't she, surrounded by all these chemicals—we'd have to find a way to steer her around them...

My vintage T-shirt landed in my lap, thrown there with some force. Jeans and jumper followed, then my socks, one at a time, bunched up like snowballs. Kip was hopping across the floor of the van, erection subsiding, one leg into his jeans. "Get dressed," he ordered, grabbing his boots. "Oz, quick. Now!"

"What for?"

"A sighting! Come on."

"Oh, man." I flopped back onto the bed. "I'm on holiday. Your bare arse is enough of a sighting for me. Come back here, and I'll make you a fry-up when I'm done with you."

I'd given him pause for thought, quite some accomplishment at a moment like this. He stopped, second boot in hand. "I have to see her," he said wistfully. "But you stay there if you want."

No. I had to see this with him. I was beginning to understand that I couldn't pick and choose—that if his van was my van and my world his world, his monsters had to be mine too. At least when he was this excited, lit up from inside with possibilities... "Wouldn't miss it for the world," I said, and he read my absence of sarcasm and gave me a grin that put the morning light to shame.

Together we ran down through the woods. I hadn't managed any healing miracles overnight, and he had to stop and catch his breath once, but the route was mostly downhill, and within a minute we'd reached the shore. Kip grabbed my arm to slow me up. I knew the drill by now. No crunching on the stones, and strictly no barking. Carefully we set out down the beach to join the group of watchers at the water's edge.

Most of them hadn't got as far as day clothes. Eleanor was in wellingtons and pyjamas, an anorak thrown on top and a hand clamped over Maggie the bulldog's mouth. The little creature sat upright in her arms, ears unfolded like sails. One of Sam's cameramen—I recognised him from the other day, a member of the burly team who'd half-carried me and my car off the beach—had set himself like a rock to film the water. Tears were running down his face. "Sam would've loved this," he said brokenly as Kip and I approached. "He would've bloody loved this so much."

Holly touched his shoulder. She was still out of breath from her cannonball run to wake us up. She'd taken a big loop to do it, jeopardising her own chances of seeing whatever this was. "Then we've got to do our best for him. Get the best footage we can."

"Even if we can't use it?"

"I'm not about to break my Saorsa vow. Are you?"

"No, but... My God, Holly. It's real. It's real."

The cryptid hunters of Saorsa were well trained. Not a sound arose from the little crowd, and hands were steady on cameras and binoculars. All except Kip's: my lad had been waiting his whole life for this, staked on it the future of his academic career. He couldn't unfasten the Velcro strips holding the case of his binos closed. Wordlessly I took over and did it for him, muffling the rasp of the material inside my coat.

To me, the loch looked much the same as it ever did. The breeze had fractured the surface into endless millions of wavelets. Beautiful, and a world away from yesterday's gloom, but I was more interested in the land-based life around me. Herne and Zadi had arrived: Herne in full fancy dress, glowering over the scene, his companion faded and worn, as if he had the cares of the world on his shoulders this morning. Everyone else was transfixed, silent as a football crowd before a cup-final shootout. I'd grown to like them all in the couple of days I'd spent in their weird world. I'd really liked Sam. As for Kip, I'd have given a few pints of blood to conjure up something for him in the water, but I could see nothing at all.

And then I did.

Chapter Eighteen
Paul

For almost thirty seconds, I believed. I'd read Kip's PhD proposal from start to finish after he'd fallen asleep the other day, and for nearly half I minute I experienced for myself the effect he'd described—the fundamental shift in my world view, the rush of cognitive dissonance, the beginnings of reconciliation in my head between a dream and a reality. As he'd promised, it made me see everything, all my certainties, all the small anchors and handholds I used to negotiate my daily existence, in a different light. I wasn't alone. Eleanor, shaking with sobs, had gone down on her knees.

But I was an engineer, not a biologist or a philosopher. I stared and stared. I reached for Kip's binos, and to his absolute unselfish credit he handed them over. He'd share his last breath with me, wouldn't he? He'd even let me have this once-in-a-lifetime vision.

Turning the wheel on the binos, I brought my focus in tight.

An amazing job. For a moment—because I *was* an engineer—all I felt was admiration. This monster's creators hadn't gone for large-scale special effects. They'd listened to descriptions, read the same newspaper cuttings Kip had plastered around his university digs at home. *At first I thought it was a log. I thought it was a seal, or otters swimming in a line. They say it might be a plesiosaur, don't they, or a giant serpent of some kind. They say the wind can make strange shapes in the water.* Oh, it was good. No roaring, no monstrous head going up and down, nothing stupid—just a long, flexible shape, a tube with gleaming flanks, contracting first on one side then the other, like an eel the size of a tree trunk.

But nothing made of flesh and bone could move like that, not at those dimensions. The damn thing was riding too high in the water. Whoever had done this, I hated them for getting so close but not getting it right, because any minute someone else would see it too, and then it would all be over. I looked for the propulsion system. There it was, behind a convincing leaf-shaped rear fin: the rhythmic bubbling of an outboard motor.

I handed the binoculars back to Kip. I glanced around, quickly calculating the radius for remote control. The operator had to be somewhere nearby. The person who ended this didn't have to be me, did it? Maybe whoever had set the contraption up would quit while they were ahead, take it around the headland and out of sight, and Kip and everyone else gathered here could go home for Christmas convinced they'd witnessed a wonder.

Shit. The thing was heading inland. Eleanor gave a kind of wail, and the poor pup, excited beyond endurance, sprang out of her arms and began a frantic dash back and forth along the shore. She wouldn't scare this bloody monster. I heard a warning shout somewhere off in the woods behind me. The gleaming cylindrical shape took a wild roll to the left, over-corrected and pitched to starboard. Maybe it had got caught up on one of the underground rocks. Whatever had happened, it jerked and abruptly flipped over, gears and pulleys belly-up in the sun.

A wild whoop of laughter broke from the trees. A voice, broadly accented, cracked the holy silence of the shore. "For God's sake, Mackie! Did I no' tell you to keep her out of the shallows?"

Three of them. There were three, dashing at full pelt down from the crags. They all looked pretty husky. That was good. I hated the idea of hitting someone smaller than myself. I broke out of the group, which was a hell of a lot easier than sticking around to see their expressions, and I ran to intercept the three lads crashing their way through the bushes and onto the shore. "Hoi, you lot. Just bloody stop."

They obeyed me, more out of surprise than anything else. The biggest of them skated to a halt three inches off my nose. "What's your problem, English?"

If he wanted to make it about nationality, that was grand by me. "You, dickhead. You're my problem."

"What?!"

Still more astonished than cross. I had to ramp this up. Hitting somebody off-guard wasn't my style either. Did I *have* a style? I hadn't landed a punch since junior-school playground, although Cedric had sailed close to my wind a couple of times. "Have you got nothing better to do?" I demanded. "Is that what you spend your benefit money on—bits of crap to glue together and scare the tourists around here?"

My guy took a step back. "Whoa, whoa," he said pacifically, holding up his hands. "I don't know what's biting your arse, mate, but leave it out, will you? We've got to get our gear back."

One of his friends was lairier. He stepped in front of the first guy, face rucking angrily. "What is your beef, pal? Get out of our way, or we'll put you out, and you won't like..." He paused, then shielded his eyes and focused past me. "Oh, hang on, Mack. It's no' the tourists he's worried about. It's the hippies from Saorsa. Look at 'em!"

Eleanor was still on her knees. She was weeping in desolation. "Oh, my God," said Mack, turning to stare too. "You are *no'* telling me yon bunch of lunatics bought that!"

All three burst into laughter. And that would do for me. Scarlet fireworks went up in the back of my brain, the bestial ancient part of it that dealt with flight and fight. I drew back my fist and walloped Mack right on the nose.

His two mates sprang on me. I ripped my way free of the first one's grasp, managed to elbow the other in the stomach and staggered away, just far enough to make my next swing. Man, it felt good! Something long bunged-up inside me cleared with an exhilarating pop. "Next," I gasped, and straight away there he was, the ugly bugger with the frown, outraged and ready for payback. He was quicker than Mack: flung himself at me and tackled me down, and we rolled out onto the shingle, fists flying. Chance more than skill brought me out on top, but I seized my advantage and hauled back for a punch.

Something grabbed my hand. "Oz, no! Oh, my God, no."

I was ready to fight anyone. I twisted round and promptly changed my mind. "Kip! Get off me."

"Not a chance, you nutter. Stand up. Come away from this. Come on."

He hauled me back. Other hands landed on me, stronger than his and more determined about the business of restraint: Herne, throwing a grip like a cable around my midriff. I struggled wildly. "Let me go."

"What will you do if I do that?"

"I just want to kill the bastards."

"Oz, why?" Seeing I was immobilised, Kip stepped round in front of me. He was pale with disbelief: maybe the sight of me in a punch-up had been harder to credit than a monster in the loch. "Do you know these guys?"

"You saw what they did! They... They fooled you. They fucked around with all of you, with your..." Cooling down a fraction, I began to hear myself, and a first warning tingle of shame touched my ears. "With your dreams. With... Did you see Eleanor? She was crying."

"Oh, Oz!" She materialised in front of me, the bulldog tucked down the front of her jacket. To my astonishment she kissed me, and the pup got in on the act, slobbering with excitement. "Oz, please calm down. My husband died last year, so everything makes me cry. I *hoped* I was seeing Her Ladyship, of course—we all did— but you don't have to worry. We're all right."

Was she speaking for all of them? I blinked hard. Mackie's mate must have got a couple of decent ones in: my eyebrow was bleeding. Through a red veil I examined the faces of the Saorsa hippies gathering round. Nobody looked broken. Mouths were open in surprise, and not a few were starting to smile. "Bloody hell," said Kip, glancing from me to the three lads, who were warily gathering up their scattered bits of radio-control kit from amongst the stones. "Did you get into a fight for us, love?"

I couldn't answer. My throat closed. Herne let me go, and I stumbled into Kip's arms. I laid my head on his shoulder and closed my eyes. "Oh," said Mackie, "no' sae tough now, are ye, ye wee pansy? Whit brought all that on, then?"

I was done. "It's complicated," Kip said over my shoulder, and I should've been furious that he was speaking for me, but all I could feel was relief. "A friend of ours died yesterday. Do you know Sam Bouchard?"

"Psychonaut Sam? The guy who does the programmes on mushrooms an' a' that? Och, no—is that why all the blue lights turned up here yesterday?"

"Yeah. So people are upset. To be honest, though, I'm not apologising for Oz. That was a shitty trick you pulled. We come here to get some peace, not to have our chains jerked by jokers like you."

"Well—not to disrespect your grief, but ye're not the centre of the universe, and we did'nae make the model for the purpose of baiting you. It's the midwinter festival over at Urquhart on Friday, and the organisers pay us a few quid to give the tourists a show, that's all. We were doing a practice run."

Mists parted in my skull. I'd heard voices, reasons, cockeyed ideas like this before. I raised my head. "I bet," I said unsteadily, "I bet you lot are engineering undergrads."

"Och, the beast speaks! We are, as it so happens— Strathclyde University. What's your excuse?"

I was all out of excuses. I straightened up, let go of Kip, and held out my hand. "John Osman. I'm in engineering too, or I used to be. I was way out of line. I'm so sorry."

Mackie eyed me warily as I approached. His mate was trying to hide behind him, still dabbing at a bleeding nose. Then he took my hand and shook it hard. "Spoiling for a fight, it looked like to me. If ye want to show me how sorry you are, ye can help us pull yon contraption ashore."

Least I could do. I shook hands with the other two lads as well, and the four of us waded out thigh-deep to retrieve the machine. The water was cold, but not as deadly as I'd thought it would be. Maybe Mackie was right: I had just been full of hell and adrenaline, and some of it was swilling around my system still. I didn't have time to think about it anyway, and that was another thing I'd missed from the engineering halls at uni—having bits of equipment thrust at me along with barked instructions, way too fast to leave room for contemplation. "You know," I said, struggling for balance while I heaved a length of canvas-wrapped aluminium off the rocks, "this would've been more convincing with a bit more weight on it. Something this big should look heavier, even from a distance."

Mackie's mate glared at me. "*More* convincing? You lot were seeing the second bloody coming as it was."

"Oh, I'm not saying it wasn't good. You had me, nearly."

"I ought to *nearly* your lily-white English backside for you. Did you hear that, Mack?"

"Yeah." Mackie hoisted up the monster's tail end with a grunt. "Cheeky bastard. Might have a point, though. Maybe if we loaded the central tubes a bit more—"

"What? The thing's at maximum weight for manoeuvrability anyway."

"Not necessarily. What if we took out one of the shorter tubes?"

"Aye, and that'll mean I have to sit up all night in a Baltic bloody boathouse relocating the motor. Ye didn't think about that, did you?"

I listened absently to their bickering all the way back to the shore. My attention was on Kip, who was watching our progress anxiously. He'd wanted to wade in with us, but had obeyed my forbidding frown and stayed ashore.

He seized the foremost edge of the tube Mack was carrying as soon as he could and helped him pull it up onto the beach. "Why didn't you give her a head?"

"Too much work wi' the tackle and pulleys. We only had two days to cobble her up." He grinned. "Thought about chopping the heid off the wooden one up by the road, but that would've sunk us. Don't suppose you know the fella who did that? I'd slip him a few bob to make us the same out of some lightweight sheet metal."

Now it was Kip's turn to hold out a hand. "At your service," he said. "Well, kind of. I'm not much into raising people's hopes and dashing them."

"That's your creation, up at the top?" Mackie put his hands on his hips and gave a whistle of admiration. "Believe it or not, we're no' in the business of crushing the life out of fairytales either. It was just a job. And if you two lads fancy joining us for a couple of days, we'll see you're well compensated. Dinner from the burger van outside Inverness."

After four days of self-catering, that actually sounded quite good. But Kip and I traded glances, and I gave him a small nod. "We'd love to," he said, "but we're heading off home shortly. Back to reality."

"Like either of you look as though you have a clue what that is."

"Maybe a better one than you, floating a motorised tube up and down Loch Ness for a living. Can we see how it works?"

"Be my guest." Mackie rested one end of the mockup on an upturned driftwood tree bole, and the other two hoisted their portions onto a couple of flat-topped rocks. "I'll leave you to it. We abandoned a few hundred quid's worth of radio gear up on the crags when this sodding thing capsized. Come on, lads, before one of these yoghurt-weavers goes and nicks it to buy dope."

I planted my hands on my hips. He backed away from me, making pacifying gestures in the air. I didn't think he was one bit scared of me, but it was nice to make a point. *Don't mess with my yoghurt-weavers, mate.* Once I'd seen him off, I lay down on the shingle beside Kip and squeezed beneath the belly of the monster. "What in the hell is a yoghurt-weaver?"

"Oh, you know. Someone who comes out to places like this and lives in a tent drinking macrobiotic soup whilst knitting their own hessian underwear and socks. A hippy like me, I suppose."

"I don't think you fit too well into the hippy box. Or any pre-labelled one I can come up with at all. Do you really want to know how the fake Loch Ness monster works?"

"I'm interested, yeah. I'm interested in all of this—the mechanics, the reasons your new friends gave for doing it. I'm interested in the way everyone here reacted. They didn't mind being laughed at, or laughing at themselves, but..." He wriggled his hips distractingly and pulled out a pen torch from the back pocket of his jeans. "But what are they meant to do with that other feeling they had— the moment when they thought it was real?"

I sighed. "What are you doing with yours?"

"Oh, it's different for me. I've had years of practice." He examined the length of plastic-clad cable attaching the monster's fin to the motor, then switched off the torch and shifted to look at me. "Anyway, I didn't come up here to find the monster in the first place. You know why I came."

"In that case, I'm sorry for punching Mackie in the face."

"Don't be. When you did that—went after someone for me, and not because they'd really hurt me or anything, but just because they might have trodden on my toes or torn up one of my stupid geeky fantasies... I had a bit of a glimmer."

"A glimmer? About what?"

"Well, about the thing I couldn't see before. Why someone might want to be clean."

I felt stupid. This wasn't the kind of conversation I'd ever planned on having flat on my back beneath a dripping, smelly length of pipe. "I don't get it."

"The thing is, I can't have the drugs and the booze and you as well. I'm not even asking you to tell me that's not true, Oz. I know I can't, not the life I got to love so much with you and Jules, having a home and a bit of a family and all that. And I know that's the only way addictions get controlled—if an addict finds something they want more than the drug."

I tried to focus on the drip. Oil or water? So much easier to think about that than to absorb what Kip had just said to me. What if I hadn't understood? "Are you telling me you... want me more than..."

"I know I'm not very convincing. I know I had all those things—you and Jules and everything—and I made you all into dirt by the choice I made. I threw you away."

"Jesus, Kip. No."

"Yes. And you might not be able to forget that, you see." Shit, he was crying. I tried to get a word out for him, but suddenly my own lungs and throat were locked tight. "You probably can't," he choked out, swiping a hand across his eyes. "Very probably."

I shoved up onto one elbow. The underside of a rubber paddle promptly slapped me on the back of the head, but I barely noticed. "*Kip*. For fuck sakes. I'm not about to speak for Jules—she's gold to me, even if she is a psycho brat from hell—but what was I, to weigh in the balance against all the stuff you've been trying to give up?"

His turn to look bewildered. "What?"

"I loved you from the day I met you, but I... I hardly ever really showed it. I looked down on you—treated *you* like dirt when it suited me. Told you to get out of my life when you needed help the most. I can see where the drugs and the drink would be a hell of a lot more fun."

"Don't."

"If you get to say all this hard stuff, I get to do it as well."

"Okay. But the point is... the guy I chose, the one who meant more to me than any kind of crack—it was just you. The way you were before you hit Mackie on the nose for me, before you realised all the nice stuff you just said."

"Uh-oh. Will you go off me if I'm not a selfish dick anymore?"

A ripple of laughter went through him, followed by a sob. "I don't think so. We'll have to wait and see. But I loved you from the day I met you, too."

Someone rapped sharply on the tube above our heads. I didn't care. I was lost in the wonders of Kip with all his guards down, of Kip laid wide open, kissing me without fear or restraint. He'd pulled me down, tucked a hand beneath my head. His body was warm on mine. I'd found the heart of the whole world, the place where every lonely, argumentative part of me could melt away in his acceptance, his willingness to take me as I was. But he chose that moment to hoist me back on top, and out of the very corner of my eye I caught a flash of highly polished shoes. Expensive. Out of my range, as were the nicely cut trouser legs above them. *Preppy* was probably the word...

Not letting go of Kip, I rolled us both out from under the belly of the beast. There he was, just as I'd first seen him in the bushes by the loch: immaculately tailored, not one shining hair out of place, spectacles reflecting the water's endless dance. At last I got my mouth open. "Sam!"

"Sorry," he said politely. "He never tired of failing to mention his brother is a twin. I guess he didn't foresee these exact circumstances. I'm Paul Bouchard."

"Oh." Stupid disappointment rocked me: had I really thought the psychonaut had somehow sailed back home? "I, er... I'm John Osman." *Call me Oz* seemed wildly inappropriate here, a friendly touch that died the death in the cold gleam on this stranger's specs. But nothing could really hurt me, not now, when every one of my next words would be true. "This is Joe Kipton, my boyfriend."

"Right." The new arrival put his hands in his pockets, rocked back on his heels and looked around him. "I've had an interesting morning, John and Joe. I spent the first part of it in what must be the world's smallest police station. Then I came here, where I was greeted by a man with horns and hooves, set upon by a bulldog, and directed to talk to somebody called Oz, as the last person who saw my brother alive."

"That's me. I'm Oz." Kip had pushed my T-shirt halfway up my chest: I twitched it quickly back down. "I'm really sorry for your loss."

"And I find this Oz character beneath what looks like a full-scale mockup of the Loch Ness monster, rolling about with his boyfriend." Paul stood in silence for a moment, then took off his glasses and rubbed his nose. A wide, familiar, utterly charming smile broke like midwinter dawn, transforming him. "Boy. Sammy must have *loved* this place."

Chapter Nineteen
Neon Halo

Camp Saorsa did its best to welcome Paul. I no longer thought of myself as separate from the people dashing back and forth to light a fire and fetch food, and I ran to the woodshed when told, filled a vast kettle with water and hung it on its tripod over the flames. Spiritual tea-making on a grand scale: even those few campers who hadn't turned out for a sighting of Her Ladyship wanted to set eyes on Sam's brother.

He was in some way common property. Even Mackie and his team had returned from the woods with their gear to sit awkwardly on the rocks and fallen tree trunks. Holly offered to take him to Sam's lab and trailer—which were his now, as she falteringly pointed out—but he gently turned her down, and took up a seat on a rock by the firepit with the rest of us. "What I want to say," he began, when everyone had settled, "is that although I appreciate your kindness, and your efforts to sympathise without actually saying the word *death*, I'm all right. Don't get me wrong, I loved my brother. But I never really felt separate from him while he was alive, so it's hard for me to feel it now. It's like... if I'm here, he must be, too."

"Oh," said Eleanor, eyes wide. "That's how I feel about Dan. I loved him, and he was a part of me, so how can he really be gone? I'm still so sorry about Sam, though. About his *death*."

Paul gave her a wry nod of thanks. "I'm sorry about Dan, too. Your husband?"

"For thirty years. And for ten of those years, we came to Camp Saorsa together. That's why I was a bit upset earlier, and—honestly, Oz—truly relieved when the monster turned out to be a fake. Dan would've come back and haunted me if he'd missed the real thing. You should've seen Oz, though, Mr Bouchard—ran straight up to Mackie there, and *bam*, right on the nose."

Mackie had the grace to lead a round of applause. I waved it away, embarrassment heating my face. "Please. Paul was trying to talk to us about Sam."

"Well, yes. There are a couple of things I need to say. Sam travelled all over the world in the course of his research, but he never stayed anywhere for longer than a few days, except for here. When he emailed or messaged me from Saorsa, he sounded like a man who'd found a kind of home. He talked to me about his great camera crew, about his fantastic production assistant and her rainbows, and all these people who worried about him but never ever judged him. So I'd have liked to work with you to arrange his funeral, but Sam—typical for him— requested a burial by birds."

Bemused silence fell over the group. Then, to my astonishment, I realised I knew what he meant. "Oh. Like an air burial, where you leave the body to be—well, to be..."

I had no idea where I'd gathered this piece of information, but I now wished I hadn't, and belatedly shut my mouth. But Paul was nodding, not visibly upset. "That's right. You expose the body somewhere isolated, to be eaten by wild creatures and returned into the ecosystem. That's not legal in the UK, so I'm gonna fly Sam back home."

"Wow. Is it legal in Canada?"

"No. But I'm the wealthy brother. I made my fortune while Sammy was off chasing mushrooms, and I live on five hundred wilderness acres in Alberta. We'll see who finds him first—the police or the birds. Meanwhile, I'd like to buy whatever you guys need to give him a good send-off here."

Herne shrugged. He'd been quiet until now, staying watchfully close to Zadi, who this morning looked worse than Kip, and was probably catching his cold. "That's kind of you, man," he said, "but we've got everything we need for that kind of party right here. We just hope you'll stay with us and share it."

"I will. I will." Paul took off his glasses and rubbed them distractedly on his handkerchief. "You are... *extremely* attractive, aren't you? Which puzzles me a lot, because I'm happily married with two kids at home."

Herne gives everyone an erection. I saw the message glimmering in Kip's eyes, remembered when he'd had to say it to me, and almost burst into laughter. But Paul was better than me at processing strangeness, and after a moment shook his head and went on. "There's one thing more I should say. The coroner has to investigate my brother's death, because it was sudden and unexpected. But I told him about what Sam did, and we watched a couple of his recent shows on the internet, and he agrees that in the circumstances, it certainly wasn't suspicious. And no-one here could possibly have done anything to foresee it or prevent it." He turned a perceptive gaze on me. "I know you saw him and spoke to him beforehand. But he was just doing what he always does—watching the world, recording it, experiencing the dangerous, far-out parts of it for himself. He died at work, in a way. Doing the job he loved."

Watching the world, recording it. Finally I remembered the camera card he'd given me. "Wait," I said. "He *was* at work. He was recording... Zadi, he was recording you. And neither of us could believe what we'd seen, so he gave me the memory card out of his camera and told me to look for myself. Then I forgot all about it." I shut up. Zadi had gone pale. Maybe he didn't want me spreading the news of his miracle walk. "Is it okay for me to tell Paul?"

"What did he record?"

"Well, it was on the beach yesterday. You were with Herne, and—"

"He got that? He recorded it?"

"I think so. But you have to play it back on a laptop or something else with an SD slot, so I haven't looked at it." I dug the card out of my coat pocket and got up to hand it across the fire. "I don't think I should be first to see it anyway. It should be you or Paul."

Zadi shook his head. "Give it to Paul," he said unhappily. "He can do whatever he likes with it. I thought something happened out there, but I'm not sure. Oz, is there any chance I can talk to you and Kip alone?"

"Zadi!" Herne leaned forward. He seemed to have gained height and bulk overnight, a greater breadth between his shoulders. Still he looked helpless. "We talked about this. Don't do it. Please."

"I have to, Herne. I can't just leave things this way. There's so much pain."

"For God's sake." Herne swung to face Kip. "He does this. This is what happens. Please don't let him."

"I won't," Kip said, "not if I can help it. What?"

"You know he's a doctor, right? A GP in Fort William?"

"Yes, I know that."

"Well, he tries to help people. He manages it a lot of the time, but he can't forgive himself for the ones he can't help. He brings every case home with him. He hardly rests. He hardly ever eats."

Zadi turned on him. "Herne, shut up."

"No, not this time. It was one of the reasons we broke up. But we both come to the same place for our holidays, and I kept running into him again. It's like we can't be apart, not for long, no matter how hard we try. And every so often, even here, he finds someone in pain."

233

"But I'm not in pain," Kip said. "At least—yeah, I was, a lot of it. But Oz is here now. I'm better."

Zadi got up and strode away upshore. I couldn't tell if he wanted to escape Kip or get him to follow. "It's true," Eleanor said wonderingly, watching him go. "He does do that. My first time here without Dan, he just came and sat with me. And the terrible pain—it was less while he was there, as if he'd taken some of it away."

Herne had put his face into his hands. "That's what he does. He goes into his Jesus mode, the saviour of the bloody world. We could never just have our own lives."

"I'll go after him," Kip said. "Don't worry, mate. Whatever he wants, I'm not gonna let him do anything to hurt himself. Oz, will you come too?"

Of course I would. I'd made him better, he'd said. I'd go with him to the ends of the earth. I paused for a moment on the edge of the group round the fire. Mackie and the lads seemed curiously well absorbed into the circle and were beginning the process of pouring tea. Paul, after nearly losing an eye to the tip of one of the horns, had reached cautiously in to pat Herne on the shoulder. The bulldog pup, also sensing the need for comfort, was jumping back and forth between Eleanor's lap and Holly's, sharing herself out as best she could. It would have been wrong of me to pull out my phone and take a picture of them all as they were at that moment, but I wanted to. Instead I laid the memory as deeply as I could into my brain. At some point over the last couple of hours, Kip and I *had* made the decision to go back home, to our own ideas of reality. There would never be anywhere quite like this again. I turned and ran after him up the beach.

***

"Kip, how does he do that?"

"I don't know. I guess I was always so stoned that it never seemed odd to me. Or maybe I thought he kept a set of robes behind every tree."

"Robes are one thing. How does he manage the halo?"

Zadi was waiting for us under a larch tree on the easternmost stretch of the beach. He looked as if he'd been sitting there for hours on his rock, his face serene beneath the weird, shifting light. The breeze ruffled his long white robes. We were within earshot now. "Hey," Kip called out gently. "Here I am, if you want to talk to me. But I really am okay now."

"Yes, yes. I know." Zadi beckoned us over, and we both took up seats on a fallen log in front of him. "At least, as you say, you're much better. You're an easy case anyway—brilliant, very addictive, very depressed."

The wind blowing over the loch was chilly now, bringing scents of a far-off winter sea. I turned a little to shelter Kip, and we exchanged a puzzled look. "Depressed?" I echoed. "Kip? He can't be. He's like a firework."

"No. Kip is like a cat with a firework attached to its tail, and that's a very different thing. The fireworks in question are the array of drugs and substances he's used over the years. Without them, what happens?"

Kip shrugged. "I'm not meant to be laying my pain on you, Zadi."

"Don't take any notice of Herne. Tell me the truth, if you can."

"Well, I crash. But that's not me. That's just withdrawal."

I stirred uneasily. The image of the tormented cat seemed all too accurate to me. "Weren't you the one who told me *whatever* you're feeling is real?"

Zadi turned a severe glance on me. "If Kip said that, he was quite right. But what if the crash *is* your reality, Kip? What if it's just your base state?"

Kip swallowed audibly. "I don't think I could bear that thought."

"No. What you can't bear is that *state*. You find yourself in one unbearable mood, mindset, whatever you want to call it, after another, and so you self-medicate. But what if we could alter that?"

"What—the... the base state?"

"That's right. What if you have the kind of brain that secondarily re-uptakes too much of its own serotonin? Lots of brains are like that."

"Are they, the rascals?" Kip made an effort at a smile. "What does that mean?"

"They eat up too much serotonin, the stuff they produce to make you feel good. There are plenty of meds available now to stop them from doing that. People don't like the term antidepressant, especially in communities like this one, but that makes as much sense as not splinting a broken leg. Fluoxetine is probably still the best re-uptake inhibitor we have."

"That's Prozac, isn't it?"

Zadi nodded. The radiance above his skull flared. "You got me. I know it's become a cliché. One of the reasons for that is that it works. Not miracles, and it doesn't make you high. What it might do is adjust your day-to-day reality to the extent that you might not feel so much of a need to grab an upper, a drink or an opiate or whatever you're trying to quit. We're getting some good results for addicted people this way. Would you like to give it a try?"

Kip leaned forward. I could feel the wave of hope that passed through him, a warmth inside my own skin. "Isn't it complicated?" he asked wistfully. "To get the stuff, I mean?"

"Well, initially. You'd need to make an appointment with your GP, and if you think I'm right about my base-state theory, explain to him or her the way you've been feeling and what you've been doing to cope with that. There's far less stigma attached to addiction these days. Most doctors accept that primate brains are booby-trapped to make us want more of a good thing—that addiction's a flaw in design, not in character. So, yes, you'd have a few hoops to jump through at first, unless..." His gaze became distant, and the radiance flared again. He pushed one hand into the pocket of his robe. "Here you go. Oh."

We all sat and stared at the bagel in his hand. As bagels went, it was perfect: round, fragrant, apparently still warm from the oven, to judge by the wisps of steam rising from its golden crust. I remembered I'd had no breakfast, and Zadi grinned and passed it over to me. "Help yourself. Let's see what else is in here. Okay, a tin of tuna... not as good as the smoked herring I managed for you the other day, but maybe useful for later." He tossed the tin to Kip, who caught it deftly. "And underneath all that lot—yes. Read the leaflet first, but by the time you've worked through this pack, you should be able to tell if they're making a difference or not."

I tried not to let my jaw drop as he held out a small cardboard box in Kip's direction. It was labelled and sealed, and I didn't want to look too closely at the printout, just in case Joe Kipton's name was already there, and the universe even more fucking incomprehensible than I'd imagined. "Should you... Should you be giving him those?"

"Maybe not under a tree by Loch Ness. If he'd come to see me in my surgery, those are what I'd have prescribed. Like I said, he was an easy case, Oz." Zadi laced his fingers together and cracked his knuckles. "Now for you."

I paused with the bagel en route to my mouth. "Me?"

"Yes. John Osman, talented engineer with no real financial problems. Why did he drop out of uni to become a data-entry clerk?"

Kip might have told him, I supposed. Not his style, though, to gossip about the failings of an ex. "I *did* have financial problems," I said earnestly, forgetting to worry about Zadi's sources in the need to explain myself. "My father left. I was the only breadwinner in my family."

"Speaking of bread, are you going to eat that bagel?"

A big lump had formed in my throat. "I don't think I'm hungry anymore."

"Give it to Kip, then."

"Not hungry either," Kip said loyally, edging closer to me on the log. "Go easy on him, Zadi. He was doing what he thought best."

"Your gran has her police widow's pension, as well as child benefit to help raise Juliet. She's not a wealthy lady but she's doing all right."

I got up. "That's enough," I said faintly. "You're a nice guy, and I'm grateful to you for helping Kip, but... I don't have to listen to this."

"Whatever your father's faults, it was never his intent to starve you out of your education, Oz. You've never touched the money he left. You won't even as your gran to check the balance."

I rubbed my eyes. I didn't like the boiling sensation behind them. "For God's sake. Speaking of checking things, do you mind if I..."

Zadi spread his hands. "Be my guest."

He sat placidly still while I walked up behind him. Tentatively I passed my hand through the air above his head. The first time I felt nothing. On my second try, something like an electric shock went through me. I snatched my hand back. "Jesus!"

Zadi shrugged. "Occasionally. Now, you were telling me about your dad."

I hadn't been doing anything of the kind. "I was so scared," I said, backing away. My voice didn't sound like my own. "He didn't tell us he was going. I got a call from Jules at seven o'clock in the morning saying she was all alone in the house, and all his drawers and his wardrobe were empty. She was hysterical. She thought he'd been bloody kidnapped."

"Telling people you're about to do a dreadful thing can be harder than going ahead and doing it. Then what happened?"

"I got on a bus and came home. Gran was there when I arrived. She got Jules ready for school, and she made her go, too. I don't think Jules ever forgave her. Then we found my dad's note. It felt like the world had ended."

"In many ways it had."

"Yeah, for Jules. She was just a kid."

Kip looked up. He was pale with the impact of all the things I hadn't told him. "You were just a kid, too."

"No. Well, maybe. But twenty one's different to thirteen. I had to make it better. I had to become the man I'd thought my father was, because..." I stumbled over a hidden root and came to a halt. "That was the only way to stop it from happening again. I had to."

"Oh, Ozzy."

I caught my breath. When had he last called me that? The ground swayed beneath me, the rich carpet of orange needles and the deep soil below. The wind was blowing the sky around. I only had one fixed point in all this dancing chaos. I went to Kip. He grabbed me as I folded, making room for me between his knees.

Footsteps whispered in the larch. I didn't care if the whole camp turned up with a brass band: my world had turned to a patch of Kip's jeans and the scent of the warm flesh and muscle beneath. I closed my eyes, and I let time go by in the movement of his hand over my hair. But some new, massive presence was making the air buzz and tingle, and then Herne's voice rang out, bouncing off the crags. "Zadi. It's time to come home."

"You can't change me, Herne."

"Goddess forgive me for trying. Did you find the pain?"

"Yes. I thought it was Kip, but I found it in Oz. The weird thing was, I didn't have to take it this time. Oz just ate a load of it himself, and Kip absorbed the rest."

"That makes sense. Oz is his monster, after all."

"I feel different now. And yes, I would like to come home."

A hand touched my shoulder. I dragged my pounding head up. Any minute now I'd swallow this huge dose of undigested pain, and then I'd be able to breathe again, move and speak and function. For now all I could do was clutch Kip's arms—the sacred scaffold of his embrace— and watch as Zadi laid down on the forest floor beside me a shining neon ring, the kind of glowstick thing you'd get at a concert.

He straightened up. Herne put out an arm for him and he went into it, his face suffused with wild joy. They set out together for the beach. The sunlight took them, and they were gone.

Chapter Twenty
Kip's Photo

"I never meant to be a monster, love."

"He didn't mean it that way. He meant I've been chasing round the world for something I already had, that's all."

"I think it was more than that, but okay."

I settled my head more comfortably on his shoulder. He'd brought me back to the van as carefully as a box of glass, but he needn't have worried. Everything inside the box was broken, and it was such a relief not to hold on to the ugly, unnatural forms I'd assumed. He could drop me as much as he liked, and all he'd get were diamonds. We'd had a lunch of shared bagel and the tin of tuna—not much, between two hungry lads, but it had seemed to go on and on—and then we'd gone to bed.

I was wearing the neon glowstick round my neck, and nothing else. By its light Kip was examining the leaflet that had come with the box of Fluoexetine. "I dunno, Oz," he said. He too was naked, propped with me on the cushions from the bench. "There's one little pile of drugs out in the storage hut, and they're supposed to be bad. Then there's this little pile of drugs here, and they're supposed to be good. I don't really get it."

"Yeah." I took hold of the bottom of the sheet so that I could read it too. "It does seem screwed up in lots of ways. It's like you're a... What did Sam call himself?"

"A psychonaut."

"That's right. And the only way to find out what these so-called good drugs do is to..."

"Make an experimental voyage?" He pulled out the foil strip inside the box and showed me the two empty pockets. "I know. Anchors aweigh."

"Oh. You started?" Anxiously I scanned the list of side effects. In Gran's house, being given an aspirin was a state occasion. "It says here you can get a dry mouth, an upset stomach, pain, weakness and lethargy. Sounds like a barrel of fun."

"If it's better than the barrel I'm normally in, I'm willing to give it a try."

"Good." I stroked his stomach. "Jesus, though, Kip— I wish I'd had the sense to work out you were depressed. I'm so sorry."

"How could you? I had no idea myself. But everything Zadi said fits." He tightened his arm around me. "I wish I'd tried to get past your tough-guy act about your dad."

"I swear to God, I didn't know I was putting one on." No way for either of us to know the truth there: that he'd punched a hole in me, all the way down to my earliest memories, the place where I'd first understood that I had a father and I was his son. "We've both made a good job of hiding from ourselves, haven't we?"

"Do you think it's safe to come out?"

"As long as I'm with you."

He leaned over and kissed me. "As long as I'm with *you*."

"Uh-oh. It also says here..."

"What? Break it to me gently."

"You may also experience loss of libido. Is that happening yet?"

A grin and a warm flush spread over his face. He was home to me: even at his wildest worst, a sweetness and a safety I'd never thought could be mine. "No," he said huskily. "Not yet."

***

When dusk was coming down over the loch, Kip and I went for a last walk. We'd packed up most of our gear into the boot of my car for an early start the next morning.

Down by the water, Sam's memorial celebrations were well underway. Paul must have brought some goods to the table after all: the flames were leaping high, and already the Saorsa campers were dancing around it, vivid black shapes against the orange light. We waved a promise to join the party later, then set off up the track.

The gap in the tarmac had been repaired. Kip took a moment to admire the spot where I'd left the road, and then we paused beside the wooden monster. I found a bottle top in my coat pocket, and he showed me the box with a hammer and nails inside it. Not quite the same as a coin in a fountain, but I did press a wish into the tree trunk as I hammered the bottle top into place, a hope that one day Kip and I might come back to this strange shore again. Then, with the shouts and laughter from the party fading out behind us, we began to walk.

He was much better. We didn't talk much, and I could hear his breath coming and going easily in his lungs. We passed through the village, and because he was moving beside me with all his old vigour, carried on along the lochside track beyond. Soon it would be dark, but there was only one road and we both had torches. The sunset was flaring in scarlet wings at the loch's far western reach. Kip had tucked one hand into my elbow. The last of the sunlight was touching his face. He was so lovely, so much a part of his surroundings, that a touristy impulse overcame me. "Can I take a picture of you here?"

He turned to me in surprise. Holiday snaps hadn't been my thing of late. Then, nor had holidays or any kind of fun at all. "Course you can," he said. "Make it a selfie if you want."

I liked that idea. *Kip and Oz at Loch Ness*, the image of a happy couple on social media. I shook my head. If I could capture anything of this last evening here, it would be my handsome cryptid hunter in his own environment. "I think I just want you," I said, calling up a sweeter smile than any lens could hope to capture. "Go and stand on the beach over there, so I can get the water in the background. Hurry up, or there won't be any light."

He strode away. I got out my phone, guilt and concerns from tomorrow's real world tugging at me. No signal down here, but I hadn't gone and stood on tiptoe on the hill behind Kip's van and tried for one either, had I? Not since Monday morning. When had I told Gran and Jules I would be back? I switched the camera on. Kip was making his way across the rocks to the beach. Clicking off a test shot, I caught him in mid-leap between one foothold and the next. We'd better make it fast, I thought, trying for better focus: another sudden Highlands tempest must be on its way, rustling the bushes and undergrowth on the slope to my right.

The rustle leapt into a roar. I swung round to face it, expecting a four-by-four or a quad bike to come bursting out of the gorse. The sun was gone, the air suddenly black and rank with the stink of fish. My hair tried to stand up in a stripe, from the fine fluff on my spine to the top of my skull. The ground shook. I stumbled backward a few steps—the road was clear, or I'd have gone blindly into the path of a truck—and then at last I saw.

Something the height of a single-decker bus. Something unknown to the world of half-submerged tubes, paddles and radio control: a thing of blood and hard-packed muscle, sinew and bone. The last rays of the sunset bounced off a wet flank not three yards away from me, textured like vinyl, splashed with patterns in green and brown. The hot stink grew unbearable, snatching my breath. A long neck shot skywards, and the creature—a wall or a whale of it, an unending rumbling length that tore up the rocks and the heather—shot past me towards the shore.

Towards Kip. From somewhere I found voice for a yell of warning. I started to run in the same direction. For five mad seconds I was side-by-side with the wall, and I remembered being a kid on the platform at Newcastle Central, pelting alongside a moving train to wave my dad off on one of his interminable business trips to the States. "Kip," I bellowed, and he whipped around, poised on a rock by the water's edge.

I still had my phone in my hand. I'd been ready to take my photo of him, my tourist snap. My fist clenched in spasm. Did it click? I had no time to worry—dropped it in favour of grabbing a rock to stay upright. I took one blind jump and then another, and then I was in reach. I flung out a hand and caught Kip's belt. Yanked him down and into a flying rugby tackle, six inches clear of the creature's thunderous path.

We landed in the sand. I must have knocked the wind out of him: he lay still and silent, eyes wide. I crouched over him, shielding him as best I could while the back end of the beast slid past.

It entered the water with barely a ripple or a sound. One second it filled my world from sky to sand, and the next it was gone, swallowed whole by the night-filled loch. "Kip," I whispered, patting his face. "Kip, wake up."

He didn't move. Suddenly terrified that I'd broken his skull on a rock, I scrambled away. Jules had assisted Gran and my dad with buying my last mobile phone, and although the neon-pink cover had made me cringe a fair bit over the last two years, I was bloody grateful now. There it was, glowing in a slimy crack between the stones, barely more than a long arm's reach away. Did *emergency signal only* mean I could pull a helicopter out of the clouds for Kip? Sam's angelic brethren seemed more likely to come and save him on this lonely shore...

Maybe they already had. By the time I'd seized the phone and scrambled back to him, he was sitting up, coughing and spitting out sand. "Oz," he said as soon as he saw me. He grabbed my shoulders as I crashed to my knees beside him. "Did you... Did you see..."

"I saw. Christ, it nearly ran you over! Are you all right?"

"Did you *see* it?"

"Sweetheart, take a deep breath. I saw it, I promise you. I... Hang on." My hands shaking, I tapped the screen. Million-to-one chance, surely. I'd been running, my squeeze of the shutter button no more than a spasm of fear. "Oh, my God. Look."

His grip closed over mine. Between us we managed to keep the phone still. The image was grainy and skewed through about forty degrees, but clear. There was Kip on his rock. Behind him, just rushing into view from the right, was a long grey-green neck. Beyond his shoulder, captured in a moment of curiosity: a head nearly as big as he was, and one great eye.

He gave a kind of squawk. He took the phone from me, held the screen close to his face, then out at arm's length. "You got a picture."

"Yeah. I didn't even mean to, but yes."

"You got a picture of me with the Loch Ness monster."

"I thought we had to say *Her Ladyship*."

"I know. I know. But that was... *definitely* a monster." He tucked the phone into my coat's inner pocket and pulled up the zip. "We saw the Loch Ness monster, Oz!"

Now it was his turn to tackle-hug me. We hit the sand together, rolling. Peals of laughter broke from him, so infectiously packed with mad joy that I started too. We wrestled ourselves breathless on the wet rocks. He kissed me until I saw stars, then took hold of the front of my jacket. "Oh, God. The phone!"

I had to take it out for him and show him that the picture was still there. As soon as I had signal again I would email it to myself to be on the safe side. And after that... I waited, grinning, until he'd finished his victory dance. The sun had gone down, frosty constellations beginning to prickle out of the blue. Half a mile downshore, Sam's bonfire was blazing fiercely, flames almost touching the overhanging branches of larch, reflecting in the water like an upside-down chrysanthemum. Kip ran out of juice and dropped back onto the sand beside me. "Show me again."

I would frame it and hang it over the side of the Loch Ness ferry to see him lit up like this. "Here. It's real. Look."

"We *saw* her. She was so beautiful. I don't think she's a plesiosaur, but she's way too big to be any kind of serpent. And the way she moved... Not lolloping like a seal, not sidewinding... It was powerful and smooth, and so *fast*. Oz, I saw a cryptid!"

"You really did."

"You didn't hire Mackie and his mates to rig up a fake, did you? To make me happy?"

"Kip, it nearly killed you. And how could I possibly rig up that smell?"

Fresh laughter shook him. "She did stink, didn't she?"

"Like a ton of old cod. What are you going to do?"

"About what?"

"The picture." I reeled him in. He was still shaking with excitement. "Something like that could make your career, if you want to go ahead with your doctorate proposal. Talk about a flying start."

"Yeah, but... I'm not sure I do."

"Really? You convinced me, even without what we saw here tonight."

"Did I? I'm glad about that. But I meant what I said— I really do believe the cryptids thrive if other species do, from the vultures who'll eat Sam's body to the tons of old cod right here in the loch. And if I'm gonna help look after that biodiversity, I think I've got to do it as a serious biologist. The kind who doesn't have to pretend to be a girl from Latvia to get his articles published. I don't want to only ever be the guy who discovered the Loch Ness monster."

I gave him a squeeze. "RIP Joni Petko, eh?"

"RIP. I'll miss her. She did some great work."

"What about the others at the camp? Are you going to show them?"

"I want to. God, I'd love to—especially Eleanor. Zadi and Herne too, and Holly. I feel like I owe it to them."

The sand was damp and cold. Night was coming down fast on the loch, and it was time I took my lad home. I got up, drawing him with me. Together we stood watching the surface of the water, where nothing but ripples stirred now. I listened to the hush of the twilight. "Kip, don't," I said with sudden urgency. "I know how you feel, but... don't say a word about this, not to anyone. No Saorsa oath is gonna be able to hold people back from talking about this, and if just one person speaks, then—"

"Then all this is gone."

"Yes. There *is* a monster in Loch Ness. You just provided proof. And no-one will rest until they've dredged, sonared, drained the bloody loch dry to find her again. Don't say a word."

He turned me round to face him. He said, very softly, "I love you, Oz," and then he let me go and clambered onto the nearest rock. "Thank you," he said—to the hush, to the sky, to the undisturbed perfection of the water. "Thank you, Your Ladyship. Good night."

Chapter Twenty One
WTF

There were two new faces by the fireside when we got back. All my fears about how Kip and I would manage to keep our secret went flying off into the night: one of the faces belonged to Sunil Patwardhan, and the other to my sister Jules. "It's all right," Holly called out pre-emptively at my approach. "It's okay, Oz. She's fine. We've been looking after her."

Maybe. Perhaps by Holly's standards, they really had. Nevertheless the kid had half a dozen plaits in her hair, each one tied with a rainbow ribbon, and what looked like a pint of cider in her hand. "Uh-oh," she said as soon as she saw me. "Look out. Here comes Brother Superior."

I came to a halt a couple of yards from the fire. Kip fastened a hold on my arm, but there was no need: I was paralysed, all circuits engaged in fitting my sister's presence to this background. My reflex to yell at her died away in my new, uncomfortable habit of examining my own actions first. When had I told her I'd be back? Three days, and that had been on Saturday. Surreptitiously counting on my fingers, I worked out that I was a day overdue.

Only one day, but still. I opened my mouth, but whether I'd been about to apologise or rip a strip off her I never found out. "Oz, look out," Kip said, and I turned just in time to see Sunil flying towards me. He pulled back to punch me: missed, and brought both of us down in a flail of arms and legs.

He was furious. I raised my arms to shield my face, too astounded to try and stop him. Kip tried to lift him away, but he wriggled like Eleanor's pup and came at me again. "Sunil!" Jules yelled, loud enough to shake pine cones from the trees. She leapt up, dashed over and grabbed him by the hood of his parka. "Stop it! Let him go."

"What?" He writhed in her grip. "You've been crying about him non-stop for twenty four hours. You told me to beat him up if we ever tracked him down!"

He took another swipe at me. Jules dragged him back, spun him round and dealt him a wallop with the flat of her hand. "Not literally, you twat. Don't you dare hit my brother."

Oh, this was great. I sat sprawled on the sand. The whole Saorsa crowd was assembled, gawping in astonishment. "Jules," I managed. "What the bloody hell are you doing here?"

"You didn't come home on day three. You said you would, Oz. You *promised*."

"Okay. Yes, I did, and I'm sorry." I rubbed my jaw: Sunil had landed at least one good blow. I knew one sure-fire way to appease her. "I came looking for Kip, though. Look—there he is."

"Never mind Kip. *He* didn't promise to come home on day three. You did."

Never mind Kip? This was new. Did it make me feel better or worse? "Jules, I swear, I—"

"So when you didn't turn up, I ran away from home."

Okay. New Oz—the one who knocked before entering, asked questions first then shot later, the kindly elder brother prepared to listen to his kid sister's story before hanging her up by her heels off the nearest high branch—disappeared in a flash. I got to my feet. Sunil stopped fighting in Jules's grasp and looked up at me fearfully. I folded my arms. "You did what?"

"Ran away. I told you I would, Oz."

She had, too. I remembered. "How did you get here?"

"How do you think?"

"If you tell me you hitched—"

"So what if we did? I was there to protect her." Sunil's voice was unsteady, but still he was prepared to have a go. That was nice, I thought. *Good for you, kid—you earned my respect before I threw you into the loch.* "It's my fault," he ploughed on. "Me and Jules are going out. And my family, they're Brahmin, so they don't want me seeing a white girl. My dad's going mad. That's why we ran."

"Didn't your brother marry Mandy Jackson from the fish shop?"

"Well—yeah, but..."

"You can drop the star-crossed lovers routine. Juliet Osman, are you telling me you walked out on Gran without telling her where you were—"

"Oz!"

I jerked around. Kip was crouching by the fire. He'd fished out Jules's rucksack and was holding it up. "Leave her head on her neck for now," he said. "Come and have a look at this."

"You two, stay exactly where you are." I marched over. Holly and the others swiftly made room for me, and I was sorry to be the shark in the goldfish bowl, but this was ridiculous. "She's thirteen years old, you know," I told Holly, kneeling beside Kip. "Thirteen."

"What? She told me she was sixteen and a half."

"What sixteen year old ever adds a *half* to their age? First rule for dealing with my sister—never believe a word that comes out of her mouth." I peered into the rucksack. There, folded with a precision I knew well, was a stack of freshly laundered clothing, everything a girl might need for a wintry couple of days in the country. Sticking out of a zipper pouch at the back was the return half of a coach ticket, home to Inverness and back. I pulled this out and waved it in Jules's direction. "You didn't run away. You said you wanted to come here, and Gran packed a bag for you and bought you a ticket."

She darted a glance at Sunil. Was it worse for her to be caught with her pants up? "Well, we did hitch. We did *too*," she repeated, as if I'd denied it. "A man with a great big Land Rover picked us up. He lives in some place called Flichity. We walked all the way down the hill to the loch, though. Anything could've happened to us."

"This guy with the Land Rover—did he happen to be about eight feet tall and wearing a Barbour? And did he read you the riot act about hippies and junkies when you told him where you were going?"

She put her hands on her hips. I could see her trying to find a way out, or around or through or whatever would restore a bit of drama to the scene. Then, very suddenly, she gave it all up. A grin lit her scrunched-up little face, and she doubled up laughing. "Fuck me if he didn't."

"Jules!"

"Eight foot tall, wearing a Barbour, and *och no, ye cannae go an' dwell among them hippie layaboots yonder!*" She slapped her thighs in delight at her own horrific attempt at Barbour Guy's accent. "Friend of yours, is he, Oz?"

"He is now. I hope you said thank you for the lift."

"What do you think we did? Throw rotten eggs at him? I tell you what, Oz, and this is something I never thought I'd ever say to you—I like your friends, the ones down here anyway. They're cool. They've taken care of me. I've had a sandwich, and a wash-up and a pee in the posh bathroom in Sam's trailer. And I wasn't gonna drink the cider, was I—I'm not a fool." She folded her arms, the gesture so like my own that it shocked me. "Not like some."

What I wouldn't have given for a pee in Sam's posh bathroom over the last few days! Holly gave an apologetic shrug. "Sorry, Oz. Sam was pretty lenient, but he didn't want everyone from all over the campsite traipsing through there. It was different with your sister."

I barely heard. I was tuning in to the hot glare running from Jules to Kip. "*Not like some?*" I said in disbelief. Kip had been her hero, her golden boy, her escape from all her life's boredom and miseries. God, I'd been bitterly jealous of that, hadn't I? Perversely, now that his halo had finally slipped, protective rage surged through me. "Was that aimed at Kip? Don't you dare. You've got no idea what he's been through, and even if you did—"

"Oz, shut up," Kip said mildly. He put out a hand and ruffled my hair. Then he stood up, making sure he was in her direct line of vision and fire. "She's got every right to be pissed off with me. I screwed her over completely. The only thing I could've done was stick around and face the music after my car crash, and I didn't. I ran. And we both know why she can't bear that."

Jules's face crumpled. She uttered a kind of wail. He strode to meet her, and she cannoned into him, arms outstretched. I tried to watch this unmoved, or at least with some kind of dignity: the whole camp had a ringside seat for this family drama. But my throat seized up and my vision blurred, and after a moment I stumbled over to join them.

Someone tugged my sleeve. I jerked my head up, wiping my eyes on the heel of my hand. There was Sunil, for God's sake, staring up at me in eloquent silence. He'd done pretty well, hadn't he? Punched Brother Superior, lied on command for Jules, got her up here in one piece even if they had done most of the journey in the safety of an intercity Megabus. As potential boyfriends went, I could think of worse. I put out a hand to give him a brotherly clap on the back, and he shot into the huddle, clutching me around the waist.

To my horror, the group around the fire began to applaud. Zadi and Herne weren't there, but everyone else, right down to Mackie and his friends, was present and correct and glued to the unfolding scene. Paul Bouchard probably thought it was some kind of mystery play put on for his benefit. He was spectacularly drunk, propped on both sides by his inherited friends. He pumped his fist in the air and grinned at me. "Go, Oz! Whoo!"

What the actual fuck?

***

So Jules and Sunil spent the night at Camp Saorsa. There wasn't room in Kip's van, unless we'd strung them from the ceiling, so Holly and Paul took them in at the huge RUV. Holly, overreacting to her earlier gaffe with the cider, swore on everything she held sacred that she'd bed them down at opposite ends of the trailer, and the pair of them went off with her, wide-eyed at the adventure. A night in a TV star's van, and a dead TV star at that... The Facebook bragging rights didn't get much bigger, and Jules promised me over her shoulder to message Gran straight away.

As for me and Kip, we tumbled into the foldaway bed, the day and its weirdness catching up with us. Before we pulled up the quilt, he dug out the brick-shaped clock from between the cushions and tossed it accurately into his open holdall by the door. "Oz," he said, and he didn't need to add another thing: I knew what he wanted to watch now. Not the slow flip of minutes passing by—the freeze-frame of one life-changing moment by the loch. I pulled out my phone. I changed its power settings so that the picture wouldn't fade until the batteries gave, and I propped it on the window ledge so he could see. I curled up around his back. "Does the world feel different to you now?"

"Completely. But not for..." He wriggled around to look at me, and suddenly I felt more important than Her Ladyship and all his other monsters combined. "Not for the reasons you think. I was thinking how weird it'll be tomorrow night, when you're not in my bed anymore."

I shivered. My own world would be back on its axis, spinning slowly through cold days and long nights. Desk six awaited me, if I was lucky, and my single bed in Gran's house. Suddenly it struck me as ridiculous that an able-bodied twenty two year old was living with his grandmother. "It'll feel horrible," I said thoughtfully, cradling his head in the crook of my arm. "You know what? I think I need to move out."

"Yes!" he whispered, as if his favourite local team had scored an unlikely goal. "At last!"

"Have you been thinking about it?"

"God, yes. But I was hardly in a position to push you. If you're ready to jump, though..."

"I am. Gran would be okay, wouldn't she?"

"Your gran is about the most resourceful human being I've ever met." His gaze became distant. "I feel as if neither of us has even begun to work her out. But I know you worry, and we'd only be half an hour up the road if she needed us."

If I jumped, where would I land? Kip was talking about *us*, and the familiarity of that was painful, reminding me of long-ago weekends, shared plans. "I think I've forgotten how to live on my own. Getting a flat, finding the deposit, all of that... When I moved in with Gran, I kept telling myself it was for her good. But now I reckon I was just scared."

He sighed. "Is there any way around all this? The lonely separate beds, I mean, and you living all on your own?"

He couldn't be offering what he seemed to be. "Sweetheart, I'm not a good horse to back. As a flatmate, I mean. I'm not even sure I've got a job anymore, and you can't hide me out in your university digs."

"Who said anything about flatmates? We'd be a couple, wouldn't we? And we should find a place off-campus, because I'm gonna need a job to help me fund my PhD. You too, while you take Leighton-Smythe's crammer course and finish up your degree. We'll be busy, but..." He drew me down, kissed me on my brow and each corner of my mouth, and it felt like sacred homecoming, the crowning blessing of my life so far. "I can't think of anything better. Can you?"

I could hardly speak. "All that... it can't happen overnight, though, can it?"

"No. Until then I'll just have to hide you out in my university digs."

Chapter Twenty Two
Home

In the morning, I piled everyone into my car—Kip, Jules, Sunil, with Holly squeezed into the back for a lift as far as Inverness—and we said our goodbyes to Saorsa. Everyone not too hung over to move turned out to see us off. Still no sign of Herne and Zadi, though, and I hoped that wherever they were, they were as full of hope for their second chance as I was about mine. I tried to give some dignity to our departure—Jules shrieking out of one back window and Sunil out of the other was more than enough—but by the time I'd got the car halfway up the track, I was waving with as much enthusiasm as everyone else. I even blew a kiss to Kip's wooden monster as we passed.

We had a perfect winter morning for our drive. Snow was forecast for later that afternoon, and by dusk Camp Saorsa would be vacant except for the hardcore handful who stayed there all year round. The shores would be bare and silent, Her Ladyship of the loch free to pursue her ways in peace. A glimmering flurry of flakes danced over my windscreen as I revved up the hill.

A warning or a promise? The lochside would be lovely under snow, but I was glad we'd set out early. Whorls were already dancing over the bright water. And something else was out there too. "Kip," I said, flipping the sun visor down against the dazzle, "is there an island or something out there?"

He leaned in over the handbrake. "No, there's only one island in the loch since the water level rose for the Caledonian Canal, a crannog all the way down at the southwest end. Cherry Island, they call it. There used to be another one, Eilean nan Con, which literally means the Isle of Dogs, but... Oh. That's Herne and Zadi."

"On a raft, right? Some kind of..."

"Invisible raft. I don't know. I can only see their feet on the water."

There was nowhere to stop. A timber lorry was snorting behind me. Kip and I had to settle for one last glance as we passed. Herne had finally jettisoned his horns and hooves, and Zadi looked ready for a day in his surgery at Fort William, except that he was barefoot. The pair were holding hands. They saw us, and Zadi waved. Herne, his bright grin flashing, offered a sign of peace. I sat back, shaking my head. "Oh, man. I have seen everything now."

I was wrong, of course. Sunil and Jules—Holly, too— had taken surprisingly little interest in the miracle on the loch. Already they'd found something to squabble about. A phone was getting passed back and forth across the back seat, a discussion conducted in loud whispers. These rose to poorly muffled shouts as we set off over the moors towards Inverness, snagging at my attention until I couldn't stand it anymore. The timber lorry had gone, so I pulled into a passing place, braked hard and brought us to a stop. I turned round, hooking my arm over the back of my seat. "I am *trying* to *drive*."

Jules stared at me, open-mouthed. "Ooh. You do sound like Dad."

A few days ago, that would've cut me to the bone. I'd have denied it six ways to sunset. "Is that a problem for you?"

"Don't get pissy, Oz. If you want to know, I liked it when he used to pull over to rip our heads off. It made me feel safe."

I took this in. I didn't want to air more family laundry in front of poor Holly. As for Sunil, he had better get used to it. Accepting that very little in my life was going to happen at a convenient place and time, I said, sounding a bit mournful to myself, "I did try to do some of the things he used to do. I was there, Jules. And I earned a wage."

"Yeah. But the thing is, you didn't need to. You weren't my dad, and I wasn't expecting that. I wanted my brother, stupid goofy Oz." Before I could react—clearly coming to a decision, the upshot of whatever quarrel had engaged her and Sunil all the way up from the camp—she held out her mobile. "Still, looks like I've got no shortage of brothers now."

I took the phone from her. A photo filled the screen. A woman was sitting on a garden bench. On either side of her sat two dark-haired, smiling boys, in their early teens from the look of it. Distractedly I heard Holly ask if this was a good idea, and I guessed that her opinion had been sought and discarded already. Kip took hold of my wrist so he could look at the picture too, and I was so bloody glad of him, of his warm and anchoring touch. "Who are these people, Jules?"

Something in his tone gave her a warning. He'd always extended her infinite rope and patience, but the games stopped when she turned her wrath on me. "Sunil made me do it," she said nervously. "He said it was a good idea."

Sunil gasped. "I so did not too, Juliet Osman! *You* wondered if they were on Facebook. *I* only helped you find them. And I've been telling you all the way up this hill that he's not in the mood and you should wait, and so did Holly, so there."

Poor kid. She looked genuinely scared. She was testing the size of the rockets she could launch and still keep her family and friends. It wasn't my job to stop her—just to be as bomb-proof as I possibly could. I took a deep breath. "Is this Dad's other family? The ones in California?"

"Yes." Tentatively she pointed at the screen. "That one's Eric and that one's Luke. They look nice, don't they?"

I didn't know. I was too busy dealing with the fact that they looked like me, if I'd ever had the chance for a serious suntan. In the photo, the sky was a deep glowing blue. The tree in the background was some kind of palm. Suddenly the world got bigger for me, inside and out. "They're older than I thought. I thought they were just little kids."

"Oh, no. Dad's been running a second family for years and years. Think about it, Ozzy—all those business trips, and how he had this fantastic job that took him all over the world, but we never had quite enough money to pay our bills at home."

"I didn't think you took any notice of that."

"I did, though. I should've known the jig was up when he blew all that cash on your twenty first."

So should I. He'd been saying goodbye. The thought bounced painlessly off my new inner shields, the ones Kip had built for me. "You've talked to these boys? You've been in touch?"

"Sunil said I should." She paused while Sunil gaped at her and gave her a gentle push, then regrouped. "*I* wanted to. I got in touch. And I was scared at first that they might not know about us, and I might be screwing things up for them and their mam, but here's the kicker. Are you ready?"

I wasn't ready for any of this. "What?"

"He's gone and left them too. Eric told me all about it. There might be a *third* family, Oz." Suddenly, out of the blue, she put a hand on my shoulder. "It's not us he left. There's nothing wrong with us. It's just what he does."

I tried to take this in. I knew she was right, and somewhere inside me a dark place lit up, fresh ideas blowing through it like the morning breeze. "Which... Which one is Eric?"

"The older one there. Our half-brother. And the mam is that one there. She's *really* nice, Oz. She's got nothing against us. She wishes she'd known about us before. She says that she always wanted a daughter, and now she feels like she's got one in a way."

"Jules, slow down. I know you're excited, but... we don't really know these people."

"I know. I'll take it slowly, I promise. But it's good, isn't it? This is a good thing."

I looked at the faces of the smiling, sunny family. The woman—my father's second wife, *the mam* as my motherless brat of a sister had called her, a scrape of yearning in her voice—met the camera's eye fearlessly. All three shared a loving, intelligent gaze—mine, I supposed, if I'd ever looked at myself in a mirror like that. "Yes," I said at last. "It's good."

***

After dropping off Holly, we did a straight run to Lower Shilby. Kip had made a few calls to April's mobile, and I could feel the scrape of his nerves when neither Letty nor her strange little guardian picked up. I didn't blame him. Even housebound, Letty with an internet connection could cut a swathe of chaos through his life. He caught my eye the next time he hung up, and I read there his relief that whatever he would have to face in Kipton Manor, he wouldn't be doing it alone.

I was just surprised that he wasn't facing a barrage of questions from Jules. She and Sunil were surreptitiously holding hands in the back seat—as if I couldn't see them with a tilt of my rearview mirror—and either she was learning some discretion or her new romance was distracting her, because she sat in more-or-less silence all the way past the Spar and the chip shop to Lady Letitia's front door. "Give me five minutes alone with her," Kip said, clearly puzzled too. "For God's sake don't go anywhere, any of you—I might need all the backup I can get."

I watched him unfasten the door and disappear inside. I drummed my fingers on the wheel for a few moments, then drew a breath to try and explain to my nosy kid sister why we'd brought Kip to this desolate place to see his mum. Or maybe I should go for a diversionary tactic, ask her more about Eric and Luke and the mam...

Before I had the chance to decide, Kip shot back out of the house. He was white as a sheet. He ran round to the passenger side, pulled open the door and dropped into the seat. "She's not there."

"What? Where would she go?"

"Nowhere I can think of. There was only a note. Look."

He held out a scrap of paper. I took it from him, squinting to make out the loops and whirls of the handwriting.

Dear Oz. When you get this, come home.

I turned the note upside down, held it up to the light. I didn't think those actions would help, but they bought me a bit of time. "Is this your mum's writing?" I asked, knowing the answer already. "Or April's?"

"Neither. What does it mean?"

Loops and whirls, the outward expression of a devious old brain. "Juliet," I said at last. "You know when you didn't really run away, and our gran packed your knickers and socks and bought you a coach ticket to Inverness?"

She turned her face towards the window, as if none of this could possibly be any business of hers. "What about it?"

"When she did all that, did she say anything about getting you out of the way for a couple of days?"

"Might of."

"Might *have*. And might you, by any unlikely chance, know why?"

She suddenly wriggled into the middle of the seat, pushing Sunil aside. "What does the note say, Oz?"

"You can see for yourself. She wants me to go home."

"Then why are you busting *my* arse for instructions?"

I gave up. I put the car into gear. Kip was caught somewhere between puzzled and scared stiff, and the best I could do for him was keep his bewilderment short. "Don't worry," I said with a confidence I was far from feeling. "I'm sure Letty's fine. It's just Gran, off on some scheme or other. We'll be home in twenty minutes, and I'll get it all sorted out."

I managed the drive in fifteen. From the outside, the shabby police house in its wind-whipped meadow looked exactly the same as when I'd left it four days ago. I bumped the car to a halt by the kerb, and I twisted round to address Kip, Jules and Sunil in turn. "Right, you three. Just for once, listen and don't argue. I am going in, and you are sitting here until I get back. Do you understand?"

Sunil rolled his eyes. Jules stuck her tongue out at me. Only Kip nodded, all fight knocked out of him by fear. He'd been working his whole adult life to shield his mum, to keep her tucked into the one frail shell he could maintain. Every time he went home, he must have dreaded this one exact scenario: empty rooms, a flown coop, Letty on the loose or scooped up by forces he couldn't control. I put one hand to his face and kissed him, unconcerned by the juvenile audience in the back. "Don't worry. Everything will be okay."

I jogged up the front path. The door was on the latch, as if I was expected, so I pushed it open. I stopped in the hallway. Voices were coming from the living room, a comfortable purr of conversation. I didn't have to open the door to see who was in there because, for some reason, Gran had installed a smart new one made of glass panes, most of them clear, a few with fish-eye distortion. No matter which type I chose, the scene was bloody unbelievable.

A scraping sound came from above me, making me jump. High up in the landing ceiling, the hatch to the loft was open. Something was hanging down from it—not the vast bat my confused vision first reported but the top half of a very small, upside-down girl. "Hi, John Osman," she said, grinning broadly, hair swinging. "I'm up here."

"So you are. Hello, April."

271

"I've got a window. It's only little and I have to stand on a chair, but I can see people coming for miles. I saw you."

"Okay."

"I've got *stairs*. You can pull 'em up after you, and then you close the trapdoor. Like this."

She hoisted herself back up through the hatch. The cover banged neatly into place and she was gone, perhaps only my dream of a precocious lost child hiding out in my grandmother's loft. When she showed no signs of reappearing, I gave up and went back outside.

Jules and Sunil shot past me on the path. Both were half-choked with giggles at their own daring, but I didn't care. Sunil had a mum and a dad of his own, and although I would do all I could all my life to help Jules, she wasn't my problem and never had been. Kip had only got as far as swinging his legs out of the car. I dropped to one knee on the kerb in front of him. "How are you feeling, love?"

"I don't know. Scared, I think. But looking at your face... I don't need to be, do I?"

"No, you don't, I promise. Do you think your new meds are making any difference?"

"A bit, maybe—things don't seem so up-and-down crazy anymore."

"I'm sorry you lost the ups."

"Don't be. They were too wild. It was like being on a roller coaster that occasionally shoots into space, but most of the time..." He ran his hands into his hair, struggling for words. "Most of the time it just crawls along underground. So, yeah—I feel like I'm out in the light, and maybe part of that's the new crack, but I'm pretty sure the rest of it's you."

My sinuses prickled. "Serious?"

"Deadly."

"You're feeling a bit more stable, then?"

"I need to be, don't I?"

"Yes. Because Gran runs a nice loony bin, but it's a total nuthouse all the same."

His eyes widened. "Wow. You'd better escort me inside."

So I took his hand, and together we walked into my gran's extraordinary house. No point in trying to prepare him, so I led him down the hall, gave a warning tap on the new glass door and opened it wide for him.

There on the far side of the blazing gas fire sat Letty. She was propped up in an armchair, but there all resemblance to her living room in Lower Shilby ceased. She was neatly dressed in clothes I recognised as my mother's, a little dated but clean and a good fit. Somebody had washed and cut her hair, and provided her with huge wooden knitting needles, which she was valiantly plying while she talked. And in the other armchair was my gran. "Shush, Letty," she said, and Letty obediently stopped in midsentence and smiled. "Hello, Kip. Hello, Oz."

I waited for Kip to speak, but he'd ground to a halt, one hand clenched on the door handle. "Hello, Gran," I said. "Do you want to bring me and Kip up to speed?"

She nodded benignly. "I ought to, oughtn't I? The first thing I have to say is to you, Oz, and it's an apology really. When your mother died, that was one thing. You still had your dad to look out for you. When he ran off too, things changed. I had to make sure that nobody else hurt my boy."

It took me a moment. "Your boy? Me?"

"Who else, for heaven's sake?" She leaned forward in her chair as Jules and Sunil clattered down the hall from the back door. "Juliet, you and your young man can make tea for everyone now. There's custard creams in the barrel."

I waited for an argument from Jules, but none came. She only stuck her head around the door for long enough to beam at Kip, then she bounced out again, and I heard her dragging Sunil off in the direction of the kitchen. "Jules is already up to speed, isn't she, Gran?"

"Why, yes. I needed her help, you see. But I'm not done with my explanation."

"For what?"

"For why I background-checked your boyfriend's family. You mustn't take it personally—it's different for Jules and Sunil, because I've known the Patwardhans all her life."

At last Kip stirred. "You... checked *my* background, Gran?"

"I'm afraid so. You and Oz broke up, but I knew that wouldn't last long. And I loved all your stories about Sir George and Lady Letitia, but of course they couldn't be true. I had to make sure you weren't hiding anything that might be harmful to Oz."

"I was, though." He swallowed with an effort. "I was. I'm sorry, Ma! How could we pass any kind of background check?"

"It depends what the checker is looking for, I suppose. All I needed to know was that our new in-laws were happy, with nothing to grieve them. Because if they weren't, then Oz would grieve too."

"But we've got everything to grieve us."

"You had, I know. So I thought I'd put some of it right."

Kip rubbed his eyes. "I don't understand. How did you even find her?"

"She's in the phone book, Kip. Not the fancy internet thing but the one they still push through your door. I could tell you were telling the truth about your mum's name, and there just aren't that many L Kiptons to choose from."

"I made you ex-directory, Ma! I phoned up and de-registered you. How are you back in the book?"

Letty had returned to her knitting. Now she looked up tranquilly. "I phoned and told them we'd done it by mistake. I *like* to be in the book, Kip. I enjoy your stories about me too, but the phone book makes me feel real."

Poor Kip. He'd striven so hard to turn her into a beautiful fiction. "What did you do?" he asked Gran hoarsely. "Ruck up at her house and take her away?"

"More or less. Juliet and I hired a taxi and went along, just to see. Now, we happened to find some young chaps from the village amusing themselves by sitting on her wall, shouting and carrying on, which must have been terrifying for a lone lady indoors, especially one like Letty here, who doesn't necessarily know what's real and what isn't. So I let them have the sharp end of my brolly..."

"Gran!"

"And Letty and I had a talk, and it turned out that she, all her belongings and that odd little creature she's been living with—April, isn't it?—fit very nicely into the back of the cab. So off we went. I sent Jules and Sunil off to find you. To get them out of the way, because I needed to talk to Letty's doctor, and arrange a visit from a social worker, and then of course we had to fix up a bedroom and make the loft space nice for April."

It was like being hit on the head by a well-meaning jackhammer. "A bedroom?" I said belatedly. We only had three of those, and unless Gran or Jules intended moving out... "*My* bedroom?"

"Look me in the face, John Osman, and tell me you came back from Camp Saucer intending to sleep in there tonight."

I couldn't, of course. I intended to sleep with my lover in a cramped university bed, limb to limb and heart to fast-beating heart. And it didn't matter now because tears were running down his face, all the things that had grieved him suddenly lifted away. He let go his grip of the door handle, stumbled over and knelt in front of Letty. "Are you *living* here, then, Ma?"

She nodded. "I do seem to be, Kip. Yes."

"And do you like that?"

Proudly she showed him her knitting: two rows that looked more Tate Modern than arts and crafts. "That old lady over there showed me how."

"We could call this Cthulhu's Web, Ma!" He sat down on the carpet and turned to Gran. "But how on earth will you manage her? I love her, but she's... I don't even know where to start with the problems she has. She can't go an hour without a hit of some kind, and only a third of that's legal."

"That's right," Gran said serenely. "We know about the other two thirds—don't we, Letty? The doctor's taken a good look at her, and he agrees that we can't drop her off the edge of a cliff. So she has the right prescriptions now for the things she *really* needs, and April keeps those in the loft with the pull-up stairs. As for the rest—I like my Facebook groups, and of course I'll miss Trouble With Angry Teens, but I think I'll be too busy now to be online. Jules can use the internet at Sunil's house, and I've given her my laptop. So there's no world-wide web in this house anymore, is there, Lady Letty, and we'll just see how we get along without."

Kip wiped his eyes. "Oh, God. She'll go nuts."

"Juliet? Far from it. She's been a very good girl."

"No, not Jules. My ma. You don't know what she's like."

"No more does she know about me. We'll find out, and I doubt it will be easy. But your ma has some things she didn't have before, Kip. Ordinary things— entertainment and company, children going back and forth, knitting and visits and tea parties. Oh, and constant supervision." She bobbed her head in satisfaction. "That glass door's a big help. Come on in, Juliet and Sunil. Just put the trays on the big table there beside Letty, and she'll do the rest."

Kip twitched in panic. "She can't, Gran. She'll break stuff. She..."

"Oz, come and take Kip out of the way. He's like you, isn't he—he has to look the gift horse in the mouth."

So I went and I gathered him off the floor. He clenched his fists in my Black Sabbath T-shirt and hung on while Letty, to our absolute amazement, wobbled up out of her chair and began to pour the tea.

Chapter Twenty Three
My New World

Annoyingly, after all that, I didn't take well to renewed student life. I'd loved giving notice on desk six, of course, although Cedric had taken the edge off that for me by shaking my hand and sincerely wishing me well. Who'd have thought?

But not all the burdens I'd shouldered had been bad. A pay check at the end of each month had changed not only my view of the world but of my own place in it. Two weeks into the new year and my crammer course—after a surreal Christmas with Gran, Jules, the Patwardhans and April—Prof Leighton-Smythe brought me news of undergrad vacancies at EON, with training on the job. Maybe he'd noticed my bewilderment among the rowdy lads who drank all night and came slouching, late and unrepentant, into study groups which felt like life-or-death to me.

EON hired me, to my delight and Kip's. A long commute, but the starting salary was good, and we moved into a sunny flat off-campus. He was hip-deep in his new PhD proposal, a study of plant-and-animal biodiversity along the route of the Caledonian Canal, to include Loch Ness, and plenty of trips for fieldwork.

A new world was unfolding for us both. The old one seeped into it, of course. Kip told me he'd never be the kind of recovering addict who could do things by halves, and our home was an alcohol and drug-free zone, though a haven for a thousand other pleasures. He just took one day at a time, promising himself and me each morning that he'd stay clean until the next. He took a lunchtime bar job in the city—thriving best, as he had at Saorsa, in a place where his old temptations flew plentifully around— and proved it, steadily, day by day.

I was due to start full-time at Kielder at the beginning of February. Kip's proposal was due by the same date. Before then, we had some plans. Kip had heard from Cryptid Kenny that a new anomalous big cat had been sighted in a forest in North Wales. Not a stray Maine Coon this time, Kenny swore, and so we were going to take a look. Kip's new Mazda was tanked up and ready to fly. We'd bought it between us, so he had a newer model this time, and by standing on the forecourt looking grim while he talked to the dealer, I'd even managed to swing him a year's warranty.

The night before our departure, we watched the Sam Bouchard memorial show on the internet. Paul was presenting, skinny and handsome in his blazer. When he spoke of his brother's death, he came across as brimming with a kind of sacred hope. He was filming from a secret location, and over the high land in the background, huge birds circled and swooped.

The highlight and finale of the piece was Sam's last recording. Loch Ness was too well known for anonymity, but Paul had blurred Zadi's face, describing him only a friend of Sam's from a small community in Scotland. And so the world saw a man walk on the water, while a horned god, his face also blurred out, stood watchfully on the shore.

Kip's head was on my shoulder. "He did it," he said wonderingly while the credits rolled. "There weren't any rocks for him to stand on there. He just walked out."

"He did more than that when we saw him on our way out of Saorsa. Herne, too. Do you ever get the feeling that they held whatever magic there was between them?"

"And neither of them could do it properly on his own? Yeah, I get that." He rubbed his face against my sleeve. "I dunno, Oz. If Jesus and the ancient god of the wildwood can make friends again, do you think the world might be a different place?"

I rested my chin on the top of his head, then kissed his curls. He never expected answers to his broader questions from me: just wanted to hear them out loud, and in our warm silences let his own thoughts flow, form and grow. "The thing is," he said at length, "I can see footage of Zadi's first walk. We could rewind it and have another look now. On our way out of Saorsa, we just drove past. I'm *way* more of a realist than I ever thought I'd be, way more of a biologist and less of a dreamer. I almost feel like I should hand in my cryptid hunter's badge."

"Don't do that. I'm looking forward to my first ABC."

"And you're so much more of a poet."

I couldn't resist. "If I am, I didn't know it."

He groaned in disgust. "Not like that. I mean that you see things, interpret them, in ways I'd never have imagined. Like Herne and Zadi holding some kind of magic between them. That's amazing." The evening was chilly despite our open fire, and he shifted deeper into the curve of my arm. "I hope we get years and years to find out how different we both are. Decades."

"Centuries," I agreed. I held him tight for a moment, then disentangled and leaned in to hit pause on my laptop. I scrolled Paul's broadcast back to the lochside scene, found the best frame I could and pressed print-screen. "Hold on a sec. I know what you mean about footage. I'm not too much of a poet for that."

We already had some photo paper in the printer. I ran off a copy of the freeze-frame and took it through to our pinboard in the kitchen. There among the appointment cards and bill reminders were two other photographs: my favourite, an unlikely capture of Kip in mid leap between rocks in rich red sunset light, and the second was our life-changing shot of Her Ladyship. We'd kept that one hidden for a while when friends came to visit, but somehow that made it all the more obvious, more likely to fall out of whichever book or magazine we'd tucked it into for the occasion. When we put it up in plain sight on the board, hardly anyone noticed. If they did, they'd give a whistle or a laugh and dismiss it as a prank by one of Kip's cryptid-spotting mates. After a while we'd left it there. He liked to see it every day, in much the same ordinary, daily-bread way he liked to see me.

Yes. Her Ladyship and me. Kip's monsters.

About the Author

Harper Fox is the author of many critically acclaimed M/M romance novels, including Stonewall Book Award-nominated *Scrap Metal* and *Brothers of the Wild North Sea*, a Publishers Weekly Best Book. To find out more about Harper and see updates on her current writing projects, please visit www.harperfox.net.